The Loner:
KILLER POKER

3-26-xt

J. A. Johnstone

PINNACLE BOOKS
Kensington Publishing Corp.
www.kensingtonbooks.com

Chapter 1

Conrad Browning knew he was asleep. That didn't make the dream he was having any less of a nightmare.

In the dream, two children ran ahead of him. Their laughter had a taunting quality to it. He hurried after them, trying to catch up. He should have been able to do that easily, since they were only three or four years old, but somehow they stayed just out of his reach.

Then, still laughing, they looked back over their shoulders at him, as if to beckon him on.

He could see they had no faces, and horror washed through him. Where happy smiles and bright eyes should have been, he saw only smooth, empty, hideously blank flesh.

He came up out of sleep with a strangled yell. Cold sweat beaded on his face.

"Sir? Mr. Browning? Are you all right?"

Arturo's familiar voice grounded Conrad and gave him something to hang on to. His chest heaved and his heart pounded madly inside it. He covered his face with his hands for a moment.

When he lowered them, he was able to say, "Yes, Arturo, it was just . . . just a bad dream."

"I surmised as much, sir."

Conrad drew in a deep breath. His pulse wasn't racing quite so crazily, but a feeling of revulsion still gripped him.

A holstered Colt, with the attached shell belt wrapped around it, lay on the ground beside his bedroll. He was glad that instinct hadn't made him grab the gun when the nightmare jolted him out of his sleep. He might have fired it without meaning to and hurt Arturo.

The tall, slender servant was sitting on a fallen cottonwood with a Winchester across his knees. A few feet away, the little creek where they had made camp gurgled along. A million stars shone in the black sky above them. It should have been a peaceful night . . .

But Conrad Browning was anything but at peace.

He ran his fingers through his close-cropped, sandy hair, then wiped the clammy beads off his face. He tried to tell himself he was sweating because the night was warm, but knew that wasn't true.

And just because he was awake didn't mean the nightmare was over.

"Is there anything I can do for you?" Arturo asked.

Conrad shook his head. He pushed the tangled bedroll aside and stood up. "I'm awake, so I might as well go ahead and take over standing guard."

"It's still more than an hour until I was supposed to wake you."

"Yeah, but like I said, I'm awake." Conrad held out his hand for the rifle. "And this is a chance for you to get a little extra sleep."

"Well . . ." Arturo considered the idea for a moment, then handed the Winchester to Conrad. "All right. I am a bit weary. Thank you, sir."

"No thanks necessary," Conrad assured him.

Arturo stood up and stretched. He was several inches taller than Conrad and fifty pounds lighter. His slender build made him look frail, but Conrad had discovered that Arturo Vincenzo was considerably tougher and stronger than he appeared. Technically, Arturo was his butler, valet, and traveling companion on their quest, but they were more like brothers in arms, having faced deadly danger together on numerous occasions.

The campfire had burned down to embers. Conrad didn't bother stirring it up before he took Arturo's place on the log.

Cottonwoods that were upright and healthy lined the creek banks. Their leaves rustled slightly in the night breezes. Conrad sat and listened intently, while Arturo stretched out to sleep.

The horses were picketed nearby. Conrad frowned as the animals began to shift around and stamp their hooves. Something had spooked them. A coyote, maybe, or even a wolf. He didn't know what dangers might lurk on the plains of eastern Colorado.

Something was out there. His instincts told him that much, and he had learned to trust them.

"Hello, the camp!"

The voice came out of the darkness, but didn't surprise Conrad. He had already decided they were about to have visitors, even though it was the middle of the night.

Arturo sat up and reached for the pistol next to his bedroll. Conrad came to his feet. There was no reason to think they were about to have trouble, but there was also no reason not to be careful.

Conrad heard the sound of several horses approaching the camp. He called, "That's far enough. What do you want?"

The hoofbeats stopped. The man who had spoken before said, "We were ridin' by not far off and heard somebody yell out. Everything all right here, friend?"

Conrad's mouth tightened. It bothered him that somebody had heard his horrified cry. "Yes, we're fine, but thank you for your concern."

"Wouldn't happen to have some coffee left in the pot, would you? We've been ridin' all night."

Though he hadn't been raised in the West, it was where Conrad made his home, and Western hospitality demanded that visitors be welcomed. "Come on in," he told them, adding quietly, "Arturo, stir the fire up." His voice dropped even more. "And keep your pistol handy, just in case."

Three dark shapes bulked up out of the night, turning into three men on horseback as they came closer. Conrad didn't point the Winchester at them, but he kept the rifle aimed in their general direction.

Little flames began to dance as Arturo stirred the campfire back to life. The light they cast showed three hard-faced, unshaven men who looked tired as they reined their lathered mounts to a halt. They had been riding hard and fast.

"All right to light and set?" the spokesman asked.

Conrad nodded. "Go ahead. Any coffee left in the pot, Arturo?"

"Some," Arturo replied. "I'm not sure it's fit to drink by this point, however."

The man who seemed to be the leader of the trio grinned as he swung down from the saddle. "It'll do fine by us. We're much obliged."

Just because they looked like hardcases didn't mean they were, Conrad thought. They could be drifting cowhands or even ranchers. There were some vast spreads on the Colorado plains, and some cattle barons didn't believe in putting on airs.

On the other hand, they could just as easily be owlhoots on the run from the law. Considering the low-slung guns they wore, that was probably more likely.

Arturo set the coffee pot at the edge of the fire. "We should let that warm up a bit. That can only improve what's left."

One of the strangers took the reins of the horses from the other two men, leaving them with both hands free. Conrad made a note of that fact.

He knew the leader was studying him and Arturo. The man didn't seem too impressed with what he saw. Arturo wasn't the least bit threatening in his appearance, and Conrad was just a young man, fairly tall and well built, but in nondescript black trousers and a white shirt open at the throat, he wasn't anything special.

The man looked over at their horses. The big, blaze-faced black gelding Conrad rode was a fine animal, and the four horses making up the team that pulled Arturo's buckboard were pretty good, too. The pack mule didn't really count.

"You know, if you fellas are interested, maybe we could work a trade."

"What sort of trade?" Conrad asked, although he was certain he already knew the answer to that question.

"Our horses are about played out, and we really need to keep movin' as soon as we've had a cup of coffee. How about we swap you our mounts for three of your animals?"

Conrad shook his head. "Sorry. We're used to these animals. We'd like to keep them."

Anger flashed in the man's eyes, but he kept a grin on his face. He looked at Arturo and said, "Is that the way you feel about it, amigo?"

Arturo was still hunkered by the coffee pot. "Whatever Mr. Browning says is fine with me," he replied.

"Your boss, is he?"

"My employer."

Conrad said, "That's none of your business."

The man held up his left hand, palm out. "Oh, now, no offense meant, friend. Just makin' conversation. You sure we can't interest you in swappin' horses?"

"I'm certain," Conrad said.

The man who wasn't holding the horses spoke up. "Ah, hell, Kingston, why all this pussyfootin' around?"

"Take it easy," the leader shot back. "How's that coffee comin' along there, Arturo?"

"It should be getting warm now." Using a piece of thick leather to protect his hand, Arturo grasped the pot's handle and picked it up. "If you have cups—"

"Just hold on," the man called Kingston said. "We need to finish our business first."

"We don't have any business to finish," Conrad said. "Drink your coffee and move on."

"Well, now you don't sound friendly at all. Where are you headed? Denver?"

"That's right."

Kingston shook his head. "That's gonna be a long walk."

"We don't plan on walking."

"Well, you're gonna have to, because we're taking your horses, and we're not leaving ours, either. With that many spare mounts, we can outdistance that posse without any trouble. You and Arturo there can either hoof it, or you can stay right here permanent-like." Kingston started to move his hand toward the butt of his gun. "The choice is—"

Conrad shot him in the face.

Chapter 2

The rifle in Conrad's hands was angled up slightly as he fired from the hip. When the slug struck the man in the right cheekbone, just above the corner of his mouth, it bored through his brain and exploded out the back of his head in a shower of blood, gray matter, and bone fragments. The other man yelled a curse and grabbed for his gun as Kingston's blood sprayed across his face.

The revolver hadn't cleared leather when Arturo uncoiled from the ground and threw the coffeepot into the man's face. The man screamed and staggered back as the hot metal seared his flesh.

Conrad worked the Winchester's lever and brought the rifle to his shoulder. He waited a second to make sure the man wasn't going to give up. When the man jerked his gun from its holster, Conrad squeezed the trigger and drilled a bullet into the man's chest. At that range the slug had enough impact to throw the man backward into the horses.

The third man struggled to control the horses as they began to spook from the shooting. Conrad levered the Winchester again and swung the barrel toward him.

"Give it up!" Conrad called.

For a split second, the third outlaw thought about it.

Then he dropped the reins, shouted, "Go to hell!", and clawed at the gun on his hip.

Conrad and Arturo fired at the same time. The bullets ripped through the man's body and spun him around. He thudded to the ground, face-first.

Without anyone holding their reins, the thoroughly panicked horses belonging to the outlaws bolted off into the darkness with their reins trailing.

Conrad watched them go and smiled faintly. Slowly, he lowered the rifle and took a deep breath. The air was thick with the smell of powdersmoke and death. He knew he ought to be used to it, but he wasn't sure he ever would be. "They must have stolen those mounts pretty recently," he said. "Otherwise they would have been used to the sound of gunfire by now."

Arturo said, "Excuse me, sir. I think I'm going to be sick."

"Go ahead," Conrad told him.

Arturo stumbled away from the campsite. Conrad heard him retching. There had been a time when the sudden outbreak of bloody violence would have affected him that way, too.

Maybe he was getting used to the killing after all.

He levered another round into the rifle's chamber—

something he should have done sooner, he reminded himself—and checked to make sure the three men sprawled on the ground were dead. He was pretty sure they were, but it took only a minute to confirm.

Arturo came back, looking pale and shaken. He wiped the back of a hand across his mouth. "My apologies, sir."

"No apologies necessary. You handled yourself very well."

"I've learned by observation, and I've had a good teacher." He gestured at the corpses. "I take it these men were desperadoes?"

"One of them said something about a posse being after them, so yeah, it's a good bet. I'll check their clothes and see if I can find anything that'll tell us their names."

It was an unpleasant chore, and an unproductive one as well. He didn't find anything in the pockets of the men except some greasy, folded greenbacks, a few coins, matches and cigarette makings, a tattered deck of cards, and a poker chip.

"If they had any loot from their crimes, it must have been in their saddlebags," he said as he straightened from the task. "Not much to show for a life of crime."

"What do we do with them?"

Conrad glanced at the stars. "It'll be light in another three hours or so. We'll bury them then. In the meantime, let's drag the bodies over there in those tall weeds. I don't want to spend the rest of the night looking at them."

When that was done, Conrad told Arturo to go

back to his bedroll and try to get some sleep, as he'd been trying to do when the three strangers rode up.

"I'm not sure I'll be able to sleep after that," Arturo said.

Conrad smiled. "Try, anyway. I'll finish out the night on watch."

"Well . . . all right. But if you need me, don't hesitate to wake me."

"I won't."

Despite what Arturo had said, within minutes his deep, even breathing indicated that he had dozed off. Conrad sat down on the cottonwood log again and tried not to think too much about what had just happened. If he allowed himself to brood about every act of senseless, wanton violence that had intruded itself into his life over the past couple years, he wouldn't have time for anything else.

And he would probably go mad.

Conrad Browning had been living the happy, peaceful life of a successful businessman in Carson City, Nevada, married to a beautiful young woman named Rebel and managing the worldwide holdings of the vast business empire he had inherited from his mother, when tragedy struck. Rebel was kidnapped and murdered, and his former fiancée, Pamela Tarleton, had been behind the evil plan.

He had uncovered that fact and attained some small degree of vengeance for Rebel's death, but only by abandoning his old life and taking up a new identity, that of the wandering gunfighter called Kid Morgan.

He came to that naturally, because his father was Frank Morgan, the famous—or infamous, depending on how you looked at it—gunfighter known as The Drifter.

Attempting to put his past behind him, The Kid had decided that Conrad Browning was no more. His new identity might be fictional, but he embraced it. During the time he had spent wandering in and out of trouble he'd first met Arturo, who was working for a man who wound up being a deadly enemy to Kid Morgan.

Eventually The Kid had learned how hard it was for a man to give up who he had been. Pamela Tarleton was dead, but one of her relatives had tried to carry on her campaign of hate against Conrad Browning, and in the course of that, Conrad had uncovered Pamela's plan to strike out at him from beyond the grave.

According to the letter she had written to him, she had given birth to twins, a boy and a girl, and Conrad was their father. The children, who would now be three years old, were hidden away somewhere in the West. Somewhere he would never find them, the letter boasted.

Shaken to the core by the revelation that he was a father, Conrad wasn't going to give up easily. Recruiting Arturo to help him, he had returned to Boston, where he had been engaged to Pamela, learning where and when she had given birth. She had left Boston with the infant twins and headed west. Conrad was able to pick up her trail that led to Kansas City and then across the plains. Following the route of the Union Pacific, Conrad and Arturo were traveling by horse and buckboard, stopping at every settlement to ask if anyone had seen a woman traveling with two small children and a nurse, several years earlier.

The odds against discovering where Pamela had hidden the children were long ones, but Conrad intended to keep searching. The Browning business empire was still thriving. Money was no concern, and neither was time.

His children were out there somewhere, and he intended to find them.

Conrad let Arturo sleep until the sky was gray with the approach of dawn. He built up the fire and put fresh coffee on to boil, then took bacon from their supplies in the back of the buckboard and got it sizzling in a pan. When the bacon finished frying, he would use the grease to cook up some flapjacks.

The good smells woke Arturo. He pushed himself up on an elbow and yawned. "I would have prepared breakfast, sir."

"I know that," Conrad said, "but I cooked for myself for a long time when I was out on the lonely trails. I don't mind."

Arturo sat up and rubbed the sleep out of his eyes. "I must say, having seen you in the midst of glittering high society, it's difficult to believe that you also spent so much time living like . . . like . . ."

"Some sort of owlhoot?" Conrad asked with a smile.

"Basically, yes."

"There's something to be said for solitude. Seemed like every time I got around people too much, I wound up in some sort of scrape. Usually a shooting scrape."

"Ah. Then what you're saying is . . . the more things change, the more they stay the same."

Conrad laughed. "That pretty much sums it up. Whether I'm Conrad Browning or Kid Morgan, people are all the time shooting at me."

Arturo looked toward the weeds where they had put the bodies of the dead outlaws. "Indeed."

"We'll have breakfast first. Then we'll take care of that little chore."

"Yes, of course. Wouldn't want to dig graves on an empty stomach, would we?" Arturo climbed to his feet and went over to the fire. "Why don't you let me finish that? You're more skilled at tending to the horses."

"Sure." Conrad tried not to chuckle. Sometimes he wondered who exactly was in charge, him or his so-called servant.

The horses had plenty of grass to graze on, so Conrad took them over to the creek one by one and let them drink. While he was doing that, Arturo finished preparing breakfast. The smell of coffee and bacon made Conrad forget that he was a little tired.

They would push on toward Denver, once they had finished the burying. He had been to the city that lay in the shadow of the Rocky Mountains many times. Denver was a big place. If Pamela had hidden the twins there, finding them wasn't going to be easy.

So far in the quest, Conrad had been able to uncover enough clues to keep him on the trail. More than once, he'd had a feeling Pamela had left those clues on purpose. She had wanted him to keep searching. She'd realized how much torment he would be in knowing that his children were out there somewhere.

Arturo poured the coffee. He handed a cup to Conrad, then knelt by the fire to dish up the bacon and flapjacks. The sun was barely peeking over the horizon.

With a sudden thunder of hoofbeats, a large group of riders surged out of the reddish-gold glare and galloped up to the camp.

Chapter 3

Conrad hadn't strapped on his Colt yet. The coiled gunbelt and holster laid on the ground next to his bedroll. His Winchester leaned against the cottonwood log, nearby but not within fast reach. All he had in his hand was a cup of coffee.

He grimaced as the riders reined in and the cloud of dust raised by their horses' hooves drifted over the camp. "You fellas are in too big a hurry. You've got dust in our breakfast."

Since the sun was behind them, the riders were mostly in silhouette. Conrad could tell they were looking for trouble. They carried their rifles across the saddles in front of them. Since he couldn't very well shoot it out with them, he would have to rely on talk instead.

"Who're you two?" one of the men demanded in a rough voice.

"I could ask the same of you," Conrad said. "After all, this is our camp, and you're the visitors." His mouth tightened. "Or intruders might be a better word."

"Don't get smart with me, boy. I'm Sheriff Lucas Pevner, and I'm on the trail of three no-good bastards who robbed the bank in Stillwater."

The thought that they might be the posse mentioned by the outlaws a few hours earlier had been in the back of Conrad's mind. He turned and gestured casually with the tin cup in his hand toward the tall weeds.

"The men you're looking for are right over there, Sheriff."

Pevner moved his horse so he blocked out the rising sun. He was that big. Conrad could see the lawman's rough-hewn face, with a drooping white mustache.

"What in blazes are you talkin' about?" Pevner demanded. He turned his head. "Danny, check it out."

One of the posse members urged his horse forward. A brawny young man who wore a deputy's badge, he rode over to the weeds and reached down with his rifle, using the barrel to push some of the growth aside.

"Son of a— They're here, all right, Sheriff. Looks like all three of them."

"Dead?" Pevner asked like he couldn't believe it.

"Dead as they can be." Danny turned around with a disgusted look on his face. "The ants are gettin' to 'em."

Pevner took off the battered old Stetson he wore and scrubbed a big hand over his face. Then he clapped the hat back on his head and glared at Conrad. "What happened here?"

"They rode in a few hours ago and tried to steal our horses. We didn't let them."

"Didn't let 'em," the sheriff muttered. "Do you know who those hombres are? I mean, were?"

"One of them was called Kingston," Conrad said. "That's all I remember."

"Bully Kingston, they called him," Pevner said. "Killed at least four men that we know of. The other two were almost as bad. And you're claimin' a dude like you and this skinny drink of water shot it out with 'em and killed all three of 'em?"

"We didn't want them to take our horses," Conrad said.

Pevner blew out a sigh, causing his mustache to flutter. "All right, Danny," he said to his deputy, "you and some of the boys drag 'em out and wrap 'em up in blankets. We'll take them back to Stillwater with us."

"We might not want to do that, Sheriff," Danny said. "It's gonna be a mighty hot day, and like I said, the ants are already startin' to get to 'em . . ."

Pevner sighed again. "You're right. We'll plant the bastards right here." He looked around at the creek and its grassy, tree-lined banks. "It's a prettier place for eternal rest than the varmints deserve, that's for dang sure."

Conrad said, "We're obliged to you, Sheriff. Arturo and I were going to bury them, but you and your men can save us the trouble."

Pevner swung down from the saddle. With his size and lumbering movements, he reminded Conrad a little of a bear.

"Who are you, mister?" the lawman demanded.

"My name is Conrad Browning. This is my friend Arturo Vincenzo."

Pevner glanced at Arturo. "Foreigner, eh?" He turned back to Conrad. "What are you doin' out here, Browning?"

"We're on our way to Denver." He didn't volunteer any other information.

"You said Kingston and his men wanted to swap horses with you. What happened to their mounts?"

"They spooked and ran off when the shooting started. That's the last we saw of them. They probably didn't go very far. You can probably find them if you want to look."

Pevner nodded and looked over his shoulder. "Danny, see if they got the bank loot on 'em."

Conrad said, "I can save your deputy the trouble, Sheriff. I searched them already. The money they took from the bank must be on their horses, because they don't have it."

Pevner gave him a suspicious frown. "Is that so? It wouldn't be that you already found the loot and claimed it for yourself, would it?"

Conrad thought about being proddy but decided it wasn't worth the time and trouble. He waved a hand at the buckboard and said, "There's all our gear. You're welcome to go through it if you want. I can tell you right now, though, that you'll find some cash. That's our traveling fund."

"How much cash?"

"A couple thousand dollars."

Danny let out a surprised whistle. "Some travelin' fund."

"Kingston and them took eight thousand from the bank," Pevner said. "Maybe you done already stashed the rest of it and just kept out a couple grand."

Conrad couldn't keep the irritated edge out of his voice. "Why don't you send some of your men to look for those horses first, Sheriff, before you go around accusing somebody who's actually done you a favor?"

Pevner glared at him a moment longer before jerking his head in a curt nod. "All right. Did you see which way they went when they stampeded?"

"North." Conrad nodded his head in that direction.

"Phillips, Martin, Webster, go take a look and see if you can find them horses," the lawman ordered.

"While they're doing that, Arturo and I are going to have our breakfast." Conrad looked at the coffee in his cup and made a face at the skim of dust floating on its surface. "That is, if it's still fit to eat."

He didn't offer to share their food with the posse. He and Arturo were running a little low on supplies, and what they had would have to last until they reached Denver.

Besides, Pevner's attitude rubbed Conrad the wrong way. He could understand why Frank had told him that a lot of lawmen were full of themselves and hard to get along with.

A couple posse members had brought along shovels. It was a smart thing do when chasing outlaws. Chances were, somebody would usually need burying before the pursuit was over.

Pevner told his men to start digging. "Not too close to the creek," he added.

When Conrad and Arturo finished breakfast, Conrad started to hitch the team to the buckboard while Arturo cleaned up. Pevner came over to the vehicle, still glaring, and demanded, "Where the hell do you think you're goin'?"

"I told you. Denver."

Pevner shook his head. "Not yet, you ain't. Not until we account for that missin' bank money."

"You searched our belongings while we were eating," Conrad said. "You should be satisfied by now that we don't have it."

"You're stayin' right here until my boys get back with them horses. Then we'll just see what happens."

Conrad's jaw tightened. He expected the three men Pevner had sent to look for the outlaws' horses to be back soon. It was easier to wait for that than to argue, but it didn't mean he had to like it. "Fine. For the time being."

Pevner snorted.

Conrad walked over to his bedroll. He reached down toward the coiled gunbelt, intending to strap it on.

"Don't do that," the sheriff snapped. "Step away from that gun, Browning."

Conrad turned toward him, struggling to control his anger. Ignoring the warning look Arturo gave him, he began hotly, "Sheriff, you—"

"The fellas are comin' back," Danny broke in. "Looks like they got those horses with 'em."

It was true. The three posse members were riding in from the north, leading the three horses the outlaws had ridden in on the night before. As they came up, Conrad saw that the saddlebags on each animal appeared to be well stuffed.

Eagerly, Pevner opened one of the pouches and stuck his hand in it. He had a thick wad of bills clutched in his fingers when he brought them out. "Looks like the loot's here, all right," he said. "Danny, get it all out and count it." Pevner cast a hard glance toward Conrad. "If there's six grand, we'll know that somebody was lyin' to us and had already collected his share."

"You said three men robbed the bank, Sheriff," Conrad said. "There are three graves over there."

"Yeah, well, maybe you was the mastermind behind the whole thing, mister."

Conrad bit back the angry words that wanted to spring to his lips. It would all be over soon, he told himself.

It didn't take Danny long to count the money he pulled from the saddlebags. "Eight thousand, one hundred, and sixty-seven dollars," he announced a few minutes later. "I reckon that matches up with what Mr. Madison at the bank told us those fellas got away with, Sheriff."

Pevner nodded and sighed. "You're right, Danny." He turned and stuck out a big paw toward Conrad. "No offense, Browning. I reckon you're in the clear."

Conrad wasn't that eager to accept his implied

apology, but he shook hands anyway. He supposed the sheriff had only been doing his job.

"You'll finish burying them?" he asked.

Pevner nodded. "We sure will."

"Then Arturo and I will be on our way as soon as we can get ready to travel."

"That's fine. Headed for Denver, you say?"

"That's right."

"You ought to be there in another couple days." Pevner paused, then added, "Unless you run into somebody else who wants to shoot you."

"I wouldn't rule it out," Arturo said.

Chapter 4

No one tried to kill them, despite Arturo's veiled prediction, and they made better time than Pevner had said. It was late in the afternoon of the next day when they reached what folks had started to call the Mile High City.

The Front Range of the Rockies lay ten miles west of Denver, but because of the thin, clear air the mountains appeared to be close enough to reach out and touch.

"It's a spectacular sight," Arturo commented from the buckboard seat as he and Conrad entered the city.

"Denver's a pretty place, all right," Conrad agreed. He rode the blaze-faced black alongside the vehicle. "I want to go see my lawyers first. Their office is on Colfax Avenue, not far from the capitol."

"Do you have attorneys on retainer in all the large cities, sir?"

Conrad smiled. "Just about. It takes a lot of paperwork to keep all those business enterprises going, and I sure as hell don't want to have to do it."

He wore a black coat to go along with the black trousers and had a string tie cinched around his neck. Silver conchos studded the hatband of his black Stetson. He looked like a successful rancher, or possibly a gambler or gunman.

They passed the federal building, the state capitol, and the U.S. Mint. All of them were impressive structures. So was the six-story brick office building where Conrad's lawyers were headquartered.

Arturo parked the buckboard on the cobblestone street in front of the building. "I'll wait out here and keep an eye on our supplies, sir."

Conrad nodded. "That's a good idea. Denver's gotten to be a big enough town that you can't trust people like you can in a little settlement."

The building didn't have a hitch rail for saddle horses in front of it. Most people traveled around town in buggies or carriages these days. Conrad dismounted and looped the black's reins around the brake lever on the buckboard. That would work well enough.

He went inside, through a lobby with a brilliantly polished granite floor, and up a wide set of stairs with gilded banisters. Quite a few men were walking and talking in the lobby, all the while puffing on expensive cigars. Their footsteps and voices echoed from the high ceiling. The smell of rich tobacco smoke hung in the air.

On the second floor, Conrad came to a heavy wooden door with pebbled glass in its upper half. Painted on the glass in gold letters were the words HUDSON, BURKE, AND HARDY—ATTORNEYS AT LAW. He turned the gold-plated knob and stepped into an expensively appointed outer office with a gleaming wooden floor.

The woman behind the desk was putting a cover over her typewriter. She looked up at him and said, "I'm sorry, sir, but we're about to close for the day."

Conrad took his hat off and smiled. "It's I who should apologize for coming in so late, Miss . . . ?"

He noticed she wasn't wearing a wedding ring.

She hesitated but then supplied her name. "Sullivan."

"Miss Sullivan." Conrad didn't recognize her from his previous visits and knew she probably had been hired since the last time he was there. She was very attractive, probably about twenty-five, with honey-blond hair pulled up on top of her head.

Conrad went on, "I need to speak to Mr. Hudson if he's here, please."

Ellery Hudson was the senior partner in the firm and the one with whom Conrad had dealt most often.

"I'm afraid that's impossible without an appointment," Miss Sullivan said without addressing the question of whether or not Hudson was in the office. "If you'd care to make one, Mr. Hudson has some time available at the end of next week . . ."

Her voice trailed off as Conrad shook his head. "This is important," he said. "I need to speak to him right away. Tell him it's Conrad Browning."

Carefully plucked blond eyebrows rose in surprise. Obviously, Miss Sullivan recognized the name. She hesitated and then pressed a button on her desk.

"Yes, Rose?"

The woman's voice came out of a black box on Miss Sullivan's desk. Conrad looked at it with interest. He knew it had to be one of the new inter-office speaking devices he had heard about. They were based on the same sort of apparatus as a telephone and were being installed in some of the offices back east. He hadn't expected to see one in Denver.

But it would be a new century before too much longer, he reminded himself. Things changed. Progress, or what passed for progress, was inevitable.

Rose Sullivan leaned forward and spoke into the box. "There's a man out here who insists on seeing Mr. Hudson, Mrs. Moorehead. He says his name is Conrad Browning."

Conrad smiled again. That was a name he knew. Julia Moorehead was Ellery Hudson's private secretary.

"Ask him to wait right there," she said.

Miss Sullivan looked up at Conrad. "If you'd care to wait a moment . . ."

"I heard," he told her, still smiling. He hung his hat on a rack just inside the door but didn't have a chance to sit down in one of the padded leather chairs before the door to the firm's inner sanctum opened and Julia Moorehead came out.

She was a handsome, middle-aged woman who had been Hudson's private secretary for a number of years. A decade earlier, nearly all the secretaries and clerks in law offices and other businesses had been men, but that was something else that was changing with the times.

"Mr. Browning," Julia said as she held out a hand to Conrad. "It's so nice to see you again."

"You, too, Mrs. Moorehead." He took her hand for a moment. "Is Ellery here?"

"Yes, I told him you were here and he said to bring you right on back." Julia glanced at Miss Sullivan's desk and added, "You can go on home, Rose."

"I don't mind staying for a while. Someone might need something typed." Rose was looking at Conrad with frank interest now that she had seen the reaction his name provoked. Clearly, he had to be an important man, and important men often were wealthy.

Conrad recognized the look Rose gave him and didn't want to encourage it. He had been a widower long enough that he was no longer in mourning—at least not officially—but he had more important things on his mind than romance.

"That won't be necessary," Julia said. "I can type anything that needs to be typed."

"Oh. All right." Rose didn't bother to hide her disappointment, any more than she bothered to hide the invitation in her eyes when she looked at Conrad.

Julia closed the door behind them and led him along a corridor lined with doors. "I apologize for that, Mr. Browning," she said quietly. "Rose has something of a predatory nature."

"Don't worry about it."

She paused. "I was so sorry to hear about what happened. I don't believe I ever met your wife, but I'm sure she was a wonderful woman."

"She was."

"We were all very upset when we heard that you'd been killed, too. It was such a relief to find out later that that report was incorrect."

She didn't know how close he had come to letting Conrad Browning stay dead. But those days were over.

Julia opened a set of double doors at the end of the hall. "Here he is, sir." She stepped aside to let Conrad enter Ellery Hudson's private office.

It was the largest office on the floor, with cross ventilation and an excellent view of the snowcapped mountains from one of the windows. Ellery Hudson came out from behind a big desk with his hand extended.

He didn't look like one of the most prominent attorneys in the country. He was a short, somewhat pudgy man with wispy, fair hair. His eyes behind rimless spectacles were pale blue. His mild appearance concealed a keen legal mind and a nature that could be ruthless when called for.

"It's good to see you again, Conrad," he said as the two men shook hands. "I'm terribly, terribly sorry for your loss."

"Thank you, Ellery." Conrad sat down in the plush leather chair in front of the desk while Hudson resumed his seat behind it.

"I'll leave you gentlemen alone," Julia murmured.

Conrad lifted a hand to stop her. "No, please stay." He glanced at Hudson. "If that's all right with you, of course."

"Whatever you prefer. I certainly have no secrets from Julia. She knows more about what goes on around here than I do."

"And that's often a good thing," she said with a smile.

"Indeed." Hudson clasped his hands together on the desk in front of him. "What can we do for you, Conrad?"

"First of all"—he took a deep breath—"I have a story to tell you."

Julia sat in a chair to the side while Hudson leaned forward. The two of them listened intently as Conrad explained everything that had happened during the past two years, starting with Rebel's kidnapping and murder. Julia put her hand over her mouth to stifle a gasp of horror several times as he filled them in.

When he reached the part about the twins and how Pamela had concealed their very existence from him, both of his listeners looked shocked and then angry. Conrad told them about his search for the children so far.

When he was finished, Julia said, "How could any woman use her own children as pawns in such a warped attempt at vengeance? I can't believe it!"

"Obviously, Pamela was capable of almost anything," Conrad said. "Warped though it certainly is, Pamela's plan has been effective. She intended to torment me . . . and she's succeeded."

Hudson said, "And now your search has brought you to Denver. How can we help you, Conrad?"

"My hunch is that Pamela probably stayed either in

one of the best hotels in town, or with friends. I need to find someone who remembers when she was here, and whether or not she had the children with her."

"Because if she didn't . . . ?"

"Then I've come too far and overlooked the place where she left them. But if the twins were still with her, the hiding place is either here in Denver or somewhere farther west. She was booked through all the way to San Francisco on the train."

Hudson nodded. "Yes, that makes sense. We have operatives who can investigate for us. It shouldn't take long to blanket all the best hotels in the city and find out what you need to know. A few days, perhaps."

"That's what I was hoping you'd say, Ellery." Conrad smiled. "I knew I could count on you."

"We'll do everything we can," Hudson promised. "Discreetly, of course. That goes without saying."

"Of course."

"In the meantime, what are your plans?"

Conrad shrugged. "I don't have any. Arturo and I have been on the trail for quite a while. I suppose we'll find a place to stay and rest while your men conduct their investigation."

"I'll telephone the Lansing House and have them reserve their best suite for you."

"That'll be fine. I'm obliged to you."

"Conrad . . ." Hudson hesitated. "Have you thought about what you're going to do when you find the children, as I'm sure you will?"

Conrad frowned. "What do you mean? They're my children. I'll take them and make a home for them somewhere. I've been drifting for a while, but then it'll be time to settle down."

"What if Miss Tarleton gave them to some family to adopt?"

Conrad's frown deepened. "You mean . . ."

"I mean those people may have been raising the twins as their own for the past three years. They may not want to give them up."

Conrad sat forward in the chair. "But they're *my* children."

"You might have to prove that. You might even have to go to court to claim them."

"How can anybody prove such a thing?" Conrad flung out a hand in irritation. "And who would go to court over it?"

"You never know. I'm just trying to make you aware of the possibilities."

Conrad sighed as his anger left him. "You're right. And I appreciate your concern, Ellery. Right now, though, all I can think of is trying to find them."

"I understand. When the time comes to deal with that, you'll have plenty of people on your side to help you."

They stood up, and Conrad shook hands again with Hudson. As he turned to go, Julia Moorehead took his hand as well and said, "I hope you find them, Mr. Browning. I'm sure you will."

"Thank you."

Rose Sullivan was gone from the outer office when he went back through it on his way out of the building. Just as well, because his mind was whirling and he didn't need any added distractions. He had been concentrating so much on locating the children that he hadn't given much thought to what would happen after he found them. Hudson was right; it might not be as simple as he wished it could be.

But a few more added problems wouldn't make him give up. Not by a long shot. He would figure out what needed to be done and—

"Mr. Browning." The voice intruded on his thoughts. "There you are."

He looked into the smiling, eager face of Rose Sullivan.

Chapter 5

Conrad nodded and touched a finger to the brim of his hat. "Hello again, Miss Sullivan."

She wore a gray jacket that matched her skirt over her starched white blouse. A white scarf was tied around her hair. She looked trim and pretty, but Conrad wasn't in the mood for female company at the moment.

"Did you finish your business with Mr. Hudson?" she asked.

"Yes, I did."

"I hope he was helpful."

"Very," Conrad said.

"He can be an old grump sometimes, but he's an excellent lawyer. You won't find any better in Denver."

Conrad chuckled in spite of himself. "I'm aware of that. I've known Ellery for quite a while."

"I'm sorry, I know I should recognize your name, and it certainly sounds familiar, but I haven't really been working at Hudson, Burke, and Hardy for that long, and—"

Conrad held up a hand to stop the flow of words tumbling from her mouth. "That's quite all right, Miss Sullivan."

"Why don't you call me Rose?"

Conrad ignored that request and tugged on his hatbrim as he said, "I really have to be going now."

She put out a hand, resting it on his forearm. "If there's ever anything *I* can do to be of service to you, I hope you won't hesitate to let me know, Mr. Browning. I try to keep up with everything that goes on at Hudson, Burke, and Hardy, you know. Anything you tell me will be held in the strictest confidence."

"I'll remember that." He hoped she wasn't going to force him to be rude to get away from her.

"I'm sure we'll be seeing each other again."

He nodded. "I'm sure." He would have to visit Hudson's office again while he was in Denver, maybe quite a few times, so it wouldn't hurt to stay on friendly terms with the determined young woman who worked there.

And she was certainly pleasing to look at, if nothing else.

When he started across the sidewalk toward the buckboard, she let him go with a smile and a flutter of her fingers. "Good afternoon, Mr. Browning," she called after him.

Conrad returned the smile and waved at her.

When he reached the buckboard, Arturo asked from the seat, "Who was *that*?"

"A young woman who works in Ellery Hudson's

office. Hudson's going to lend us a hand in our search. He's also made arrangements for us to have a suite at the Lansing House." Conrad untied the black's reins and swung up into the saddle. "I know where it is. Follow me."

The Lansing House was a small but extremely elegant—and expensive—hotel in downtown Denver, not far from the famous Tabor Grand Opera House built by the tycoon Horace Tabor to impress his wife Elizabeth, better known as Baby Doe. Wealthy businessmen who valued privacy and discretion often stayed at the Lansing when they were visiting Denver, and more than one million-dollar deal had been arranged in the hushed confines of its comfortably appointed salon.

Service at the Lansing was excellent as well. Conrad told Arturo to park the buckboard in front of the hotel and leave it there, along with their bags and supplies. "Everything will be brought in and taken up to the suite," he assured Arturo, who looked dubious. "There's a livery stable in the next block that will take charge of the horses."

"If you say so, sir."

They went inside, where a doorman wearing a uniform as fancy as that of a Prussian archduke met them and ushered them through the lobby to the desk. Conrad had stayed there a few times before, and the doorman remembered him, calling him by name.

So did the clerk, who said, "No need for you to check in, Mr. Browning. Mr. Hudson called and said that you were to have the suite we keep reserved for his firm's clients."

"Thanks. This is my friend and business associate, Mr. Vincenzo."

The clerk nodded. "It's a pleasure to meet you, Mr. Vincenzo. If there's anything we can do to make your stay in Denver more pleasant, please let us know."

"Of course," Arturo said. "Thank you."

A bellboy rode the elevator with them up to the third floor and showed them to the suite, which had two bedrooms, a luxurious sitting room, and indoor plumbing. When the bellboy was gone, Arturo said to Conrad, "You didn't tell them I was your servant."

Conrad shrugged and tossed his hat onto a desk. "Didn't seem to be any need to. We're partners, Arturo. We've been through too much together to worry about such things."

"I see." Arturo frowned. "Does this mean you're no longer going to pay me?"

Conrad threw back his head and laughed. "No, that's not what it means. I'm just not going to worry about a bunch of meaningless protocol and phony manners."

Arturo regarded him for a long moment and then nodded slowly. "You're very different from Count Fortunato, sir."

"I should hope so. Nobility or not, Fortunato was a crazy, evil son of a bitch."

"You'll get no argument from me, sir."

* * *

Conrad changed into a brown tweed suit, also donning a silk cravat and a diamond stickpin before they went back downstairs to have supper. The food in the dining room of the Lansing House was as good as any to be found east of San Francisco, and Conrad enjoyed the dinner they ate that evening. After the meal, he lingered over a snifter of brandy.

"Do you have any plans for this evening?" he asked Arturo.

"Plans?" Arturo blinked in surprise. "Why would I have any plans? I've never been here before."

"Well, I have. Come on. I'll show you some of Denver's night life."

"Are you sure that's a wise idea, sir?"

Conrad drained the last of the brandy. "We don't have anything else to do while we wait for Ellery to carry out his investigation. Denver's too big for us to wander around the town asking folks at random if they remember seeing Pamela and the twins."

"You have a point there," Arturo admitted. "Where are we going?"

"A place called the Palace."

"This so-called Palace isn't a house of ill repute, is it?"

Conrad chuckled. "Hardly."

They left the hotel and walked a few blocks northeast to the corner of Blake and Fifteenth Streets, where an imposing two-story brick building sat, taking up almost the entire block. A big sign on the front of the building proclaimed it to be the Palace Variety Theatre and Gambling Parlor. More signs plastered up around the entrance announced that famous vaudevillian Eddie Foy was scheduled to perform there the next week.

"If we're still here, maybe we can take in the show." Conrad pointed at the signs with a thumb. "Tonight we'll just pay a visit to the gambling parlor."

"I've never been very fond of gambling," Arturo said.

"You don't have to bet on anything. I used to enjoy it, but somehow it doesn't seem quite as exciting anymore."

Losing what he had lost, and then living a life where it seemed he was constantly wagering his life instead of money he would never miss, certainly had changed him, Conrad mused as he and Arturo went inside and up a broad set of marble stairs to the big gambling room on the second floor.

Despite that, he felt his pulse quicken a little as familiar sounds engulfed him: cards slapping down on green felt, the click of a roulette ball as the wheel whirred and spun, the clink of bottles on fine crystal, the laughter of women, the hearty talk of men. In his younger days, Conrad had spent a lot of time in places just like that, including the Palace. Those memories were still part of him.

A huge gas chandelier hung from the ceiling in the center of the room and cast its light through hundreds of glass prisms over the various tables and gambling layouts. A long mahogany bar polished to a high sheen ran along one wall. Waitresses in elegant, low-cut gowns delivered drinks to the players engaged in the games. The room was crowded, and everyone seemed to be having a fine time.

"Let's get a drink," Conrad suggested with a nod toward the bar with its gleaming brass footrail.

"If you say so, sir," Arturo agreed.

"Forget that 'sir' business. Tonight we're just a couple of pards out on the town."

Arturo cocked an eyebrow as if he found that a very unlikely proposition, but he didn't argue.

They hadn't reached the bar when a man stepped in front of them to stop them. His waist was thickening and his hair was thinning with middle age, but he was still a solidly built, impressive individual. A dark brown mustache curled on his upper lip. He had a cigar clamped between his teeth, but he removed it to say, "Conrad? Conrad Browning? Is that you?"

Conrad grinned with the pleasure of recognizing an old friend. "Hello, Bat," he said as he extended his hand.

Bat Masterson gripped Conrad's hand. "Good to see you again, son. I heard you were dead."

"Not hardly."

"How's your pa? I mean, your father."

"Frank was fine, the last I heard from him. He's still drifting, so we don't see each other very often."

Masterson nodded. "Frank Morgan never could stay in one place for very long. We were alike in that respect, only he's even more fiddle-footed than I am. Did he ever tell you about the time he helped me track down some killers while I was still packing a badge in Kansas?"

"No, I don't think I've heard that story."

Masterson clapped a hand on his shoulder. "I'll tell you sometime. It's quite a yarn." He smiled at Arturo. "Who's your friend?"

"Arturo Vincenzo," Conrad said. "Arturo, meet Bat Masterson."

"The famous lawman?" Arturo asked.

"Retired," Masterson said as his smile widened into a grin. He shook hands with Arturo. "Pleased to meet you, Mr. Vincenzo. You don't sound Italian, if you don't mind my saying so."

"I was educated in England, among other places."

"Ah, a citizen of the world! Good man. Come on, you two, let's have a drink."

"That's where we were headed," Conrad said. As the three men walked toward the bar, he waved a hand to indicate their surroundings and asked, "Do you still own this place, Bat?"

Masterson shook his head. "No, no, I sold it several years ago. Got tired of arguing with the city fathers who seemed to believe it's some sort of den of iniquity. I moved down to Creede for a while and just came back to Denver a couple years ago. I was a little surprised to see the place still operating, but I come here when I can. Old times' sake, you know."

"I'll bet it's still a good place to find a high stakes game."

"The best." Masterson frowned in thought. "In fact, there's a game coming up that might interest you. As I recall, you like to play some cards now and then."

Although Conrad was aware of Masterson's reputation as a buffalo hunter, lawman, and gun handler, he knew the man primarily as the owner of various gambling halls, including at one time the Palace in Denver.

With a shake of his head, Conrad said, "I didn't come here to gamble, Bat. Things have changed."

"Yeah, I heard you've had some bad luck. Some mighty bad luck. I'm sorry, son."

Conrad nodded. "I'm obliged for that."

They had reached the bar. Masterson said, "Well, if you change your mind, let me know. The buy-in to this game I'm talking about is pretty steep, but I'm sure you can afford it."

Masterson signaled the bartender and ordered three cognacs for them. The drinks had just come and Conrad was picking up his snifter when someone jostled him heavily from behind. About half the cognac splashed across the bar.

Instinct made Conrad swing around angrily. He was about to tell the man who had bumped into him to be more careful, when he saw a gun barrel rising toward his face and heard the unmistakable metallic ratcheting of the weapon's hammer being drawn back.

Chapter 6

Gasps sounded around the bar as Conrad's left hand flashed up and closed around the gun barrel. He wrenched upward on it at the same time his right fist smashed into the face of the man who was trying to shoot him. The gun went off with a deafening roar that echoed through the room and left a stunned silence in its wake.

The man's head rocked back from the force of Conrad's punch, but he didn't go down or let go of the gun. Bellowing in rage, he bulled forward, ramming his shoulder into Conrad's chest and driving him against the bar. A wave of pain went through him as he was bent backward.

The man was big enough and strong enough to snap Conrad's spine unless he did something in a hurry. Keeping his grip on the gun barrel, he slashed the side of his other hand into the man's throat.

That did the trick. The man let go of the gun and staggered backward, gagging and clutching at his neck as he struggled to breathe. He wore a black

Stetson and black Western-cut suit, and his deeply tanned face was rough-hewn under graying hair.

Several men wearing range clothes surged forward from the crowd, probably friends of the man who had attacked Conrad. The situation might have gotten uglier if Bat Masterson hadn't stepped in just then.

With a pistol held rock-steady in his hand, in the loud, commanding voice that had helped bring law and order to numerous frontier towns, Masterson said, "That's far enough, gents. Rance got himself into this trouble. It's his lookout, not yours."

"Damn it, Bat, he's our boss," one of the men objected. "We've got to back his play."

"Come ahead, if it's worth a bullet to you."

The games had all come to an abrupt halt. Every eye in the place was on the confrontation at the bar.

The man who had started the trouble was still rubbing his neck, but had caught his breath and was able to talk. In a pained rasp, he said, "Back off, boys. You don't want to go up against Masterson."

"He can't kill us all, boss," one of the men said.

Masterson smiled. "Are you willing to bet your own life on that, friend?"

"Damn it, I told you to take it easy," the man called Rance said. "Get on out of here. We'll find some friendlier place to drink and play some cards."

"You're the one who tried to shoot me, mister," Conrad pointed out. "If anybody made this place unfriendly, it was you."

"I wasn't gonna shoot you," Rance said in a surly voice. "Just teach you to have a mite of respect for your elders—and betters."

Conrad smiled coldly. "You're older than me, anyway." He was still holding Rance's gun by the barrel. Flipping it around, he caught it easily by the butt, and opened the cylinder. He tilted the gun up and turned the cylinder so the bullets slid out and fell to the floor, clattering as they landed.

Rance's face darkened with anger, but he held his temper.

Conrad put the empty gun on the bar and kicked the shells away.

"Why don't you come back and get your gun later, Rance?" Masterson suggested. "They'll hold it for you here."

"Fine," Rance said bitterly. "I'm no shootist like you, Masterson. Never claimed to be. But there'll come a day when somebody takes you down a notch." He glared at Conrad. "You and this fancy-pants kid both."

With that, Rance turned around and stalked out of the Palace's gambling room. His men had pulled back a little but hadn't left. They followed him down the stairs, but not without casting some mighty hostile glares toward Conrad and Masterson first.

Masterson didn't lower his gun until they were all gone and a buzz of sound had begun to grow in the room again. Then he reached behind his back and slid the pistol into a holster he wore under the tails of his coat. "That was a near thing. Rance McKinney isn't a good man to cross, and his men are almost as loco as he is. Or can be. He's not always quite so proddy."

"Friend of yours?" Conrad asked.

Masterson grunted and shook his head. "Not so's you'd notice, but we're civil enough to play a little poker together from time to time. Rance fancies himself pretty good at it."

"Is he?"

Masterson shrugged. "That depends on who he's playing against."

"What was the idea of pulling a gun on me? He's the one who ran into me and spilled my drink."

"He's a high-handed son of a gun. He probably meant it when he said he was going to teach you a lesson. Just turning around to challenge him when he bumped into you like he did was enough to set him off."

Conrad shook his head. "He's lucky somebody hasn't shot him before now."

"Rance owns one of the biggest spreads in Colorado, and he's always got that crew of curly wolves with him. People tend to step well away from him when he comes around."

"I don't remember him from the last time I was here."

"He moved into the area about five years ago. Bought the old Double Star ranch from Milt Tompkins and started gobbling up all the range around it."

Conrad shook his head. Five years earlier, he hadn't had much interest in ranching, so he didn't remember the spread Masterson mentioned. It didn't matter. McKinney was gone, and Conrad didn't intend to have anything more to do with him.

He turned back to the bar and found that the bartender had mopped up the spilled cognac and replaced the drink with a fresh one. "Thanks." He nodded to the man. "I'm sorry about the disturbance."

"It wasn't your fault, sir." The bartender smiled. "Anyway, it doesn't take long for things to get back to normal in here."

That was true. The mood in the Palace was as jovial and high-spirited as it had been when Conrad and Arturo went in a short time earlier. No blood had been spilled, so the patrons had gone back to having fun.

Conrad sipped his cognac and looked at Arturo. "What do you think of the place?"

"I think that wherever you go, trouble seems to follow you there," Arturo said bluntly.

That made Bat Masterson laugh. "Yeah, he really is a chip off the old block!"

Despite Arturo's comment, no more trouble broke out while they were at the Palace. Conrad enjoyed catching up on old times with Masterson, and as they left later, Masterson said, "If you change your mind about that high-stakes game, let me know. You can find me in here or one of the other usual places."

The next day, Conrad paid another visit to Ellery Hudson's office. He knew it was probably much too early to expect any results from Hudson's investigation, but he couldn't sit around the suite at the Lansing House doing nothing.

Rose Sullivan smiled brightly as Conrad came into the outer office. The place was busy. The door behind Rose's desk was open, so he could look along the hall and see lawyers and clerks passing back and forth as they went about their work.

"Hello, Mr. Browning," Rose said. "Mr. Hudson told me to tell you—if you came in—that he's in the law library."

"He wants to see me?" Conrad was a little surprised.

"I think so." Rose got to her feet. She wore a pale blue blouse over a black skirt and looked as lovely as she had the day before. Her blue eyes were just as bold, too. "I'll show you."

Conrad thought he remembered where Hudson, Burke, and Hardy's law library was, so he started to say, "I can find it—"

"No, I wouldn't hear of it. I'll escort you, so you won't get lost." She came around the desk and took his arm.

He was too much of a gentleman to pull away from her, letting her link arms and steer him back out the pebbled glass door into the outer corridor. He was sure it was no coincidence that the soft warmth of her breast pressed against his arm as they walked around a corner to another door. It had pebbled glass in the upper half, too, but no writing on it.

Rose opened the door and led him into a hallway. A door off that hall led into the vast, high-ceilinged law library. The smell of fine paper and rich leather bindings would have been pretty heady stuff to a bibliophile, Conrad thought.

Ellery Hudson stood in front of one of the tall bookcases that lined the walls. He had just slid a thick volume back into place and was reaching for another one when Conrad and Rose went in. He looked over his shoulder and said, "Ah, there you are, Conrad. I was going to telephone you at the Lansing if you didn't come in." He nodded to Rose. "Thank you, Miss Sullivan. That'll be all."

She let go of Conrad's arm with obvious reluctance. "If you need anything else, Mr. Browning, don't hesitate to let me know." She lingered as long as she could without annoying Hudson.

When she was gone and the door had closed behind her, the lawyer chuckled. "I'm sorry, Conrad. Our Miss Sullivan appears to be something of a fortune hunter. I didn't know that about her. She's dealt with many well-to-do clients before without acting like that. But perhaps not many who have youth and good looks to go along with their money."

"I'm not here to talk about my money or good looks," Conrad said with a wry smile. "I was just curious to know if you'd found out anything yet."

"Not really. However, I mentioned to Violet that you were in town, and she suggested that you come to dinner at our house tonight."

Violet was Hudson's wife. Conrad had met her a few times and thought she was a nice enough woman, but he didn't relish the idea of spending the evening with the Hudsons.

"Ellery, I don't know—"

"Of course, when I say dinner, I may be understating the case a bit. There'll be fifty or sixty people there."

The idea of attending a party at the Hudson mansion was even less appealing. Back in Boston, Conrad had ventured into the high society circles he used to frequent, but that had been to help him find out more information about Pamela and her activities.

Of course, the same tactic might work there, he realized. Pamela had friends in Denver from the time of her engagement to him, and she might have visited some of them when she came through the Mile High City three years earlier. Conrad hadn't considered that possibility before.

Hudson went on, "I thought that someone who's there might be able to tell us something about Pamela."

Conrad smiled. "Great minds work alike, as the old saying goes, Ellery. The same thought just occurred to me."

"So you'll come?"

"I will. What time?"

"Eight o'clock. I'll send a buggy for you." Hudson frowned. "There's just one thing. Violet won't like it if there's an odd number of guests. We'll have to come up with someone to accompany you."

"And by someone you mean a lady?"

"Of course. Violet's a great one for pairing everyone up. The problem is, I can't think of anyone who'd really be suitable right now."

Conrad smiled. "Maybe I can."

Chapter 7

"You want me to go with you to a dinner party at Mr. Hudson's house?" Rose Sullivan asked with a surprised but happy smile on her face.

Hudson cleared his throat as he stood in front of Rose's desk with Conrad. "This was Mr. Browning's idea, not mine," he said, as if he wanted to be on record about that.

"I think it'll be fine, Ellery," Conrad said. "Will any of your guests actually know Rose that well?"

"I'm sure some of them have seen her here in the office. . . ." Hudson shrugged. "But if she wore her hair down, say, and was in an evening gown rather than business attire . . . we could tell people that she's Violet's niece or cousin, something like that, visiting from back east."

A frown replaced Rose's smile. "You want me to pretend to be somebody I'm not?"

"Just for this evening," Conrad said. "And it would be very helpful to me."

"Well . . . is this part of my work, Mr. Hudson?"

"Of course I can't order you to do it," Hudson said quickly. "But it would be a favor to us, and Mr. Browning and I would appreciate it."

"Then certainly I'll do it." Rose got to her feet. "And I won't disappoint you, Mr. Browning." A worried look suddenly came over her face. "But I don't have a gown that would be all right for something like that."

"Julia can help you," Hudson said. "The two of you can go out and buy whatever you need. Have the bills sent here to the firm."

"That would be wonderful." Rose smiled again. "I'll go tell Mrs. Moorehead right now."

As she bustled down the hall, Hudson looked over at Conrad. "Are you sure about this?"

"It'll be fine, Ellery," Conrad assured him. "And it'll be an evening Rose never forgets."

Hudson grunted, as if that might not be such a good thing.

Conrad went back to the Lansing House and told Arturo about the plan. "I'll see to it that your best suit is cleaned and pressed, sir. And if I may be so bold, perhaps you should pay a visit to the barber."

"Getting a little shaggy, am I?" Conrad laughed. "All right. I'll do that."

Conrad spent the rest of the day getting ready for the dinner party. In his mind, he went over the people he knew who were important figures in Denver's society circles, trying to remember if any of them had been particularly close to Pamela. He thought of several people he definitely wanted to talk to that evening. Even if they weren't close,

Pamela might have gotten in touch with them when she passed through Denver three years earlier.

By the time the buggy picked him up at the hotel shortly before eight o'clock that evening, he didn't look anything at all like Kid Morgan anymore. Elegantly dressed, carefully barbered, smelling a little of bay rum, he carried himself with the casual arrogance of the very wealthy. The people he would be seeing at the party would expect that of him.

But in the back of his mind, he unexpectedly found himself thinking that he would have been happier in some lonely trail camp far from civilization, drinking Arbuckle's and eating bacon and beans next to a campfire. He couldn't help but wonder if The Kid was now the real person, and Conrad Browning only a pose.

He put that thought out of his head. Conrad Browning was the father of those two children, so Conrad Browning he would be.

The buggy's driver was a burly, middle-aged black man. "Good evening, Mr. Browning."

"Good evening. We'll need to pick up Miss Sullivan——" Conrad stopped short. "Blast it. I don't know where she lives."

The driver smiled. "Mr. Hudson provided me with her address, sir. That's where we're going next."

"Excellent." Conrad nodded. "Ellery usually thinks of everything. I suppose that's what makes him such a good lawyer."

"Yes, sir."

The driver sent the buggy rolling over Denver's

cobblestone streets and pulled up a short time later in front of a boarding house.

"Is this it?" Conrad asked.

"Yes, sir. Miss Sullivan should be ready. Would you like me to fetch her?"

Conrad stepped down from the buggy. "No, I'll get her. I'm her escort for the evening, after all."

He went up the walk to the boarding house's porch. The building was a gabled, three-story Victorian and appeared to be fairly new. It even had a bell-push next to the front door, instead of a knocker. Modern progress was everywhere in Denver.

A middle-aged woman answered the door. She smiled at Conrad and said, "Oh, my goodness. You must be Mr. Browning. Rose has told me all about you." She stepped back. "Please, come in. I'm Mrs. Sherman, her landlady."

As Conrad went into the foyer, he took off the soft black hat he was wearing. "I'm very pleased to meet you. Is Rose ready?"

"I'm sure she is. I'll just go and let her know you're here."

Mrs. Sherman started toward the stairs, but before she could get there, Rose appeared at the second-floor landing. She started down the stairs, being careful in her descent.

The long-sleeved, dark blue gown hugged Rose's body closely enough to show it off to her advantage, and the square-cut neckline was low enough to reveal the start of the valley between her breasts. The glittering necklace she wore drew even more attention to that area. Fine white lace at the cuffs and neckline of the gown set off the dark blue color of the material. Her honey-blond hair hung down around her shoulders with an attractive wave now that it wasn't pulled up on her head in a more conservative arrangement.

Conrad waited at the bottom of the stairs for her, and as she reached them, he held out a hand to her. As she took it, he said, "You look lovely, Miss Sullivan."

She blushed prettily. "Under the circumstances, shouldn't you call me Rose, Mr. Browning?"

"All right," he said with a smile. "And I'm Conrad."

"Of course . . . Conrad."

Her voice was a little husky as she said his name. He felt himself reacting to her. He was only human, after all.

But he was also engaged in important business, and Rose had a part to play in that business. "Shall we go?"

"Certainly. Just let me get my shawl."

Mrs. Sherman stepped forward holding a lace shawl. "It's right here, Rose. My, don't you and your gentleman friend look fine tonight, just fine!"

Conrad didn't bother correcting the landlady about him being Rose's "gentleman friend." He didn't know what she might have told Mrs. Sherman about what was happening, and it didn't really matter. As long as Rose did her job and gave him a chance to find out what he wanted to know, that was all he cared about.

With Mrs. Sherman beaming and clasping her hands together in front of her, Conrad and Rose left the boarding house and walked out to the buggy. He linked his arm with hers as he did so. Might as well get used to acting like they were a real couple, he told himself.

The driver didn't waste any time getting the buggy rolling briskly through the streets, and it wasn't long before they pulled up in front of the mansion that belonged to Ellery and Violet Hudson. It was similar to the boarding house where Rose lived, but it was built on a much larger and grander scale. If it had been daylight, Conrad might have been able to count all the gables, but he probably wouldn't have bothered. A flagstone driveway led through a large lawn dotted with shrubs, flower beds, and trees, and the brightly lit house made a pretty picture as the buggy approached.

A number of other buggies and even some old-fashioned carriages were parked in front of the house, where the drive made a circle around a big flower bed. Guests were climbing out of some of those vehicles.

When the driver brought the buggy to a halt, a liveried butler was there to help Conrad and Rose get out. Conrad hopped lithely from the buggy and motioned the man away, then turned back to take Rose's hand. She smiled in appreciation of his gallantry.

Another servant was at the door to greet them and take Rose's shawl, which he turned over to a maid. The man led the two of them into a large, luxuriously appointed room where people with drink in their hands were mingling. Laughter and talk filled the air, just like it would have in a saloon, but it was a much more subdued sound.

Once again Conrad was struck by how strange it all seemed to him. At one time in his life, he had spent many of his evenings in settings just like that one. It seemed like an entire lifetime ago, as if someone else besides him had lived through those experiences and somehow the memories had intruded into his brain.

"Conrad, there you are!" Ellery Hudson emerged from the crowd to shake his hand. Then he turned to Rose, put his hands on her shoulders, and leaned forward to kiss her cheek. "And Rose, you're looking as lovely as ever."

She looked shocked, until Conrad leaned close to her and whispered, "You're supposed to be a member of the family, remember?"

Rose smiled brightly, gave Hudson a hug, and said, "Ellery, darling. How are you? How's Violet?"

"Anxious to see you," Hudson said as he slipped out of her embrace. "She's right over there." He pointed to an attractive brunette in a green gown. "Why don't you go say hello to your cousin, dear? I'll join you in a moment."

"Of course," Rose murmured.

As she moved through the crowd, smiling and gracious, Hudson said quietly to Conrad, "Quite a little actress, isn't she?"

"She is," Conrad agreed.

"I've been talking to people about you," Hudson went on. "You know how this crowd likes to gossip. Whenever I brought up your name and said that you were going to be here tonight, nearly everyone brought up the tragedy that befell you, if I may speak frankly."

"Please do," Conrad said with a nod.

"Everyone's very glad that it turned out you weren't killed after all."

Conrad smiled tightly. "That's good to know."

"A few people brought up Pamela as well. They remember when the two of you were engaged."

"Do any of them remember her being here three years ago?" Conrad asked. His heart began to beat a little faster as he waited for Hudson's answer.

"Actually, one man did remember her paying a visit to Denver about the time we're interested in." Hudson put a hand on Conrad's arm. "But brace yourself, Conrad. He didn't know anything about the children."

Conrad felt a surge of disappointment. He swallowed it and told himself that was just the beginning. Whoever the man was, he might know more than he realized, especially if he had spent any time with Pamela while she was there. "Who is it? I want to talk to him."

"That's the odd thing about it . . . I don't believe you even know him. He didn't live in this area when you and Pamela were engaged. He became acquainted with her when she was here the last time. I'll introduce you."

Hudson guided Conrad through the crowd. As they approached a knot of men standing in front of a huge fireplace that wasn't lit at that time of year, he heard loud laughter coming from them, evidently prompted by something one of the men had said. That man stood with his back to Conrad, his broad shoulders seeming to stretch the expensive fabric of his coat.

"Excuse me," Hudson said as he and Conrad stepped up to the group. "Conrad, I'd like for you to meet Ransom McKinney—"

The big man swung around in response to the lawyer's voice. Conrad recognized him instantly.

The man was the son of a bitch who had attacked Conrad in the Palace gambling room the night before.

Chapter 8

The smile on McKinney's face disappeared. An angry scowl replaced it as his fingers tightened on the glass he held. "You! What are you doing here?" He looked like he was ready to throw the glass into Conrad's face.

Conrad was ready to move fast if McKinney tried anything.

Hudson frowned. "Is something wrong here?"

"Damn right there's something wrong," McKinney said into the uncomfortable silence that had fallen. "Judging by the fact that this hombre's here, you need to start inviting a better class of guests to these little get-togethers of yours."

Hudson began to look angry. "Now see here, I don't care how much money you have, Ransom, you can't—"

Conrad put a hand on the lawyer's shoulder to stop him. "Don't worry about it, Ellery. He's just blustering, like an old bull pawing the dirt."

McKinney said, "An old bull who can trample you into that dirt, you little——"

"That's enough," Hudson cut in. "Enough, do you hear me? I won't stand for this. If you want to continue as my client, Ransom, you'll apologize to my friend. You may not know it, but this is Conrad Browning."

Clearly, McKinney was enough of a businessman for the name to mean something to him. His shaggy gray eyebrows went up in surprise for a moment, then his eyes narrowed. "*You're* Conrad Browning?"

"That's right," Conrad replied coolly.

"Then maybe both of us jumped the gun a mite." McKinney shifted his drink from his right to his left and extended the right. "Sorry, Browning. For the trouble last night and for anything I said here tonight."

"You two have met?" Hudson asked.

"That's right." McKinney chuckled. "He's the one who gave me this bruise." He motioned with the hand holding the drink to a small purple mark on his face.

McKinney's right hand was still held out. Conrad took it. "Apology accepted, McKinney." He didn't think the rancher's words were sincere and still didn't trust him, but didn't want to continue the scene in Ellery Hudson's house.

Hudson heaved a sigh of relief. "For a moment there, I thought we were going to have fisticuffs."

"Or a gunfight." McKinney chuckled.

With an owlish look of surprise, Hudson said, "Ransom, you're not *armed*, are you?"

"Damn right I am," McKinney answered. "I never go anywhere without packing iron. I learned that lesson a long time ago." He pulled back his coat to reveal the gleaming ivory handle of a small revolver resting in a shoulder holster under his arm.

"How about you, Browning?" McKinney asked.

"I came to eat dinner, not trade shots with anybody," Conrad replied . . . which didn't really answer the question.

In fact, he had a short-barreled .32 tucked into a holster under his coat at the small of his back, the same sort of rig Bat Masterson had been wearing in the Palace the night before. Conrad had been carrying the .32 then, as well, but he hadn't needed it since Masterson was there.

"Let's all settle down," Hudson suggested. "I'm glad this was just a misunderstanding."

The room was big enough that some of the guests hadn't even been aware of the confrontation. Those who were had gone back to their socializing.

Hudson went on, "Ransom, could we talk to you for a moment?"

"You mean you and Browning?" McKinney shrugged. "I don't see why not."

The three of them headed for a quiet corner. Hudson said, "Ransom, do you remember when I was asking you earlier about a woman named Pamela Tarleton?"

"Sure I do." McKinney tossed back his drink and grinned. "She's a little spitfire, that one. Mighty good looker, too. I wonder if she'll come back to Denver one of these days."

"That's very unlikely," Conrad said. "She's dead."

McKinney's fingers closed so tightly on the glass Conrad was sure it would shatter. Breathing harshly and obviously upset, McKinney said, "What do you mean, she's dead?"

"She was killed about a year and a half ago. It was an accident." Conrad didn't mention that she had been trying to kill him at the time.

"That doesn't hardly seem possible," McKinney muttered. "She was so full of life when she was here . . ." He stared down into his empty glass for a moment like he was remembering, then lifted his eyes to Conrad. "How did you know her?"

"I was engaged to her at one time."

"Really?" McKinney shook his head. "She didn't mention anything about that. Hell, I'm sorry for your loss, Browning. I didn't know anything about it."

He still didn't, Conrad thought. Pamela's death hadn't been a loss for him. It had been justice of a sort . . . an unsatisfying sort, because Rebel was still gone.

And so were his children, although he had known nothing about them at the time. Putting his mind back on the matter at hand, he said, "That's all right. How did the two of you meet?"

"I saw her in a restaurant here in town one night, having dinner by herself. She looked lonely, so I went over and asked her if she'd like some company. I could tell by looking at her that she was a mighty fine lady. I'm just an old cattleman with a lot of the bark still on me, but I've never been one to sit back

and wait when I see something worth going after."
McKinney paused. "No offense."

"None taken. We weren't engaged at the time.
What happened?"

"Well, the two of us hit it off. I was quite a bit
older than her, and like I said, rough as a cob com-
pared to her, but she said she enjoyed talking to me.
She suggested we get together again while she was in
town, so we did. We had dinner a few more times."
McKinney shrugged again. "But that's all that happened, Browning. I give you my word on that."

Conrad waved that away. "How long did she stay
here?"

"A week, maybe ten days. Then she said she had
to travel to San Francisco." McKinney sighed. "I
never saw her again after that."

"And she was alone, you said?"

"That's right. I never saw anybody else with her."
The rancher frowned. "I've been answering your
questions, Browning, but I've got to admit I'm curious. Just what is it you're after?"

"I'm just trying to clear up . . . a family matter. I'm
sorry. I'm really not at liberty to say any more."

For a second McKinney looked like he was going
to lose his temper again, but then he said, "All right.
I suppose I can accept that. Don't reckon I have any
choice but to accept it."

"Thanks." Conrad nodded.

"Anything else I can do for you?"

"No, that's all. I'm obliged to you for your help,
McKinney."

The rancher gave Conrad a curt nod but didn't

say anything else. He headed back over to the men he'd been talking to earlier.

Conrad and Hudson stayed where they were for a moment. "I'm sorry," Hudson said. "I was hoping he could tell us something about the children. But just because Pamela didn't mention them to him, doesn't mean that they weren't here in town with her."

"I know. She was traveling with a nurse, so it's possible the nurse was taking care of them whenever Pamela met with McKinney." Conrad paused. "He seems a strange sort to show up at one of your dinner parties."

"He's definitely rough around the edges, like he said. But he's a client, and it seems to be important to him that he at least try to fit in. To be honest, though, he seems like he'd be a lot more at home in some place like the gambling room of the Palace Theater."

Conrad chuckled. "As a matter of fact, that's where we met last night."

"Really?" Hudson asked, his eyebrows arching.

"I'm afraid I'm a lot more disreputable character than I used to be, Ellery."

"I doubt that. Not that you used to be disreputable, that's not what I mean—"

Conrad held up a hand to stop him. "We'd better go see how your wife and Rose are getting along. Violet may not appreciate being left to manage the masquerade on her own."

"She doesn't mind," Hudson assured him. "I told her your story, and she was eager to help."

They found Violet Hudson and Rose Sullivan on the other side of the room. Rose was smiling and looked like she was having a wonderful time. She clutched Conrad's arm and whispered, "Thank you for bringing me tonight. I've always dreamed of being in a place like this, associating with fine people like these."

"I'm sure you're a fine person yourself."

"Nothing like this."

A few minutes later, a servant called everyone to dinner. The table in the dining room was long, covered with a snowy cloth of fine linen, and set with beautiful china and crystal. The food was excellent, the wine was even better, and Conrad should have been enjoying the meal.

Instead he kept thinking about the things Rance McKinney had said about Pamela. He glanced along the table at the rancher, who was with a beautiful woman with midnight-black hair. Conrad didn't know her.

McKinney's words had carried the ring of truth, but Conrad's instincts told him there was more to the story, something McKinney hadn't told him about the time he had spent with Pamela. Ellery Hudson had talked to all the other guests and had come up empty. Conrad trusted the lawyer. The only lead they had was McKinney, and even though the rancher seemed to be a dead end, for some reason Conrad didn't believe that.

He wanted to know more, which meant he was going to have to figure out some way to spend more time with McKinney. That prospect didn't appeal to him at all.

When dinner was over, everyone went back into the other room for brandy and dancing. A group of musicians played softly and skillfully. When Rose asked in a slightly breathless voice if they could dance, Conrad didn't have the heart to refuse her. They swept around the room in a waltz, and he had to admit she was a good dancer, very graceful and light on her feet.

Her beauty made her popular, too, and when one of the male guests cut in, Conrad let her go. She smiled and wiggled her fingers at him as the man twirled her away. She was having the night of her life, and Conrad was glad for that.

As for himself, he sought out Ellery Hudson again. When he had the lawyer off to the side where they could talk quietly, he said, "I think McKinney knows more than he's telling us."

"Conrad, you heard him. He had dinner a few times with Pamela. That's all. If there actually was more between them . . . well, knowing those details isn't really going to help anything, is it?"

"That's not what I'm talking about. I just have a hunch he's not telling us the truth. Not all of it, anyway." Conrad stroked his chin as he frowned in thought. "Bat Masterson told me that McKinney is quite a card player. Maybe I need to sit in on a game with him."

Hudson looked around as if he was afraid he was going to be overheard. "I think McKinney plans to play in that big tournament Masterson is putting together."

"Wait a minute. Bat said something to me about a high-stakes game, but he didn't say anything about a tournament."

"It's going to be thirty or forty of the biggest high rollers this side of San Francisco. I've heard a lot of gossip about it. It's supposed to last for several days, maybe as long as a week, depending on how long it takes to narrow down the field to the top four players."

Conrad felt his interest growing. "Bat didn't say anything about that. McKinney's going to play?"

"That's what I've heard. A man who likes to gamble as much as he does, I don't see how he could resist."

"No, I don't, either."

"If you really think he can tell you more about Pamela, that would be a way to get closer to him, Conrad. You can learn a lot about a man over a poker table."

Conrad nodded slowly. "You certainly can."

"I've heard that the buy-in is going to be awfully steep, though. Ten thousand dollars is the rumor."

"I can handle that," Conrad said with a little laugh.

"Of course you can. Would you like for me to make arrangements for the cash with the bank?"

Conrad didn't think about it for very long. "Yes, Ellery, I would. I'm taking cards in this game . . . and we'll see just what sort of player Ransom McKinney really is."

Chapter 9

There was a large garden behind the Hudson house, and after a while the French doors were opened so the guests could stroll outside or continue dancing on the large flagstone terrace if they wanted to. Rose came up to Conrad, took his hand, and asked, "Can we go out to the garden? It's a lovely night."

Since he already knew there was a connection between Pamela and Rance McKinney, and since he had decided to take part in the poker tournament with the rancher, Conrad didn't see anything else he could accomplish there. He might as well make the evening as enjoyable for Rose as he could.

"Of course." He squeezed her hand. "Come on."

He led her onto the terrace, which was softly lit by lamps spaced out on the stone railing around it. They could still hear the music, so he took her in his arms and swept her around the terrace several times. As they danced, she moved closer and closer to him until she was leaning against him and her blond hair rested on his shoulder. He was all too aware of the soft warmth of her body in his arms.

The music came to a stop. Rose lifted her head a little, looked up at him, and breathed, "Conrad . . ."

He didn't try to stop her when she kissed him.

He had been with one woman since Rebel's death, the bounty hunter Lace McCall. He knew better than to believe he would spend the rest of his life like a monk. He knew, too, that he could have Rose Sullivan if he wanted her.

He didn't believe she was just after his money, although that was a large part of what had drawn her to him in the first place. If she had any genuine feelings for him, it wouldn't be fair to her if he took advantage of those feelings, knowing that he didn't return them.

Or maybe she was just acting, playing the part of Violet Hudson's cousin who had come with him to the dinner. He didn't think that was the case, but it was possible, he supposed.

Either way, nothing serious was going to happen between them tonight, he told himself, no matter how hot and sweet Rose's lips were as she kissed him. He kissed her back. He couldn't seem to stop himself.

He forced himself to pull away and said quietly, "Rose, this isn't necessary. It isn't part of the role you're playing."

"I know that, silly. Don't you like it, Conrad?"

"Of course I do," he replied truthfully. Kissing Rose Sullivan was one of the most pleasant things he had done recently. "But it wouldn't be right for me to force you into—"

"Conrad, you're not forcing me into anything," she broke in with a note of exasperation in her voice. "I want to do anything you want to do." She laughed softly. "But if you'd rather go slow, I understand. Why don't we take a walk in the garden? There's plenty of moonlight."

He wasn't sure that was a good idea, but he said, "All right. I suppose we can do that."

She slipped her hand into his as they went down several marble steps from the raised terrace and started along a flagstone path that wound through the big garden. A few couples were dancing on the terrace, and Conrad wouldn't have been surprised if there were lovers taking advantage of the moonlight in the garden. The shrubbery that grew thickly in places could have concealed any number of things, but he didn't intend to stray off the path with Rose.

It was a perfect night for romance, with a warm breeze making the limbs of the trees rustle softly. The moon Rose had mentioned floated in the heavens, a silvery ball surrounded by millions of stars against a backdrop of ebony night. The sweet fragrance of flowers filled the air.

At one time, strolling through a beautiful garden like that with a lovely woman like Rose would have been a wonderful evening for Conrad Browning, but he had a hard time not thinking about Rance McKinney and wondering if that son of a bitch knew more than he was telling about Pamela.

Rose came to a stop in a patch of deep shadow

cast by a pine tree that grew close to the path. Conrad stopped as well and turned to face her as she rested her hands on his shoulders.

"Conrad, you really don't have to worry. I'm a grown woman, and I know what I'm doing. You know I'd do anything for you."

"You've already helped out plenty. I think we should go back inside." His resolve wasn't wavering, but at the same time, he didn't see any point in continuing to have her alluring temptation thrown in his face.

"Just a few more minutes. I . . . I'm enjoying pretending that a man like you could really care for a girl like me."

He bit back a curse of frustration. She was playing on his sympathy and he knew it, but that didn't mean the tactic was any less effective.

In the darkness, he felt the warmth of her breath on his face. "Conrad . . ." she whispered.

Leather scraped softly on the stone path behind him.

The sound was close enough to set off alarm bells in his head. His instincts took over. Pushing Rose toward the tree, he said sharply, "Get down!" He whipped around and saw moonlight reflect off cold steel as a dark shape thrust a long-bladed knife at him.

Conrad twisted to the side. The blade went past him, and the man wielding it was thrown off balance by the miss. He took a stumbling step closer, bringing him well within reach of the right fist Conrad sent smashing into his face.

The blow staggered the man but didn't stop him from trying to rip Conrad's belly open with a backhanded slash of the knife. Conrad jerked out of the way of the blade.

"Rose, run!" he called to her as he tried to stay between her and the attacker. "Get inside, now!"

She didn't respond, and he didn't know if she was all right or not. At the moment he didn't have time to check on her. The man with the knife caught his balance and came at Conrad again, thrusting and slashing. Conrad had to give ground, backing along the flagstone path.

One of the stones suddenly shifted under his foot, and it was his turn to lose his balance. He went over backward, landing on the grass at the edge of the path. He felt the .32 digging into the small of his back, but he didn't have time to reach for it. The would-be assassin leaped at him, knife upraised for a killing strike.

Conrad's hand fell on the loose flagstone. He grabbed it and jerked it in front of him as the knife plunged down at him. The blade hit the stone with a loud clang. The man grunted in pain at the unexpected impact. The knife was ripped from his fingers and clattered away on the path.

With both hands on the flagstone Conrad shoved it up into the man's chest, using it as a weapon. The man fell to the side, gasping for breath.

Conrad could have used the flagstone to crush the man's skull, but he wanted to ask the man some questions. Tossing the stone aside, he used his fist to smash another blow to the man's jaw.

The man's knee came up and dug hard into Conrad's belly, knocking the breath out of him, and giving the man time to throw a punch of his own. A bony fist landed on Conrad's cheek and rocked his head back. Stars swam in front of his eyes, not just overhead in the night sky.

The man bucked up, toppling Conrad onto his back again. Heaving himself off the ground, the assailant swung a foot in a vicious kick. Conrad got his hands up in time to grab the man's ankle. A heave of his own sent the man crashing to the ground.

He lunged after the attacker. Hands gripped Conrad's coat and threw him to the side. As he rolled across the grass, the man came after him. Conrad thrust his hands up and locked them around the shadowy figure's throat. At the same time, the man grabbed him by the neck and started to squeeze.

It was a race to see which of them could choke the other into unconsciousness—or death—first.

Suddenly the man lurched forward. In the bright moonlight Conrad saw his eyes widen, then bug out in shock and pain. His grip on Conrad's neck loosened, the fingers falling away from bruised flesh.

Conrad let go as well. The man made a high, keening sound and toppled to the side, landing face-first on the ground. Sticking up in the center of his back was the handle of the knife he had used to try to kill Conrad. The heavy blade was completely buried in his body.

Rose stood there, both hands pressed to her

mouth. "Oh!" she cried. "Oh, my God! What have I done? What have I done?"

Conrad climbed to his feet and took her in his arms, holding her trembling body against him. "Maybe saved my life, that's what you've done."

"But I . . . I k-killed him!" She pressed her face against his chest and began to sob.

Conrad patted her a little awkwardly on the back. He had never been very good with crying women. He didn't know what to do or say to comfort them and get them to stop crying.

A rapid patter of footsteps came from the direction of the house. Ellery Hudson called, "Conrad? Conrad, are you out here?"

Conrad turned, keeping an arm around Rose's shoulders, and raised his voice, saying, "Over here, Ellery!"

He saw a light bobbing. Someone was bringing a lantern. Hudson and half a dozen other men hurried up to them. Rance McKinney was one of the men, Conrad noted.

The light from the lantern fell on the man sprawled facedown with the knife in his back. The sight made several men gasp in horror and surprise.

Hudson said, "Good Lord! What happened?"

Conrad prodded the corpse's shoulder with a foot. "This man tried to kill me. It's thanks to Rose that he didn't."

She sniffled. "Oh, no, I . . . I didn't really . . . I just saw him ch-choking you, Conrad, and his knife was lying there, and I picked it up and . . . and . . ."

A fresh round of sobbing shook her.

Conrad held her while McKinney strode forward and knelt beside the body. "We'd better make sure he's really dead," the rancher said harshly. He took hold of the man's shoulders and rolled him onto his back. Conrad made sure that Rose couldn't see the twisted, lifeless face staring up into the lanternlight.

"Does anybody know him?" Hudson asked.

Murmurs came from the assembled men, indicating that they didn't. As Conrad held Rose, he studied the man's face. The would-be assassin's features were coarse and beard-stubbled, and his clothes were threadbare.

"A damn thief, from the looks of him," McKinney said. "He probably saw the way the house was lit up and figured there was a party going on. Snuck into the garden and thought he could rob one of the guests."

"I think you're probably right, Ransom," Hudson said. "I've already called for the police. They'll be here soon. They may recognize him."

Conrad said, "Maybe some of you men could stay with the body. I think I should get Miss Sullivan back inside, away from . . ." He didn't finish his sentence, but a slight motion of his head toward the dead man made his meaning clear.

"Of course, of course," Hudson said quickly. "Ransom, if you can keep an eye on—"

"Sure, go on," McKinney said. A couple of the other men volunteered to stay with the corpse as well.

Conrad and Hudson took Rose into the house, keeping her between them. She was pretty unsteady on her feet. She'd had a big evening, all right,

Conrad thought, maybe the biggest of her life . . . including killing a man.

Violet Hudson and the rest of the dinner guests were waiting anxiously inside the French doors. When Violet saw how pale and shaken Rose was, she hurried to take charge of the young woman. "This poor dear needs to go upstairs and lie down with a cool cloth on her head." She put an arm around Rose and led her to the wide, curving staircase.

Rose glanced back at Conrad as she started up the stairs with Violet. She tried to summon up a tear-streaked smile, but it was a pretty feeble effort. Conrad returned the smile and gave her a firm nod.

One of the other guests asked "Ellery, do we need to stay?"

"What? Oh, no, no," Hudson said. "The police are coming, and I'm sure they'll want to talk to Mr. Browning and Miss Sullivan, but they shouldn't need anyone else."

With that, the guests began taking their coats and wraps and filing out, eager to be away from the scene of violence and possible scandal. In a matter of moments, Conrad and Hudson found themselves alone.

The lawyer sighed. "I promise you, Conrad, my dinner parties aren't usually occasions for such excitement. As a rule, they're pretty quiet affairs." He looked closely at Conrad. "You aren't hurt, are you?"

Conrad shook his head. "A few bumps and bruises, maybe, but I managed to avoid the knife while that hombre was trying to cut me open."

"Hombre?" Hudson repeated with a slight frown.

"Oh, that's right. You've spent a lot of time in the Southwest recently, haven't you?"

Conrad nodded slowly. Hudson could believe that if he wanted to, but Conrad knew the truth. When danger reared its head, Kid Morgan was never far away.

Chapter 10

Rose was much more composed by the time the police were ready to talk to her. "Yes, Mr. Morgan and I were walking in the garden when that man came out of the shadows and attacked us from behind," she told a detective in a brown tweed suit and a bowler hat.

That wasn't exactly how it had happened, Conrad thought, but close enough for the purposes of the investigation.

"You stuck that knife in him after he dropped it, miss?" the detective asked.

Rose winced at the blunt question, but she nodded. "That's right. The man had Mr. Morgan pinned on the ground and was choking him. I . . . I didn't really think about what I was doing. I just saw the knife lying there on the walk and picked it up and—"

"I think that's enough," Hudson said. "It's obvious what happened here, Detective."

The man nodded and closed the notebook in which he had been scrawling words as Rose answered his questions. "I believe you're right, Mr. Hudson. The man was a thief, but he picked the wrong fella to rob."

"Do you know who he is?" Conrad asked.

"Not really," the detective replied with a shrug. "I hate to say it, but there are plenty of varmints like him in Denver. The town's not near as wild as it used to be, but we still get our share of outlaws drifting in. The undertaker's wagon should have carried this one off already. I'll go and check."

Rose shuddered a little at the mention of the undertaker, Conrad noted. She was still pale, and he knew that despite the circumstances, the fact that she had taken a human life probably would continue to weigh heavily on her for a while.

The detective told them he'd be in touch if he needed any more information and said good night. He went out the French doors into the garden, where a couple uniformed officers stood holding lanterns at the scene of the attack.

Conrad put a hand on Rose's arm. "I can take you home now."

Violet Hudson was sitting nearby. She stood up and said, "Nonsense. Rose doesn't need to be alone tonight. We have plenty of room here. She'll spend the night in one of our guest rooms." Violet frowned at her husband. "And she won't be at work tomorrow unless she feels like it, either."

Hudson held up his hands in surrender. "Of course, dear. Whatever you say."

Violet put an arm around Rose and led her upstairs again.

Hudson took a cigar out of his vest pocket, offered it to Conrad, then lit it himself when Conrad shook his head. "Quite an evening." Hudson blew out a cloud of smoke.

Conrad nodded. "That's right. But at least we learned a little."

The lawyer frowned in confusion. "What's that?"

"We learned that McKinney was around Pamela quite a bit while she was here and may know more than he's letting on." Conrad smiled. "We also learned it's not wise to turn your back on Rose Sullivan when there's a knife close at hand."

Hudson grunted and shook his head. "I never would have expected such a thing of her." He paused to take another puff on the cigar. "Did she really save your life, Conrad? Or did you have things in hand?"

"It's hard to say," Conrad admitted. "I think I would have been able to overpower the man if Rose hadn't done what she did . . . but I don't know that for certain."

"Well, then, we'll give her the benefit of the doubt and consider her a heroine. Maybe that will make it easier for her to get over what happened tonight."

"Maybe," Conrad said.

He told Hudson good night and went out to the buggy where the driver waited. "I heard about all the excitement, Mr. Browning. Are you all right?"

"I'm fine," Conrad told him. Instead of sitting in the back, he climbed onto the buggy's front seat next to the driver and nodded for him to get the vehicle moving. The driver slapped the reins against the backs of the two horses hitched to the buggy.

"What really happened back there in the garden, if you don't my askin'? One of the other drivers said somebody tried to kill you."

"The man wanted to rob me," Conrad said.

Or had he? That question suddenly crossed Conrad's mind. He thought back over exactly what had happened. He had been holding Rose Sullivan and she had been about to kiss him. Then he had heard the faint scrape of the man's boot leather on the flagstone walk.

If not for that tiny warning, that little sound some people wouldn't have even heard, a second later the man would have driven the knife deep in his back. Conrad supposed it was easier to go through a man's pockets and rob him after he was dead, but if the thief had succeeded in killing him, then he would have been forced to kill Rose as well, to keep her from crying out and screaming for help.

Would a robber have been willing to murder two people just to steal a few dollars?

Of course things like that happened, Conrad reminded himself. People had been murdered for pennies, for their clothes or their shoes or for no good reason at all. But that usually happened when they were fighting back against being robbed.

The man had been set on killing Conrad right from the first. That much was clear from the way he had attacked. He hadn't threatened or demanded money.

He had just gone for the death blow.

The would-be assassin was a stranger to Conrad. He couldn't think of a single reason the man would have wanted to kill him.

But Pamela had wanted him dead—years ago. She had come up with the elaborate scheme to torture him by withholding the knowledge of his children's birth and then letting him know about it after they were hidden away. She had also made arrangements to have him killed when he started searching for them. It was all a big, vicious game to her, he thought. Set out a goal—the twins—and give him the clues he needed to keep him on the trail, but set up death traps for him along the way. If those traps were successful, then he would die knowing he had failed to find his children. If they weren't, they would make him more determined than ever to continue the search. Pamela had known him well enough to predict that reaction from him.

Was the attempt on his life just another in that series of traps orchestrated by Pamela? He didn't know the answer to that question, but couldn't help pondering it.

"Sir? Mr. Browning?"

With a little shake of his head, Conrad realized that the driver on the seat beside him was talking to him. The buggy had stopped moving.

"We're here, sir. The Lansing House."

Sure enough, they were. The buggy had come to a stop in front of the hotel.

"Thank you." He took a coin from his pocket and pressed it into the driver's hand, despite the man's protests that it wasn't necessary.

"You be careful now, Mr. Browning," the driver told him as he stepped down from the buggy. "I got a feeling there are still folks out there who wish you harm."

"I know there are." Conrad smiled. "But they're going to be disappointed."

He went through the hushed, beautiful lobby and up to his suite. Arturo was in one of the armchairs in the sitting room, reading a newspaper. He put it aside and immediately stood up. "How was your evening, sir? Did you find out anything?"

"Maybe," Conrad said.

Arturo smiled. "And I take it no one tried to kill you?"

"Well, actually . . . ."

Arturo's smile disappeared and his eyes widened. "No!"

Conrad nodded. "Pour us a drink, Arturo, and I'll tell you all about it."

Conrad slept late the next morning. In the afternoon, he went to Ellery Hudson's office and found Julia Moorehead at the desk in the outer office. There was no sign of Rose.

"Mr. Browning, it's good to see you," Julia said as she got to her feet. "I heard about what happened last night at Mr. Hudson's house, of course. How are you today?"

"I'm fine," Conrad told her with a smile as he took off his hat and held it in front of him. People who were acquainted with him in the business and society part of his life didn't seem to understand that somebody trying to kill him wasn't all that unusual. "Do you know how Rose is doing?"

"That poor girl. I talked to Mrs. Hudson on the telephone this morning. She said Rose is still very upset. I can understand why she feels that way. It's why I've taken over here this morning." Julia's voice took on a slight note of disapproval as she added, "No offense, Mr. Browning, but your idea turned out not to be such a good one."

"I don't know about that. I'm still alive, and I might not have been if not for Rose."

"Well, I suppose there is that to consider . . ." Julia's manner became more businesslike. "What can we do for you this morning?"

"I came by mainly to check on Rose. Is Ellery free?"

Julia shook her head. "He's in conference with a client, and then he has to be in court in a little while."

"That's all right." Conrad put on his hat. "Just tell him I stopped by."

"Of course."

Conrad left the law office. He slipped his watch from his pocket and checked the time as he emerged from the building. It was only two o'clock in the afternoon, but he had a hunch there was a good chance he would find Bat Masterson at the Palace Variety Theatre and Gambling Parlor.

That hunch turned out to be correct. The famous former lawman and current gambler was sitting at one of the poker tables, cards in hand, playing in what appeared to be a low-stakes game with three other men. The pot in the center of the table didn't add up to much. Masterson was just keeping in practice, Conrad thought as he caught the man's eye and nodded toward the bar.

"I'm out, gentlemen." Masterson squared up his cards and dropped them facedown on the table. He pushed back his chair and stood up.

When he joined Conrad at the bar, Conrad said, "I hope I didn't cause you to throw in a good hand, Bat."

Masterson chuckled. "Actually, I probably would have won. But did you see that pot? Chicken feed. I've lost more than that betting on whether the next woman through the door will a blonde, a brunette, or a redhead."

"I hope the news I have for you will more than make up for it. I've decided to play in this poker tournament you're organizing."

Masterson arched his eyebrows. "Really? I *am* glad to hear that."

"You're glad that you'll have ten thousand more dollars in the kitty."

"Well, that, too, of course. But you're a good player. You'll bring some excitement to the game." Masterson frowned as a thought appeared to occur to him. "Say, you're not doing this in hopes of getting back at Rance McKinney, are you? He's going to be part of the tournament."

"Actually, McKinney *is* the reason I decided to play. But not because of what happened in here a couple nights ago."

He had thought about it, and decided to take Masterson into his confidence. He knew his father trusted the man, and Frank Morgan's opinion was good enough for Conrad. Quietly, as they lingered over schooners of cold beer, he told Masterson about the real reason he had come to Denver and the conversation he'd had with McKinney at Ellery Hudson's house the night before.

Masterson tugged at one side of his mustache as he frowned in thought. "You believe Rance McKinney knows more about Pamela than he's saying?"

"My gut tells me he does."

"I don't believe I ever met the lady, but from what I know about her, she and McKinney strike me as an odd pair."

Conrad nodded. "There's no doubt about that. But if there's one thing I've learned in the past couple years, Bat, it's that Pamela would use anybody she could to help her get the revenge on me she wanted."

Masterson nodded. "Yes, I can see that. I heard about what happened at Ellery Hudson's house last night."

"It's not in the newspaper, is it?" Conrad hadn't looked at the papers yet.

"No, no, Hudson has too much influence in this town for that. He wouldn't want everybody knowing that a guest at one of his dinner parties was almost murdered in his garden. But I have my sources. Every old lawman does."

Conrad didn't doubt that.

Masterson went on, "Do you think it's possible

your former fiancée had anything to do with that fellow trying to stick a knife in your back?"

"I thought of the same thing. It wouldn't surprise me a bit."

"Considering what you've told me, I wouldn't be surprised, either. And Rance McKinney was there."

Conrad nodded. "Indeed he was."

Masterson lifted his schooner of beer, took a long swallow, then used a fancy handkerchief he took from his breast pocket to pat foam off his mustache. He gave Conrad a long look. "There aren't going to be guns blazing over the tables in that poker tournament I'm putting together, are there?"

"I can't promise anything."

Chapter 11

The tournament was scheduled to begin the next night. Conrad intended to lie low at the Lansing House until then.

Masterson had given him all the details. The tournament would take place in a large private room at the Palace. The buy-in was ten thousand dollars, as Conrad already knew. There would be eight tables with six players at each table, for a total of forty-eight, slightly lower than had been rumored. The men would draw lots to see who played at each table.

The games would continue until everyone at each table was cleaned out except for one big winner, however long that took. Food and drink would be provided, as well as places to sleep if proved necessary.

Once the eight winners were determined, the second round would consist of two tables with four players at each. Again, the games would continue until there were two big winners and everyone else was wiped out.

Then those two winners would meet in the final game.

"That could take weeks," Conrad had said.

Bat Masterson had shaken his head. "Not the way these hombres play. A lot of them like to take big plunges, so they win big . . . and lose big. I think it'll take less than a week to determine a winner."

"Who will walk away with more than half a million dollars."

"Probably closer to a million. You know what they say about the rich getting richer. . . . You'll do all right, Conrad, if you just keep your wits about you."

Conrad had nodded. "I intend to."

He didn't care about the money he might win or lose. His lawyers—Ellery Hudson in Denver, Charles Harcourt back in Boston, Claudius Turnbuckle and John Stafford in San Francisco—would care. They would probably be horrified at the risks he was prepared to take in order to find his children. But none of that mattered.

Not as long as his dreams were haunted by those nameless, faceless images running away from him . . .

On the afternoon of the day the tournament was to begin, a knock sounded on the door of Conrad's hotel room. Arturo went to answer it, calling through the door, "Who is it?"

"Rose Sullivan," a woman's voice answered.

Turning to look at Conrad sitting comfortably in one of the upholstered wing chairs, Arturo raised his eyebrows to inquire if Conrad wanted to let her in.

Conrad didn't hesitate. He nodded.

Arturo swung the door open and murmured, "Miss Sullivan, please come in."

Rose looked quizzically at him as she stepped into the room.

Conrad got to his feet and made the introductions. "Rose, this is my friend, Arturo Vincenzo. Arturo, Miss Sullivan."

Arturo clasped her gloved hand. "The pleasure and the honor are mine, Miss Sullivan."

"Thank you."

"Might I take your hat?"

She shook her head in response to Arturo's question. "No, thank you. I won't be here long." She wore a dark blue skirt and jacket, a white blouse, and a hat of the same dark blue shade. Her hair was pulled up on her head again. She carried a black handbag.

"Then perhaps something to drink?"

She shook her head again.

Arturo looked at Conrad. "I'll be in my room if you need me." He withdrew discreetly from the sitting room.

Conrad came over to Rose and clasped her hands. She asked, "Is he your servant?"

"A good friend," Conrad said again. "How are you, Rose? You're looking a lot better."

It was true. Most of the color had returned to her cheeks, and her hands weren't trembling at all as Conrad held them.

"I'm all right," she said with a slight smile. "Mrs. Hudson has been very helpful. I think I would have fallen completely apart if it weren't for her. But I went back to my own place today. And tomorrow I'm going back to work."

"Are you sure you're ready for that?"

She nodded. "It's for the best. But I wanted to see you first and make sure you were all right. Mr. Hudson told me where you were staying. I hope that's not a problem."

"Not at all," Conrad assured her with a smile. "Come over here and sit down."

He took her handbag from her before she could protest and set it on a spindly-legged side table that was actually a valuable antique. With a firm hand on her arm, he ushered her over to a divan and sat down beside her as she took a seat.

"I was curious," she said, "if the police have found out any more about . . . about the man who tried to rob you."

Conrad shook his head. "If they have, they haven't said anything to me about it. I doubt if they'll ever find out who he was. Just some sneak thief."

It was better to let her think that than to tell her he suspected the man had been sent there specifically to kill him. Rose's part in the affair was over. He wasn't going to put her life at risk again.

"Is everything else all right?" she asked.

"Yes, of course."

"That's good. Mr. Browning . . . or is it all right if I still call you Conrad?"

"Conrad is just fine," he assured her.

"I don't know exactly why you wanted me to pretend to be Mrs. Hudson's cousin the other night, Conrad, but I'm sure it had something to do with whatever it was that brought you to Denver." She took a deep breath. "I want you to know if there's anything else I can do to help you, I'm more than willing."

He was shaking his head before she finished making the offer. "You've done plenty. More than enough. And it could have gotten you hurt."

"I'm not worried about that. I wouldn't worry about that . . . as long as I was with you."

Conrad frowned. He would have thought she'd realized it was dangerous to be around him. But she was offering to put herself right back into the line of fire. "I'm sorry, Rose. Do you trust me?"

"Of course I do, Conrad."

"Then believe me when I tell you it's better that you're not involved in this anymore. Just go back to your job at the law office and don't worry about me or my problems."

She pouted. "Just like that?"

"I'm afraid so."

"Oh, all right," Rose said with a sigh. "I suppose if that's the way it has to be . . . But I have one request, Conrad."

"Whatever it is, I'll be happy to do it, if I can."

As soon as the words were out of his mouth, he thought he might have been too hasty. It all depended on whatever favor Rose came up with to ask of him.

"I'd like for you to take me to dinner."

He smiled. "That I can do."

"At the best restaurant in Denver."

"Of course. Just name it."

She mentioned a steak house where many of the cattle barons from Colorado and elsewhere ate. The poker tournament at the Palace didn't start until ten o'clock that evening. There would be plenty of time for him to have dinner with Rose first.

"I'll pick you up at seven," he promised as they both stood up.

"I'm looking forward to it." She stepped closer to him, came up on her toes, and brushed a kiss across his cheek. "Until then, Conrad."

He handed her handbag to her, then showed her to the door and watched as she went down the hall toward the stairs. A door opened and closed behind him, and Arturo said, "So you have a dinner engagement with the lady before the poker games begin?"

Conrad grinned over his shoulder. "Why, Arturo, you old eavesdropper."

"Part of my job is to look out for your best interests, sir."

"And I appreciate that. But I'm not too worried about having dinner with a beautiful blonde."

The real danger would come later, he sensed, when he sat down across a poker table from Rance McKinney.

Conrad used the buggy that Arturo had been driving since they left Kansas City. He didn't take Arturo along or hire a driver, handling the team himself as he drove toward Rose's boarding house that evening.

Mrs. Sherman was happy to see him, beaming as

she let him into the house and offered to take his hat. He hung on to it and asked, "Is Rose ready?"

"I'll see. The darling girl was all atwitter when she came in this afternoon and said she was going to dinner with you tonight." Mrs. Sherman put her hand to her mouth. "Oh, dear, I probably shouldn't have said that."

Conrad smiled and leaned toward her. "Don't worry, I won't say anything."

Rose wore a red gown, light jacket, and hat when she came downstairs. She looked as lovely in that outfit as she had in all the others Conrad had seen her wearing. While Mrs. Sherman looked on happily, he took Rose's arm and led her out to the buggy.

When he had the buggy rolling easily through Denver's streets, he made conversation by asking, "How long have you lived here?"

"Not long, actually. About three months."

"Where did you live before that?"

"St. Louis. I was born and raised there, in fact."

"What made you leave, if I'm not being too inquisitive?"

Rose laughed. "Not at all. My parents were both gone, I didn't have any other family there, and I decided I wanted to see something of the West. It was an adventure, I suppose you could say."

She had probably gotten more adventure than she bargained for, he thought, but he didn't want to remind her of what had happened in Ellery Hudson's garden.

"You've done well for yourself, getting a job in the

city's top law firm in that amount of time," he commented.

"I was lucky. Mrs. Moorehead told me that the girl who had the job before me took sick and passed away suddenly." Rose caught her breath. "Oh, that sounds terrible, doesn't it, to call such a thing lucky?"

Conrad shrugged. "Someone's bad luck is nearly always someone else's good luck. I suppose that's the world's way of balancing things out."

"Maybe so, but I still wish I hadn't said it."

"Don't worry about it. I know what you meant."

They arrived at the restaurant a short time later. The dining room had booths made of dark, thick wood. The place just *felt* expensive, but Conrad didn't care about the cost.

The meal was excellent: thick steaks, mounds of German fried potatoes, a fine wine. It occurred to Conrad that he shouldn't be eating such a heavy meal. The poker tournament would be starting in just a few hours, and he needed to be alert, instead of feeling like he ought to take a nap.

Rose's company perked him up. She talked brightly and animatedly, obviously enjoying herself. After what she had gone through in order to help him out, he was glad he could give her a fine evening. But she would have to understand that he might never see her again.

When they were ready to go, he linked arms with her as they walked out to the buggy. Rose leaned her head against his shoulder. "It's been such a lovely evening, I hate for it to end," she said wistfully.

"Conrad, do you think we could go for a drive before you take me back to Mrs. Sherman's house?"

Conrad thought about it for a moment, then nodded. "I don't see why not." Denver's city government recently had begun widening many of the streets and planting trees in the center of them. It would be a picturesque drive, and the night air might refresh him and make him more alert for the poker tournament.

He helped Rose into the buggy, then got the team moving and swung the vehicle into one of the recently widened boulevards. The trees were in bloom, filling the night with their fragrance.

"It's beautiful," Rose said.

Conrad had to agree. He was about to say so when he heard hoofbeats behind the buggy. It sounded like a couple riders were about to overtake the vehicle.

At first he thought they just wanted to pass him, but the horsebackers split, one galloping up on each side of the vehicle. Both men wore black bandannas pulled up over their faces as they pointed revolvers into the buggy.

Rose let out a sudden scream.

Chapter 12

Conrad hauled back on the reins as hard as he could with his left hand while his right flashed behind his back and reached under his coat for the .32. The team lurched to a halt, their harnesses preventing them from rearing.

One of the gunmen yelled, "Out of the buggy! Out of the buggy *now!*"

Rose screamed again and clutched at Conrad's arm, inadvertantly keeping him from pulling his gun.

He couldn't start trading lead with those two, anyway, he realized. Not with Rose in the buggy where a stray shot might kill her.

"Hold your fire," he told the men as they struggled to keep their horses under control while continuing to aim their guns at him.

"Get out of there," the other man ordered. The bandanna over the lower half of his face muffled his voice, but the words were clear enough. "Get out and hand over all your money, mister, or that pretty girl with you won't be so pretty anymore."

So it really was a robbery, Conrad thought. The men must have been watching the restaurant, waiting for one of the wealthy patrons to leave.

Or was it? he suddenly asked himself. Maybe what they were saying was just for Rose's benefit, so after he was dead, she could tell the authorities the killing was a hold-up attempt turned deadly. Either way, those two hombres were going to regret what they were trying to do . . . just as soon as he was sure that Rose was out of the line of fire.

He wrapped the reins around the brake lever but didn't set it. He held out his hands so the gunmen could see them. "Take it easy. I'm getting out. Just leave the lady alone."

"Sure," one of the men said with a sneer in his voice. "We just want your money and any other valuables you got, mister. We'll take the gal's handbag, too."

Conrad climbed down from the buggy. "Whatever you want, that's fine. You boys sound like you ought to be out robbing stagecoaches."

"Ain't no stagecoaches no more," the man on the right said. He sounded a little wistful.

The man on the left snapped, "Shut up. No more talking than we have to. Now, mister—"

"Hyaaahhh!" Conrad yelled, snatching off his hat and slapping it against the rump of the nearest horse. He leaped away from the vehicle as the horses lunged forward, dragging the buggy behind it. He caught a glimpse of a startled Rose being thrown back against the seat as the team took off.

The next instant, the .32 was in his hand, spitting

fire and lead. The short-barreled gun cracked twice as Conrad put both bullets in the chest of the man closest to him. As that man slumped backward in the saddle and struggled to stay mounted, his companion opened fire. Conrad heard a bullet whip past his ear as he dived to his left. He fired twice more as he was falling.

One of the slugs went through the left shoulder of the second gunman. He howled in pain and twisted in the saddle. His gun hand dropped, then he forced the weapon up again. Conrad wanted to take the man alive, but it didn't look like the varmint was going to give him much choice in the matter.

Lying on his side in the street, he fired again just as the gunman jerked his trigger. The heavy revolver boomed, but the slug smacked harmlessly into the cobblestones. Conrad's bullet fluttered the bandanna mask as it passed through the cloth and angled sharply upward through the man's neck into the base of his brain. Blood gushed from the wound.

Choking and gasping for breath through his ruined neck, the man toppled out of the saddle and crashed to the street.

Still on his horse, the first man was obviously in great pain as he hauled the animal around and put the spurs to it. Conrad scrambled to his feet and tackled the wounded man, dragging him out of the saddle. They fell, and the impact broke Conrad's grip on the man. They rolled apart.

Managing to hold on to the .32, Conrad came up on his knees and pointed the gun at the other man. "Don't move!"

The man had lost his gun. He lay on his belly, struggling to get both hands under him so he could push himself up. The light was bad, but Conrad saw that the bandanna mask had slipped down, revealing a coarse, pain-twisted face.

"You . . . you . . ." he gasped. Choking out something unintelligible, he finished, ". . . bitch!"

Covering the man with the .32, Conrad said coolly, "I've been called worse than a son of a bitch before, amigo."

The man didn't hear him. His head slumped back to the ground with an audible thud as his forehead struck the street. Conrad stood up, moved over to him, and carefully checked for a pulse without finding one.

Both outlaws were dead. They wouldn't be answering any questions about whether that had been a real hold-up attempt . . . or something else, something even more deadly.

Conrad heard police whistles blowing. He didn't want to spend hours talking to the authorities. The poker tournament was supposed to start in less than two hours. He turned and looked for the buggy. It had come to a stop about fifty yards up the street, where the momentary panic of the horses had run out of steam.

He grabbed his fallen hat out of the street and hurried toward the vehicle, anxious to make sure Rose was all right. Maybe she would understand it wasn't such a good idea to spend much time around him.

When he reached the buggy, he saw her slumped to the side on the seat. "Rose! Rose!"

He holstered the .32 at the small of his back and sprang onto the seat next to her. Taking hold of her shoulders, he turned her toward him. Her eyelids fluttered, and she moaned. At least she was alive, he thought.

"Rose, can you hear me? Are you all right?"

"C-Conrad?" she whispered.

"Yes. Are you hurt?"

With his help, she straightened up. She blinked rapidly, looking confused for a second. "No, I . . . I'm all right. I think I . . . hit my head against the back of the seat . . . when the horses took off." Her fingers clutched at his coat. "What about you?"

"I'm fine. I'd like to get out of here, though. I don't want to be stuck here talking to the law."

"Those men . . . ?"

"Both dead," he told her.

"Oh, my," she said as he reached for the reins. "Conrad, I . . . I hope you won't take this the wrong way . . . but I think it might be a good idea . . . if we didn't see each other anymore."

He slapped the lines against the backs of the horses and got them moving again. "Don't worry, I understand." A bitter taste climbed up his throat and into his mouth.

Rose Sullivan wasn't the first beautiful blonde who would have been better off if she had never even met Conrad Browning. At least she wasn't dead.

Mrs. Sherman made a big fuss over Rose when she found out what had happened. "Someone tried to rob the two of you *again?*" she said in outrage as she put an arm around Rose and gave Conrad an angry frown.

"Please, don't blame Mr. Browning," Rose said. "He saved us both times."

The landlady snorted. "Perhaps it wouldn't have happened if you weren't with him. Let's get you upstairs to your room. I'll make you a nice cup of sassafras tea, dearie. That'll settle your nerves right down."

"Good night, Conrad," Rose called over her shoulder as Mrs. Sherman hustled her up the staircase.

He drove the buggy back to the livery stable in the next block down from the Lansing House, where he turned it over to the hostler. He wouldn't need the buggy again as the Palace was also within walking distance of the hotel.

Since he'd been rolling around in the street while engaged in the shootout, he wanted to change his suit before he headed for the gambling parlor. Arturo was a little surprised to see him.

"I didn't know if you'd stop by here following your dinner engagement with Miss Sullivan or not," Arturo said. His eyebrows arched as he noticed the disarray and dirtiness of Conrad's clothes. "Good Lord! Did you run into trouble *again*, sir?"

"You sound like Mrs. Sherman," Conrad commented as he took off his coat and started untying his cravat.

"Who?"

"Never mind. But to answer your question, yes, a couple men on horseback jumped us while we were driving around after dinner."

"And what did you do?"

In answer, Conrad reached behind him and took off the holstered .32. He placed it on a table.

"Of course, you shot them. Are you injured?"

Conrad shook his head. "No, I'm fine. Just wondering why it is that hombres keep trying to rob me."

"Beyond the obvious reason of stealing your money?"

"Exactly."

"And are you asking yourself why these hold-up men seem to be drawn to you while you're in the company of Miss Sullivan?"

Conrad gave Arturo a hard stare. "What do you mean by that?"

Arturo didn't back down. "I mean it's rather coincidental that the last two times you and Miss Sullivan were alone together, someone attacked you and tried to kill you."

"I don't think I like what you're getting at, Arturo."

"I don't like it either, sir, but it's something to consider."

As a matter of fact, Conrad *had* considered it, and the possibility had cropped up even stronger in his mind as he was driving back to the hotel from Mrs. Sherman's house. The idea had been reinforced by the fact that when he'd picked up Rose's handbag that afternoon, it had seemed a little heavier than it should have.

As if a gun had been in it.

When he first thought that, he had told himself

without hesitation that he was crazy. Rose was just a sweet, pretty young woman who worked in Ellery Hudson's office. That was all. He had no proof there was anything more to her than that.

Anyway, it was too far-fetched to think that she could have had anything to do with the attacks on him. She had been in danger both times herself.

Or had she? If the man in the garden had succeeded in burying that knife in his back, what would he have done then? Would he have killed Rose, too?

Or would she have congratulated him on a job well-done? Conrad felt the blood in his veins start to turn to ice as he remembered how she had been distracting him just before the attack took place.

But she had killed the attacker herself, he reminded himself. She had plunged that knife right into his back.

Because she was afraid Conrad would defeat him and question him, and the man might reveal her part in the scheme?

The only real danger Rose had been in after dinner was when the buggy's horses bolted, and that had been Conrad's doing. If he hadn't made that play, the two so-called robbers might have gunned him down as soon as he stepped out of the buggy and left Rose to tell the police whatever story she wanted.

She had grabbed his arm when he first reached for his gun, too, he recalled, an act apparently of fear . . . but maybe not.

The dying gunman might not have been calling him a son of a bitch after all, Conrad speculated.

Maybe he had been referring to Rose as a bitch because the job had gone all wrong.

Rose had admitted that she hadn't been in Denver for long. All he had for her background was her word. Sure, it was loco to think she might be playing some convoluted part in Pamela Tarleton's vengeance scheme . . .

But Pamela had made other elaborate arrangements before her death that didn't bear their perilous fruit until after she was gone.

"Sir?"

Conrad came out of his reverie and realized Arturo was talking to him. He'd been standing there motionless, his cravat in his hand, thinking about Rose and turning over all the possibilities in his mind.

"Sir, were the police involved in tonight's incident?"

Conrad shook his head. "No, since Rose and I weren't hurt, I got out of there before they could show up. I knew I had that poker game to get to, and I didn't want to stand around answering a lot of questions."

"Indeed, you have Mr. Masterson's tournament and Mr. McKinney to deal with. But questions *do* need to be asked. Why don't you let me ask them?"

Conrad squinted at him. "You mean you're going to play detective, Arturo? Like that fellow in the stories by Conan Doyle?"

"Sherlock Holmes, yes, sir. I thought that while you're busy with other matters, I could make a few discreet inquiries into Miss Sullivan's background and her activities here in Denver."

"Very discreet, Arturo, very discreet. If she's innocent . . . if she has nothing to do with any of this except being unlucky enough to be with me when those attempts were made . . . then I don't want her to know I was suspicious of her."

Arturo nodded. "Of course, sir. I'll be the very soul of discretion. Anyway, I can't get started on my investigation until tomorrow, and perhaps you'll find out what you need to know from Mr. McKinney tonight."

"Maybe," Conrad said. "I'll be surprised if it turns out to be that easy, though. I have a hunch McKinney will prove to be a tough nut to crack."

With that settled, he changed clothes quickly, made sure the .32 had five rounds in it with the hammer resting on an empty chamber in the cylinder, and set out for the Palace with Arturo's wish of "Good luck, sir," following him out of the hotel room.

He didn't want to be late for what might turn out to be the most important poker game of his life.

Chapter 13

Conrad sensed the excitement in the Palace when he walked in a short time later. Players in the tournament, along with a few employees of the gambling parlor, were the only ones who would be allowed into the private room once the games got underway, but everyone knew what was going to take place. A lot of people were talking excitedly about it. The tournament was the biggest thing to hit gambling circles in a long time.

Because of that, a large crowd had shown up to wait in the main room and catch bits of news about what was going on in the chamber where the games were taking place.

Bat Masterson was holding court, surrounded by a number of newspaper reporters scribbling notes on their pads with stubby pencils. Conrad heard him talking about sporting blood and the gallantry of competition, as if instead of a poker tournament it was the old-fashioned kind held between knights, with lances and swords and shields. The sort of tournament where blood might be spilled . . .

With so much money at stake, it might come to that, Conrad thought.

Masterson caught Conrad's eye and winked. When he was through talking to the reporters, he came over and pumped Conrad's hand.

"Ah, the fourth estate!" he said with a grin. "What would we do without them? The thought's crossed my mind that I might try my hand at journalism myself, one of these days."

"I'm sure you'd be good at it, Bat. Is everything ready for tonight?"

Masterson nodded. "Absolutely. In fact, you're the last of the players to arrive. That's why I was so glad to see you. I was afraid you might have changed your mind, or that something had happened to you."

Something had indeed come close to happening to him, Conrad thought. Close enough he had heard the bullet whipping past his ear.

But he didn't say anything about that. "Did you get my buy-in? Ellery Hudson was supposed to have the bank send it over with some armed guards this afternoon."

Masterson nodded again. "Yes, it's locked up securely in the safe, along with the rest of the money, and there are half a dozen men with shotguns guarding it. Tough men, and I trust them completely. I know that sort of loot might be a very tempting target."

Masterson opened his coat a little to reveal he

had revolvers in shoulder rigs under both arms. "I'll be on hand to help protect it myself if need be."

Conrad didn't think most would-be robbers would want to go up against the famous Bat Masterson, even for that sort of money. "What about the players? Is it all right for us to be armed, as well?"

Masterson grimaced. "I'm sorry, Conrad. But if you're packing iron, you'll have to surrender it before the games start. It wouldn't do to have somebody take offense over the way a hand turned out and start shooting."

"As long as it's that way for everybody, I can go along with it." Conrad shrugged, even though he didn't like the idea of being unarmed. Especially with the way things had been going since he arrived in Denver. "Just make sure nobody tries to sneak anything in."

"Don't worry. The only weapons in there will be cards."

A short time later, Masterson rounded up all the players and herded them toward the double doors leading into the private room. Conrad spotted Rance McKinney among them. The rancher had abandoned his town suit and wore range clothes: black trousers, black shirt, and a black-and-white cowhide vest. He had never looked comfortable in fancier duds, and Conrad had a hunch McKinney thought he might play better if he was wearing his normal clothes.

Those things didn't matter to Conrad. He was in black trousers and jacket, white shirt, and string tie. He'd been wearing his black Stetson with the concho headband when he came in, but had handed it to one of the Palace's beautiful hostesses to take care of.

Masterson collected guns and knives from the players before they were allowed to enter the room. He had quite a few pocket pistols, derringers, and even a few long-barreled hog legs before he was through, along with a number of knives of different sizes and styles. Conrad took off his holster and handed over it and the .32. If he wasn't going to be carrying the gun, he didn't see any point in putting up with the discomfort of the holster.

"All right, gentlemen, gather around," Masterson said when all the players were in the room and the doors were closed, shutting out the noise from the main room. One of the hostesses joined him, holding a huge, white, ten-gallon hat. Masterson continued, "Inside this hat are numbered chips. You'll draw one at a time for seating assignments. Thad Harper, you go first."

The man Masterson had picked stepped forward and drew a chip from the hat. It had the numeral 3 on it. Masterson pointed out which table was the third one. The other men went up one by one, and drew chips as well, spreading out across the room to the tables they had drawn. Once they had chosen their seats, hostesses appeared and asked if they wanted anything to drink. Most of the men declined, preferring to keep their heads clear, at least for a while.

Conrad drew Table 5, feeling a twinge of disappointment as he did so. McKinney had already drawn Table 2. Conrad had been hoping to be at the same table as the rancher right from the start, but knew he couldn't ask anyone to switch with him without arousing suspicion.

That meant in order to play against McKinney, he had to emerge as the big winner at Table 5. There was nothing he could do about it, so he might as well get at it, he thought.

After he had taken his seat, a lovely, smiling hostess leaned over him and asked, "Would you like a drink, sir? Wine? Brandy?"

Conrad shook his head. "No, thanks."

"A cigar?"

"Never picked up the habit," he told her, returning her smile briefly.

"If you do need anything, please let me know."

"I will," he promised, but knew what he really needed, she couldn't provide.

He glanced over at Table 2, where Rance McKinney was arranging stacks of chips in front of him. More than ever, his instincts told him McKinney knew more than he had admitted about Pamela's plans.

Conrad would be betting more than money in that tournament. The real stake was the possibility that McKinney could tell him where his children were.

While he was waiting for all the players to get settled in their seats and ready for the games to begin, Conrad looked around the room. It was quite large, maybe half the size of the main room, with thick carpet on the floor that muffled the steps of the hostesses as they moved around. The eight tables were arranged in a grid that took up most of the space in the center of the room. Around the walls were over-stuffed divans, comfortable armchairs, and smaller side tables, places where men could relax while taking a break from the competition. Gas chandeliers over the tables provided plenty of illumination, while the lighting around the edges of the room was more subdued. Paintings, mostly sedate landscapes, hung on the walls. It was a comfortable room that felt like wealth, just the sort of place where rich men would gather to play high-stakes poker.

When everyone was in place, Bat Masterson stood up and addressed the group to explain the rules of the tournament. Each man had an assortment of chips in front of him representing his ten thousand dollar buy-in. In addition, each man would be allowed to purchase up to another ten thousand dollars in chips as the games proceeded. Breaks could be called whenever all the players at a table were in agreement. Players who were cleaned out and had to leave the game would be required to leave the room as well, although there was nothing stopping them from waiting in the main room outside until they found out who the big winners were. The big winners from each table would be allowed to remain in the room while the other winners were being determined. There would be an eight-hour break between the end of that round and the beginning of the next.

"Is everyone clear on the rules?" Masterson asked. "Any questions?" When no one spoke up, Masterson grinned and said, "All right, gentlemen. Good luck to you all. Start the games whenever you're ready."

Conrad didn't know the other five men at the table with him, although a couple of them looked vaguely familiar to him. He supposed he had seen them during previous visits to Denver. They took turns introducing themselves. Conrad took note of the names—Hal Roberts, Bernard Church, J.D. Wilson, Fred Montgomery, and Edgar Pennyworth— but knew he probably wouldn't remember them in a week. They were just obstacles between him and Rance McKinney.

On the other hand, he had to beat them all in order to move closer to McKinney, so he took a little time to study them. Roberts and Wilson had the staid look of successful businessmen. Bernard Church was a little harder to read, which told Conrad that he was probably a professional gambler. Fred Montgomery was a rawboned railroad magnate; Conrad recognized the name. Edgar Pennyworth was an older man, probably sixty, with a mild, round face and a shock of white hair, who looked like he could have been a small-town preacher. He was probably the most dangerous opponent of them all, Conrad mused, simply because he didn't look like much of a threat.

When Conrad gave them his name, Montgomery said, "I thought I recognized you, Browning. Didn't you own some stock in my railroad at one time?"

Conrad nodded. "I did. Maybe I still do." He chuckled. "I don't really know. My lawyers handle everything like that."

He saw the scorn in Montgomery's eyes. He didn't think much of a man who didn't manage his own business affairs. If that led him or the others to underestimate Conrad, then so much the better.

They cut cards to see who would have the deal first. It fell to Hal Roberts, who took the deck, shuffled, and dealt with reasonable deftness after announcing that they were playing simple five card stud. That was fine with Conrad. He watched the cards fall in front of him, not touching them until Roberts had finished dealing. Then he picked them up and expressionlessly looked to see what sort of hand he'd been dealt.

The game was underway.

Chapter 14

As in nearly any game, the pace was slow and cautious at first as the players got to know one another and gauge the strength of their opposition. Conrad kept his bets reasonably small, considering the stakes, and didn't try anything fancy. He seldom bluffed, just enough to let the other men know that he was capable of it, and by the time a couple hours had gone past, he was up a few hundred dollars.

The players took a short break to stretch their legs. Edgar Pennyworth smoked a fat cigar while Fred Montgomery filled a pipe and puffed on it. Bernard Church had one drink, a short, neat whiskey.

When the six men returned to the table, the feeling in the air was more tense than it had been earlier. Things would begin to get more serious.

Midnight rolled past. The room was fairly quiet. Low-voiced conversations took place at each table as men asked for cards or commented on a just-concluded hand. The hostesses weren't being kept very busy fetching drinks, so some of them sat down, yawning, and dozed in the armchairs. Bat Masterson, as the organizer of the tournament, wasn't playing. He strolled from table to table, a cigar clenched in his teeth, and kept up with the action.

As Conrad could have predicted, Fred Montgomery was the first one to grow impatient and start taking more risks. He won a couple big pots with daring plays, but lost even more. When his pile of chips began to shrink, he called Masterson over and said, "I need five thousand more, Bat."

Masterson nodded. "Of course. Anyone else?"

J.D. Wilson, who had lost several hands in a row, also bought more chips. They turned their money over to Masterson, and one of the hostesses delivered the chips. Play resumed.

Montgomery's luck didn't change. His stake continued to dwindle. He bought his other five thousand in chips. By six o'clock in the morning, he was down to his last thousand. With an annoyed grimace, he shoved the chips into the pot to call when he, Conrad, and Pennyworth were the last ones left in the hand. Pennyworth took the pot with four tens.

Conrad saw the anger flash in Montgomery's eyes, and for a second he thought the railroader was going to lose his temper and cause a scene. Masterson hovered nearby, ready to step in quickly if there was trouble.

Then Montgomery let out a laugh and shook his head. "Looks like I'm busted. But I had a good time, so I reckon it was worth it." He pushed back his chair and stood up, taking his watch from his pocket to check the time. "The railroad office'll be open in a couple hours. I need to get in there and tell my boys to raise the cost of a ticket a little bit. I'll have that twenty grand back in no time!"

"You don't want to wait and see who wins, Fred?" Masterson asked.

"Oh, I'll be back. I don't figure you'll settle things here for a while yet."

Montgomery left, and the other men at the table took a break. The players at several of the other tables had stopped for the moment, too, including Table 2. Conrad walked over to a long table where coffee and food had been set out. Rance McKinney was there, sipping from a cup of coffee that he had sweetened with something from a silver flask he took from his pocket.

He gave Conrad a curt nod of greeting. "Browning. How are you doing?"

"Fine," Conrad said without going into detail. Actually, he was up almost seven thousand dollars. His calm, steady play had been going well. "How about you?"

"Don't worry about me," McKinney snapped. "The rest of that bunch can't stay with me."

Was that the rancher's natural arrogance, Conrad wondered, or was the bravado intended to cover up the fact that he wasn't doing as well as he'd expected? That was the potentially major flaw in his plan, Conrad thought. McKinney might not make it out of the first round, and since they had drawn different tables, the effort would have been for nothing.

In that case, he would figure out some other way

to get to the truth, Conrad told himself. It would be just a minor setback.

The food and coffee refreshed the players. No one wanted to take a longer break to catch some sleep. After a while, the game resumed.

The hours rolled by. In the windowless room, there was no way of knowing if it was day or night. Conrad took off his coat and tie and rolled up the sleeves of his shirt. The other men got more comfortable, too, as they settled in for the long haul. It was a scene that was repeated at table after table in the room. From time to time a man would let a curse rip out as the cards didn't fall his way and he saw the last of his chips being raked in by one of the other players.

Of the forty-eight who had started the tournament the night before, eight were gone by midday and several others were perilously close to being wiped out. There wasn't much noise, only the whisper of cards, the click of chips, and the strained voices of men making their bets or asking for more cards.

Sometime early in the afternoon, J.D. Wilson leaned back in his chair at the conclusion of another losing hand and said, "That's it. I'm done." The green felt in front of him was empty of chips.

"It was a good game, J.D.," Hal Roberts said. Obviously the two of them had been acquainted before the tournament.

Wilson grinned ruefully. "I hope you'll tell my wife the same thing when she finds out how much I lost. I'm not sure she'll agree that it was worth it."

He shoved back his chair. "But it was. Good luck, gentlemen."

The table was down to four players, and visible weariness gripped all of them. Pennyworth, who was the oldest, mopped sweat off his face with a handkerchief and said, "I think a longer break is in order, if you agree, gents."

Conrad, Roberts, and Church all nodded. Conrad lifted a hand to get Bat Masterson's attention. Masterson, who had been in the room the whole time, somehow looked as fresh and rested as he had when the tournament began.

"We're taking a break, Bat," Conrad said. "You'll have someone watch the table?"

"It'll be just like it is when you come back," Masterson promised. "I can guarantee that. Go through that door right over there. There are rooms waiting for you. How long do you need?"

Conrad looked at the other three men. "A couple hours?"

They all nodded.

"Someone will wake you," Masterson said. "Have a good rest, gentlemen."

Conrad and the other men adjourned to the rooms Masterson had waiting for them. The rooms were furnished simply, with nothing more than a chair, a wash basin, and a narrow bed, but that was all Conrad needed. He stripped down to his underwear, put his clothes on the chair, and stretched out on the bed. Sleep hit him like a hammer.

But just before the blow fell, he thought about Arturo and wondered what his friend had found out about Rose Sullivan.

* * *

Rose was back at her desk in the outer office of Hudson, Burke, and Hardy when Arturo arrived at the law firm that morning. She greeted him with a smile, obviously remembering him from the day before. "Mr. Vincenzo, isn't it?"

"That's right," Arturo said as he took his hat off. "How are you this morning, Miss Sullivan? Recovered from your ordeal last night, I hope?"

She nodded. "I suppose Conrad told you all about it."

"Of course."

Rose looked around and lowered her voice. "We left before the police arrived, so I don't know if it would be a good idea to speak much of it around here."

"I understand. I was just inquiring about your health."

"I had a headache last night from that knock on the head, but it's gone this morning."

"Excellent. I'm sure Mr. Browning will be glad to hear it."

"Where is he?" Rose paused. "Oh, yes, that big poker tournament at the Palace. I've heard quite a bit of gossip about it. The so-called respectable people won't admit it, of course, but they're just as interested in it as anybody else."

Arturo smiled thinly. "No doubt. Is Mr. Hudson in?"

"Are you here on Conrad's behalf?"

"I have some business to discuss with him," Arturo said, not really answering Rose's question.

"Well . . ." Rose got to her feet. "Let me see if he's busy."

Conrad had told Arturo about the telephonic communications system between the offices, but Rose didn't use the black box on the desk. Instead she turned and went through the door behind her, leaving Arturo alone in the outer office.

She probably didn't want him to hear what she was going to say about him, he thought.

Rose certainly seemed like a pleasant, friendly young woman. It was hard to believe she might have anything to do with a couple vicious assassination attempts. Yet it made sense. Conrad and Arturo had discussed the matter the previous night, before Conrad left for the Palace. Arturo had a feeling Conrad hoped he was wrong, but neither of them was willing to rule out the possibility.

He thought about going through her desk while she was out of the office, but didn't know how long she would be gone. Besides, if she was cunning enough to do the things they suspected her of, she wouldn't likely leave proof of her part in it lying around where anybody could find it.

He waited patiently, and in a few minutes Rose returned and told him, "Mr. Hudson can see you for a few minutes, Mr. Vincenzo. But only a few."

Arturo smiled again. "That's fine. Thank you."

She ushered him down the hall to the double doors where Julia Moorehead waited. Julia led him into Ellery Hudson's office while Rose returned to her desk.

"Arturo," Hudson said as he came forward. "What can I do for you? Did Conrad send you?"

"In a way." Arturo glanced at the doors, which Julia had closed behind her. She might be just on the other side of them, though, for all he knew. Or she might be in another office, listening through one of those devices.

No matter. He would just have to take a chance. "Someone tried to kill Mr. Browning again last night."

Hudson's eyes widened in shock. "Good Lord!" the mild-looking little attorney exclaimed. "What happened this time?" Before Arturo could answer, Hudson went on, "Wait a minute. Wasn't he going out to dinner last night with Miss Sullivan, before that poker tournament started?"

"That's exactly right." Quickly, Arturo told Hudson about how two men had stopped the buggy, then traded shots with Conrad, only to wind up dead. He concluded by saying, "Since we both represent Mr. Browning in different capacities, I trust that what I've told you will be kept confidential."

"Of course. But the police—"

"He didn't wait for the police. The authorities found the two dead men, I'm sure, but have no idea who made them that way."

"Good Lord," Hudson muttered. "Why, it seems like every time Conrad is alone with Miss Sullivan, someone tries to . . ."

His voice trailed off as he looked at Arturo, his eyes widening.

"Exactly," Arturo said.

Chapter 15

Thumbs hooked in his vest pockets, Hudson paced back and forth through a slanting rectangle of light that came in through his office window. "I don't believe it. I simply don't believe it. If there is any truth to the idea, then Pamela would have had to anticipate every move Conrad is making. She would have had to arrange more than a year ago to plant someone in my office, knowing Conrad would come to see me when his search brought him to Denver."

He and Arturo had been hashing out the situation for long minutes, going over everything that had happened since Conrad's arrival in Denver. Hudson was smart enough to see the possibilities, but he didn't want to accept them.

"We've seen evidence in the past that the woman was diabolically cunning," Arturo pointed out. "She left behind assassins in Boston to strike at Mr. Browning, and it's certainly conceivable that she could have done the same here. There's also the matter of her cousin Roger, who was deeply involved in her schemes. He was in St. Louis several months ago, not long before Miss Sullivan came to work for you. Perhaps he actually hired her, acting on the late Miss Tarleton's suggestion."

Hudson stopped his pacing and shook his head. "Diabolical is the word for Pamela, all right. The hell that she's put Conrad through . . . He's put a good face on it and seems to be in good spirits, but the knowledge that his children are out there somewhere must be tormenting him every hour of the day and night."

"Just as Miss Tarleton wanted," Arturo said softly.

"Yes." Hudson took a deep breath and went on in a more business-like tone, "So what are we to make of Miss Sullivan? Is it really possible that she's a hired killer?"

"I don't think we can ignore the possibility. But if she is, she'll have to bide her time and wait to strike. She can't get at Mr. Browning while he's engaged in that poker tournament."

"Which gives us some time to investigate and find out one way or the other." Hudson nodded. "I like that idea. I'll try to find out more about her background."

"And I'll keep an eye on the lady herself," Arturo decided. "Perhaps she'll meet with her confederates, or attempt to recruit some new ones if she no longer has anyone to assist her." He smiled. "After all, Mr. Browning has disposed of the first three men who tried to kill him since he got here."

Hudson grimaced. "You say that like you think there'll be more."

"Don't you?" Arturo asked in all seriousness.

As Bat Masterson had promised, after a couple hours a waiter rapped on the door of the room where Conrad was sleeping. Even though he was still tired, the break had refreshed him somewhat. He hauled himself out of the narrow bed. Washing up made him feel even better. By the time he got dressed and returned to the room where the tournament was taking place, he felt ready to go for hours.

A couple tables were empty as more players took their breaks, including the one where Rance McKinney had been playing. Conrad spotted Masterson, and went over to him. "McKinney didn't get cleaned out, did he?"

Masterson shook his head. "No, he's sleeping. Actually, I think he's well up on the other players at his table."

That was encouraging. Conrad was lagging behind both Bernard Church and Edgar Pennyworth at his table, but he was still well within striking distance.

Masterson was finally starting to look a little ragged around the edges. Conrad said, "You should probably get some rest yourself, Bat."

Masterson nodded. "I intend to. Jack Barton's going to relieve me in a bit."

Conrad was vaguely acquainted with Barton, who had been a gambler, a deputy sheriff, and a Wells Fargo agent. He was a good man, tough and solid.

He would keep the game running properly while Masterson was taking a break.

The other players had emerged from their rooms and drifted back to the table. Conrad joined them, and the game got underway again. The men had cups of coffee next to them to help keep them alert.

By late afternoon, Hal Roberts had dropped out, heaving a regretful sigh as he stood up and left the table. He mustered up a wish of good luck for the other men and went into the main room.

That left Conrad, Church, and Pennyworth. Conrad saw the look the other two men exchanged. They regarded each other as their only true competition and probably thought of him as just a rich, idle young man who was taking part in the tournament for the thrill of it.

Let them believe that, Conrad mused behind a faint smile.

He continued his calm, steady play. Church and Pennyworth paid little attention to him. He figured each man had decided his best strategy would be to dispose of the other, leaving only Conrad to beat to become the big winner of the first round.

The pots gradually rose in value. Conrad took one now and then, and the gap between his winnings and those of the other two players began to shrink. Church and Pennyworth didn't seem to notice.

Suddenly, Pennyworth made his move. He had drawn Church into betting maybe more than he should have. Church had too much money in the pot to drop out. He wouldn't have enough chips left to stay up with the other two players in the next hand. It was win or drop out for Church, so the dapper man had no choice but to shove in all the chips he had in front of him. Pennyworth called, and then, almost as an afterthought, so did Conrad.

"Three kings," Church said as he laid his cards down.

Pennyworth gave an avuncular chuckle. "Not quite good enough, my friend. Full house, sevens over treys." He leaned forward, his chubby hands reaching out to gather his winnings.

"Just a minute," Conrad said. "I'm still in this hand."

He placed his cards faceup on the table. Church and Pennyworth stared in shock at the three, four, five, six, and seven of clubs.

"Straight flush," Church muttered. "You haven't gotten a hand that good since this game started, Browning."

Conrad shrugged. "Then I guess this was a good time for it."

He reached out and raked the chips into a pile in front of him.

Church laughed. "Splendid. To tell you the truth, if I have to be cleaned out, I'd rather it was you who did it instead of this pompous blowhard." He flicked a hand across the table toward Pennyworth.

"Pompous blowhard, is it?" the older man said with a scowl. "Let me remind you, I'm still in the game, Bernard. You're not."

Church pushed back his chair. "That's true." He grinned at Conrad as he stood up. "Good luck, kid," he added, inadvertently calling Conrad by the name he had used much of the time during the past two years.

Pennyworth snorted contemptuously. "A break before we finish this off, Mr. Browning?"

Conrad nodded. "Fine by me."

He stood up and stretched, then took out his pocket watch and flipped it open. Almost eight o'clock in the evening. More than twenty hours had passed since the tournament began, and not a single big winner had emerged yet, although most of the tables were down to two or three players. Table 2, where Rance McKinney was playing, had three men left, including the rancher.

Conrad hadn't eaten much during the day. He'd been living mostly on coffee. There would be a chance to eat a good meal and get some real sleep once that round of the tournament was over.

Pennyworth was older, and the strain was taking a toll on him, too, though, he didn't show it. He was the same amiable, grandfatherly figure he had been when the game started.

Bat Masterson had returned to the room a short time earlier, looking considerably refreshed. He strolled over to Conrad. "Down to just two of you, eh?"

"That's right."

Masterson lowered his voice. "It's really not fair for me to say this, but watch out for Pennyworth, Conrad. He looks harmless, but he's a sly old dog. I suppose you've figured that out for yourself by now."

"I know he's dangerous," Conrad said with a nod.

"I wouldn't have said anything, but . . . I know this game is about a lot more than money for you, amigo. I want this whole affair to turn out well for you."

"Thanks, Bat. I appreciate that." Conrad poured a cup of coffee from the pot on the table. "I guess we'd better get on with it."

He took the coffee back to the table. Pennyworth joined him. With a disarming smile that didn't disarm Conrad at all, the older man asked, "Are you ready, my young friend?"

"Ready," Conrad said.

Pennyworth gestured magnanimously. "The deal is yours, I believe."

Conrad shuffled and dealt a hand of standard draw poker, what they had been playing most of the time. He won the hand, but the pot was fairly small. Now that it was only the two of them, maybe Pennyworth planned on playing things close to the vest for a while.

Since only two of them were left, the importance of each hand was magnified. If either of them got reckless, the game might be over in a hurry.

During one of the breaks, Conrad noticed that McKinney's table was down to only two players, the rancher and a burly man with a bald, bullet-shaped head. He didn't look like he'd be much of a poker player, but obviously he was or he wouldn't still be in the game. Conrad hoped McKinney would be able to finish him off and move on to the next round.

Before he and Pennyworth could resume their game, the bald man let out a loud oath and surged to his feet across the table from McKinney. "You son of a bitch!" he yelled as one of his ham-like hands swept up the chair where he'd been sitting. "You cleaned me out!"

With a roar of rage, he flung the chair straight at McKinney.

grabbed the roll."

McKinney.

Chapter 16

McKinney threw his hands up to shield his head from the chair. It crashed into him and knocked him backward in his seat. The bald man lunged across the table at him, making cards and chips fly into the air. Those big paws reached for McKinney's neck.

Conrad headed for Table 2 as fast as he could. He had visions of that bald-headed monster snapping McKinney's neck, making it impossible for the rancher to ever tell anything else he might know about Pamela Tarleton and her schemes.

As fast as Conrad was, Bat Masterson was equally fast, and he was closer. He reached the table a step ahead of Conrad. The gun in his hand rose and fell in a swift, chopping blow that slammed the weapon against the top of that shiny dome. The man slumped forward, senseless, his weight shaking the table as he landed on it.

Conrad grabbed the man's collar and rolled him onto the floor, where he landed with another crash.

McKinney was on his feet, and stepped toward the man, looking like he was about to kick him.

"That's enough, Rance," Masterson said sharply. "He's not going to cause any more trouble."

"The bastard like to stove my head in with that chair!" McKinney shouted. "Whatever happens to him, he's got it coming!"

Masterson didn't exactly point his gun at McKinney, but the barrel swung more in the rancher's general direction. "I said that's enough."

Several of the Palace's burly waiters had come rushing in at the sound of the commotion. They were behind Masterson ready to step in if needed. Conrad stood shoulder to shoulder with the famous ex-lawman.

McKinney glowered at all of them and muttered, "Fine. I just never could stand a sore loser, that's all." He gave Conrad an especially dark glare, as if what he had just said applied more to Conrad than any of the others.

That was puzzling, but Conrad didn't take the time to ponder it.

The man on the floor groaned and began to stir.

"Roll him onto his back," Masterson told a couple waiters.

When they had done that, Masterson hunkered next to the man and pressed the barrel of the gun he held against the man's nose. The feel of that cold ring of metal made the man's eyes widen.

"Listen to me, Hugo," Masterson said in a calm, reasonable voice. "In a minute you're going to get up and leave. You don't have to apologize, and you don't have to make any sort of restitution for the trouble you've caused. All you have to do is get out of the Palace and don't ever set foot in here again, at least not while I'm here. Do you understand?"

Masterson moved the gun enough so the man could jerk his head in a nod.

"All right." Masterson stood up and moved back but kept his gun trained on the man.

Hugo struggled to his feet, shook his head like an old bull, and turned to stumble out.

Masterson motioned for some of the waiters to follow him. "Make sure he doesn't cause any more trouble on the way out."

With that taken care of, Masterson holstered his gun and turned back to McKinney. "My apologies for the disturbance, Rance. Are you injured? Do you need medical attention?"

"I'm fine," McKinney answered in a surly voice. "You should have shot that big ox, Masterson."

Bat smiled. "To tell you the truth, I wasn't sure I could bring him down with anything less than a Greener, and a wounded beast is even more dangerous, you know." He turned and raised his voice. "Let's get back to the games, gentlemen."

Conrad went over to Table 5, where Edgar Pennyworth was standing and waiting for him. "Nothing like a little action to break up the monotony, eh?" Pennyworth asked with a smile.

"I don't think Hugo cared for it," Conrad said.

Pennyworth waved a pudgy hand. "Don't worry about him. I've seen him around. Always a troublemaker. If Bat hadn't stepped in, he might have broken McKinney's back."

That was doubtful, Conrad thought, because if Masterson hadn't stopped Hugo, he would have. It was odd how he had almost been put in the position of protecting someone he absolutely disliked.

He and Pennyworth resumed their game. The hands went back and forth, the momentary advantage flowing to one man, then the other. As the evening progressed, Conrad slowly began to accumulate a larger pile of chips. Pennyworth's jovial smile disappeared. He had thought defeating Conrad wouldn't pose much of a challenge, but he was steadily being proven wrong.

Pennyworth began raising more, taking risks like a prizefighter who has grown tired and starts flailing at his opponent. Some of his gambles paid off, but more of them didn't. He threw in five thousand at a time. Conrad matched it and upped the bet. Pennyworth called, then muttered fiercely under his breath when Conrad's cards turned out to be better.

On the next hand, Conrad hesitated. Pennyworth saw that and attacked, not realizing he had just taken the bait Conrad laid out for him. Conrad tossed away a couple cards and drew two more, prepared to fold if necessary. But the cards surprised him and filled the inside straight he was going after. Still, he raised cautiously.

Sensing that he was about to make a recovery, Pennyworth shoved half of what he had left into the center of the table. He sat back and smiled, obviously expecting Conrad to fold.

Conrad matched the bet and raised the amount that Pennyworth had left. The older man's shaggy white brows drew down in a surprised frown. His only choices were to fold, which wouldn't leave him with enough of a stake to last more than another hand or two, or call.

Like a true gambler, he called. "Three aces," he said hesitantly as he laid his cards down, hoping against hope he would somehow emerge victorious.

"Sorry, Pennyworth." Conrad placed his straight on the table. Pennyworth stared at it, all the sparkle going out of his pale blue eyes.

Then he heaved a great sigh. "Ah, well. Can't win them all, as the old saying goes." He summoned up a smile. "You played an excellent game, young man."

"Thank you." Conrad gathered in the chips. He was glad Pennyworth was being gracious in defeat. He felt an instinctive liking for the man.

Pennyworth leaned back in his chair and raised a hand. "Oh, Bat," he called. "We have a winner."

Masterson came over to the table, an expression of disappointment on his face. He thought Pennyworth had won. His expression changed to one of surprise when he saw the pile of chips in front of Conrad.

"Well done." He clapped a hand on Conrad's shoulder, then reached over and shook hands with Pennyworth. "Thank you for playing, Edgar. It's always nice to have a bit of class in a game. Are you going to be around to watch the next round?"

"Yes, I believe I will." Pennyworth nodded to Conrad. "I want to see how this young man does. I suspect his next opponents won't underestimate him as I did."

"Probably not," Conrad agreed with a smile. He gestured toward the chips. "You'll take care of these, Bat?"

"Of course. What are you going to do?"

Conrad's muscles creaked as he stood up. He didn't know what time it was, didn't know how long he had been playing. But it felt like a week.

"I think I could use some rest, and then maybe a big meal."

"We can handle that," Masterson assured him. "You can use the room you used before."

Conrad nodded. "Thanks."

As he started toward the door, he saw Rance McKinney sprawled in one of the armchairs, legs stretched out in front of him, a drink in his hand. Their eyes met for a second, and Conrad saw the cold hatred in the rancher's gaze. He still didn't have any idea what had made McKinney feel that way toward him, but he was convinced it didn't have anything to do with the slight ruckus between the two of them at the Palace several nights earlier.

No, Conrad realized, McKinney's attitude toward him had changed at Ellery Hudson's dinner party, when he had found out who Conrad was.

The only reason McKinney would have to hate Conrad Browning would be if Pamela had told the rancher about him, he thought. There was no way of knowing *what* Pamela had told McKinney, but it couldn't have been anything good.

More than ever, he wanted to face McKinney over

a poker table. He would be betting more than money. He would be betting he could work the truth out of McKinney.

Arturo didn't have any training to be a detective, and he wasn't a frontiersman used to following trails. But he thought he could manage to keep an eye on one young woman.

However, the job was turning out to be more difficult than he expected. He had waited in the doorway of a building across the street from the offices of Hudson, Burke, and Hardy and watched for Rose Sullivan as people began to emerge from the building at the end of the business day. When she came out, wearing a neat hat on her blond hair, he gave her a chance to get about half a block ahead of him and then fell in behind her, staying on the other side of the street.

He needed a pipe and one of those hats like Sherlock Holmes wore in the illustrations in the stories in *The Strand* magazine, he thought. But such a getup would just draw attention to him, he decided, so it probably wasn't a good idea after all.

The sidewalks were crowded. Arturo picked up his pace, thinking he should get a little closer to Rose, so he wouldn't risk losing sight of her. The blue gown she wore was easy to see.

Of course, he realized, it was possible she would just go back to the boarding house where she lived. In which case he would follow her again when she went to work in the morning, and trail her home in the afternoon, if he needed to. If she was going to plan another attempt on Conrad's life, sooner or later she would have to get in touch with the men who would carry out the actual attack.

Unless she had decided she couldn't trust anyone else to do the job and planned to murder Conrad herself.

Or unless she was totally innocent, which Arturo considered highly unlikely given everything that had happened so far.

He wasn't surprised when she turned down a side street and went into a small, rather dingy restaurant. A sign painted on one of the unwashed windows read LUIGI'S. Arturo's mouth tightened when he saw that. Being Italian himself, he enjoyed his homeland's fine cuisine, but doubted if a dirty little place called Luigi's, in Denver, Colorado, would offer much in the way of good food.

The smells coming from the place as he approached it were surprisingly appetizing. He went down a shadowy alley, grimacing at the thought of what he might be stepping on, and found a door at the back. A slender, balding, sharp-featured man with a soup-strainer mustache answered his knock. Arturo spoke to him in Italian. "Are you Luigi?"

The man frowned at him in apparent puzzlement. Then his expression cleared as understanding dawned on him. He answered in English.

"You just asked if I was Luigi, didn't you, amigo? Nah, there ain't no Luigi. Well, there was, but he died and I bought this place from his widow after a horse fell on me down in Raton and busted my leg so I couldn't make a hand no more. Name's Weaver, Bert Weaver. What do you want?" The man looked a startled Arturo up and down. "You're too well dressed to be a bum lookin' for a handout, that's for damn sure."

Arturo struggled to make sense of the flood of words. "I'm sorry, I thought perhaps you were one of my countrymen."

"You're Eye-talian? Could'a fooled me, ace. You sound more like one of them Limeys, or some dude from back east."

"Please," Arturo said. "I'd like a table."

"Sure, just go around front." Weaver grinned. "I'll put on my waiter hat."

"No, you don't understand. I'd like to slip into the dining room from the kitchen, if that's possible."

"Oh! I get it now. You're trailin' somebody, ain't you?"

"I really can't explain—"

Weaver held up his hands. "That's all right, you don't have to. You got an honest face, amigo, so I'm gonna trust you. Who is it you don't want to see you?"

"There's a young blond woman, very attractive, wearing a blue dress and hat."

Weaver nodded. "Yeah, I seen her come in. She's been here before. She's your ladyfriend, is she, and you think she's steppin' out on you?"

"Hardly," Arturo said, wondering what this former cowboy would think if he explained that Rose Sullivan might well be a professional assassin.

"Well, it's your business, not mine. Sure, I'll help you out. The two of us bein' close to countrymen and all. Leastways we would be if I was really named

Luigi. Lemme take a look and see exactly where she's sittin'."

Weaver motioned for Arturo to follow him into the kitchen, then went through a swinging door into the main room of the restaurant. Arturo indulged his curiosity and checked the pots on the stove. He was tempted to sample whatever was in them but put that idea aside when he saw a rat scurry across the floor.

The scrawny proprietor came back, limping a little on the leg that horse down in Raton had fallen on. He crooked a knobby finger at Arturo. "The lady's sittin' in one of the booths up front. She can't see the kitchen door from where she is. Go out through this door and turn to your left. There's a table where you can sit and see part of the booth where she is."

"Will I be able to see if anyone joins her?"

"Somebody already has," Weaver said. "A couple of tough lookin' hombres. Are they gonna recognize you?"

"That's doubtful." Arturo's pulse began to speed up. Rose was already meeting with two more hardcases, no doubt hiring them to try to kill Conrad. "Will I be close enough to hear what they're saying?"

Weaver shook his head. "Not from that table. You'll have to get closer. If you do, there's a chance she'll spot you."

"That's a chance I'll have to take." If Rose was plotting to kill Conrad, then he had to find out as much about her plans as he could. He took a deep breath and pushed through the swinging door into the main room of the restaurant.

Chapter 17

Arturo slipped into the booth Weaver had indicated first, so he could get a sense of the restaurant's layout and where Rose and her companions were sitting. The space was long and narrow, with booths along each wall and others sitting back to back and side by side up the middle, forming two aisles. About a fourth of them were occupied by customers eating Weaver's food.

There were other booths along the front wall, and it was in one of those where Rose and two men sat, evidently holding an earnest, low-voiced conversation. Plates of food were on the table to make it look like they were there for a meal, but Arturo knew it was more than that.

From his position, he could see Rose's blue gown, and got a good look at the two men. Both were rough-faced, beard-stubbled individuals, one with a thatch of rusty red hair under a thumbed-back Stetson, the other man burlier and more ape-like with a derby crammed down on his head. He seemed to be doing more of the talking. The man with the cowboy hat leaned back against the booth's seat with an indolent expression on his face.

He also wore a revolver in a tied-down holster. Arturo had been around enough rough frontiersmen to know that meant the man fancied himself to be slick on the draw. Maybe he was. Arturo seriously doubted the man was as fast as Conrad.

Not that he wanted to put it to the test.

The booth closest to the front in the center section was empty. Arturo thought if he could reach it without Rose seeing him, he might be able to overhear part of their conversation.

He pulled his hat down lower so it partially shielded his face, then stood up and moved quickly toward the first booth. But not so quickly it would draw attention to him, he hoped. He kept his head down, despite the urge to glance up and get a better look at Rose.

When he reached the booth he slid into it and pressed his back against the seat. The top of his head showed over the seat, but not enough for her to recognize him. He leaned closer and strained his ears to hear what they were saying.

Rose's voice was too low for him to make out many of the words, but he suddenly heard her say something about the Palace, the theater and gambling hall where the poker tournament was taking place. He knew she had to be talking about Conrad.

A deep, rumbling voice asked, "What time?" That had to be the man in the derby, Arturo thought.

". . . way of knowing," Rose replied. "I'll have to . . . him out."

Arturo's pulse quickened as his mind filled in the blanks he hadn't been able to hear. Rose had told the men there was no way of knowing when Conrad might leave the gambling hall. She would have to lure him out of the place.

And when she did, Arturo had no doubt the two men would be waiting to gun him down.

He had proof that Rose had been plotting against Conrad. They had been right to be suspicious of her. He needed to go to the police.

His spirits fell as he realized the knowledge he had gained wasn't exactly proof. If he went to the law, it would just be his word against Rose's. She would deny everything.

He would have to catch her in the act, which meant he would have to risk Conrad's life. He wasn't sure he could do that. Better to hurry to the Palace and warn Conrad, so he wouldn't walk blindly into the trap Rose was setting for him.

He would wait for them to leave, then go out the back way and hurry to the gambling hall as fast as he could. Conrad would be sequestered in the private room where the games were taking place, but Arturo would get word to him somehow. Bat Masterson was in charge of things, Arturo recalled. He needed to talk to the famous ex-lawman.

His nerves drew tighter and tighter as the trio in the front booth continued their conversation. He couldn't make out any of what they were saying, but he knew they were probably discussing exactly how they would go about carrying out the assassination they were planning.

Finally, they stood up. Arturo heard them moving around. He hoped Rose wouldn't walk past the booth where he was sitting, look into it, and recognize him.

Luck was with him. The front door of the restaurant opened, and he heard a swish of skirts as she went out. The two men strolled past him, and the man in the derby actually glanced at him, but neither of them had ever seen him before so he wasn't worried about them recognizing him. They walked to the back of the place and paid Weaver for the food they'd had.

The men left the restaurant without looking at Arturo as they went by. As soon as the door swung closed behind them, he was on his feet. He hurried to the back and said to Weaver, "I'd like to go out through the kitchen, if that's all right."

"Figured you might want to do that," the former cowhand said, grinning again. "Find out what you wanted to know?"

"I hope so." Arturo paused long enough to slip a double eagle out of his pocket. As he pressed it into Weaver's hand, he said, "This is for your trouble."

"Well, it wasn't much trouble, but I'm mighty obliged to you, partner. Come back any time you want to. And tell your friends about Luigi's!"

Arturo thought that was highly unlikely, but he didn't take the time to say so.

Once he was in the alley again, he headed cautiously for the street. He knew he needed to be careful. It was possible Rose was still around where she might see him. He would have to check both ways along the street before he stepped out. If he knew his way around Denver better, he might try some other route, but he was afraid he would get lost and fail to reach the Palace in time to warn Conrad.

A shape suddenly loomed out of the shadows in front of Arturo, a patch of deeper darkness that moved swiftly toward him and took on the dimensions of a man. The pistol Conrad had given him was tucked away under his coat, but as he reached for it a fist exploded against his jaw and sent him falling against the wall. Arturo struggled to remain conscious as two pairs of rough hands grabbed him and shoved him toward the street.

A fog seemed to have descended over his eyes. He couldn't see much except shifting patterns of light and darkness, but he heard a deep, gravelly voice ask, "Is this him?"

"Yes, I thought so." The reply was in the cool, measured tones of a woman.

Arturo's mind was stunned, but he recognized the voice of Rose Sullivan.

"I told you I recognized his hat over the top of that booth. He had no reason to be there unless he was sneaking around, spying on me."

"What do you want us to do with him?"

Rose didn't answer for a moment as she pondered the question. Then she said, "Put him in the carriage and bring him with us. He might come in handy, especially if Browning gets suspicious and doesn't want to cooperate."

It was amazing how much different she sounded, even though the voice was the same. The sweet young woman was gone, and in her place was a cold, calculating schemer. Arturo knew he had to get away, had to warn Conrad.

"Just make sure he can't interfere," Rose went on.

"Sure," one of the men holding Arturo said. He grunted with effort, and the next instant something hard crashed against Arturo's skull with blinding force.

He suddenly felt like he was tumbling forward into a deep, dark well. The last thing he heard, echoing in that darkness, was, "Conrad Browning has to die tonight."

Conrad hadn't stretched out to go to sleep yet when a soft knock sounded on the door of the little room. His boots were off, but he still wore his trousers and shirt. Yawning with weariness, he went over and asked, "Who is it?"

"Bat."

Knowing that Masterson wouldn't bother him unless it was for something important, Conrad opened the door.

"Sorry to break in on you, Conrad," Masterson said. "I see you hadn't gone to sleep yet. Good."

"No, but I'm pretty tired, Bat. What's going on?"

"I got word there's a lady looking for you."

Conrad grimaced. "Honestly, Bat, I'm too tired right now to be thinking about women—"

"It's not like that," Masterson broke in. "Although I must say, Conrad, you're too young to *ever* be too tired to think about women." He noticed the look of impatience on Conrad's face, and went on, "This is that Miss Sullivan you're acquainted with from Ellery Hudson's office."

"Rose?" Conrad couldn't hold in his surprise. "What the hell is she doing here?"

"She said something happened to your friend Vincenzo and she needs your help. She saw him on the street. A man had attacked him and robbed him. She says he's hurt."

Mixed emotions shot through Conrad. First and foremost among them was genuine worry for Arturo. He had planned to investigate Rose's background, and he could have been following her. It was entirely possible that a thief could have assaulted him.

But Conrad also felt a nagging suspicion about Rose. Was this a trick of some sort, designed to lure him away from the poker tournament and out of the Palace so another attempt could be made on his life?

That was possible, but if Arturo actually was hurt, Conrad had to give Rose the benefit of the doubt. He had to play along and see what was really happening, but there was no reason he couldn't be careful. "Loan me a six-gun, Bat."

"I'll do better than that," Masterson said. "I'll come along with you."

Conrad considered that for a second, then shook his head. "No, whatever's going to happen, I want it to happen. I'm tired of not being sure about certain things."

"Yeah, but if you're walking right into trouble—"

"That's why I asked for the gun."

Masterson reached under his coat and handed him one of the weapons from his shoulder holsters.

It was a Smith & Wesson .38 caliber double action revolver with a four-inch barrel. Like most short-barreled guns, it wouldn't be very accurate at more than twenty feet or so, but it packed a fairly lethal punch.

Conrad checked to make sure the hammer was on an empty chamber, then tucked the gun into the waistband of his trousers. He pulled his boots on and shrugged into his coat, leaving off the tie and his hat. "I'll be back by the time you're ready for the next round to begin."

"Just be careful," Masterson said. "You don't know what you're walking into out there."

Conrad nodded. He was well aware of the danger.

Masterson came with him as he strode through the private room and into the main room of the gambling hall. "She's waiting for you in the lobby."

Conrad spotted Rose as he started down the broad marble staircase. She saw him, too, and hurried to meet him with an anxious expression on her face. She was waiting for him when he reached the bottom of the stairs.

"Oh, Conrad," she said as one of her gloved hands clutched at his arm, "I'm so glad I was able to find you. Your friend Arturo has been hurt."

"What happened?" he asked curtly.

"I was walking home a little while ago, and I heard someone cry out behind me. When I turned around to look, I saw Arturo fighting with a couple men. They must have been trying to rob him. I saw one of them reach under Arturo's coat and yank something out." She frowned. "What was he doing there,

Conrad? Was he following me? Do . . . do you not trust me for some reason?"

Before he could answer, she waved a hand, dismissing the question. "But there's no time to worry about that now. They hit him in the head, and when he fell down they ran away. I tried to help him, but he wouldn't wake up and I couldn't find a policeman and . . . and . . ." She was starting to sound hysterical.

Conrad said, "Settle down. Take a deep breath. Where's Arturo now?"

Rose took in a deep breath as he had said and let it out in a sigh. "There was a carriage passing by. I got the driver to stop and help me put Arturo inside. I was going to try to find a doctor, but then I realized we weren't far from this place and I thought if I could talk to you, you'd know what to do."

Conrad nodded and took hold of her arm with his left hand. "Show me. We'll get Arturo the help he needs."

"Oh, thank God." Rose sounded sincere, and Conrad wanted to believe her, but he couldn't take anything she said on faith.

They left the Palace, and he saw a carriage parked at the curb a short distance away. A short, broad-shouldered man in a derby hat stood there holding the reins of the team. He called, "Did you find him, miss?"

"Yes, this is Mr. Browning," Rose said as she led Conrad toward the vehicle. "He—"

Somebody inside the carriage howled in pain and the next instant its door burst open. Arturo tumbled out, shouting, "Conrad, it's a trap! Run!"

A redheaded man in a Stetson appeared in the doorway of the carriage holding a gun. Smoke and flame geysered from the weapon's muzzle, and Arturo was thrown forward on the sidewalk as a slug slammed into him.

Chapter 18

Conrad's hand streaked to the gun in his waist-band. As it came out, the front sight caught for a second, slowing down his draw, giving the red-headed man in the carriage doorway time to swing his revolver toward him. The gun roared and spouted flame again.

He was already moving, swaying to his right. He felt the wind-rip of the slug's passage past his left ear, mere inches away from its target. The Smith & Wesson bucked twice against his palm as he triggered it.

The gunman doubled over as at least one of the bullets punched into his gut. He dropped his gun and toppled out of the carriage, landing on the sidewalk near Arturo's sprawled body.

Conrad whirled in the direction of the burly driver in the derby, but he was too late. The man had already dragged a gun from under his coat. It was lined up, ready to put a bullet through Conrad's head.

Before the man could fire, another gun cracked, coming from the direction of the Palace. The man cried out in pain and staggered as blood sprayed from the back of his right hand. The fingers opened involuntarily and the gun clunked to the ground.

Conrad could have shot him without any trouble just then, but he didn't want the man dead. He wanted him alive to answer questions.

With a popping sound, another gun went off. Conrad felt the bullet tug at his coat in another near miss. That would be Rose, he thought, finally taking a hand in the action herself instead of just planning and acting as the bait. He half turned toward her, hoping she wouldn't make him kill her.

The man in the derby roared and threw himself forward, tackling Conrad.

They both went down, Conrad landing on the sidewalk first. The man's weight coming down on top of him drove the air from his lungs and left him stunned for a second, giving the man the opportunity to grab Conrad's wrist and pound his hand against the sidewalk. The Smith & Wesson flew out of his fingers and went skittering away.

As footsteps pounded past on the sidewalk, moving fast, the man reached for Conrad's throat. Conrad twisted and hunched his shoulders to keep his attacker from getting a grip. Driving an elbow backward, he dug the point of it into the man's stomach, buying him a second to catch his breath.

Conrad got his knees under him and heaved his body up. Breaking free of the man grappling with him, he turned to swing a hard, looping right into

the man's face. The blow didn't do much good. The
man's ape-like strength allowed him to shrug it off.
He flung out a long arm and backhanded Conrad in
the jaw. The impact sent Conrad rolling across the
sidewalk.

The man bounded after him. As Conrad came to
a stop, he lifted both legs and kicked out with them,
catching the onrushing man in the belly with his
boot heels. The man's momentum carried him forward, bending Conrad's knees. He straightened his
legs and used them to lever the man up and over
him. With a startled yell, the man sailed through the
air for several feet before he crashed in the street,
practically under the hooves of the startled horses
hitched to the carriage. The animals danced around
in their harness, putting the man in danger of being
trampled.

He scrambled away from the slashing hooves, but
as he surged to his feet, Conrad was already up and
waiting. He shot a hard left into the man's beard-
stubbled face, then followed it with a right cross that
landed solidly on his jaw with a sound like an ax
biting deep into a chunk of firewood. The man went
down again, and didn't move. Conrad bent down,
grabbed his coat, and dragged his senseless form
away from the horses so they wouldn't step on him.

With that done, Conrad looked around for Rose
but didn't see her. Now that the shooting seemed to
be over, a crowd of curious onlookers was gathering.
A man knelt beside Arturo, who hadn't moved since
he had fallen to the sidewalk after being shot.

Conrad ran over and dropped to a knee beside

his friend. He glanced at the redheaded gunman, who lay not far away. Judging by the pool of blood forming under the man, he no longer represented a threat.

"Can you tell how bad he's hurt?" Conrad asked the man who was bent over Arturo.

The man glanced up. "Are you a doctor?"

"No."

"Well, I am, so give me some room. If you want to help, let's roll him onto his right side. The wound seems to be in his left arm."

That was a relief, Conrad thought. A bullet through the arm was better than one through the body. But such a wound could still be very dangerous. A man could bleed to death from a bullet hole almost anywhere in his body, and from the looks of the dark stain on the left sleeve of Arturo's coat, he had lost quite a bit of blood already.

Carefully, Conrad and the doctor moved Arturo onto his right side. The doctor took a folding knife from his pocket and used it to cut away the coat sleeve and then the shirt sleeve, laying bare Arturo's arm. The upper arm had two ugly, puckered holes in it, about halfway between the shoulder and the elbow, where the bullet had passed through the flesh.

"Your friend is lucky," the doctor said. "It looks like the slug missed the bone. Once we get the bleeding stopped and clean up that wound, I'll be able to get a better idea of how badly he's hurt. It's possible there could be some nerve damage that would keep him from using the arm properly in the future."

That was a worrisome prospect, Conrad thought, but still a lot better than it could have been.

"He'll have to be taken to the hospital."

Conrad nodded. "Do whatever you need to do, Doctor. I'll see to it that all the expenses are covered. Money is no object."

"He'll get the best care I know how to give him either way," the physician said gruffly. He glanced toward the redheaded gunman. "I'm afraid that one is beyond help."

"Considering that he shot Arturo here and tried to kill me, I'm not going to lose any sleep over that." Confident Arturo was in good hands, Conrad straightened and went back over to the man he had knocked out.

He spotted the Smith & Wesson he'd borrowed from Bat Masterson lying on the sidewalk a few feet away and was glad no one had taken advantage of the opportunity to steal it. He picked up the gun and covered the burly carriage driver as he started to stir.

The man let out a groan and rolled onto his side. Struggling to prop himself up on an elbow, he shook his head as if he were trying to clear away the cobwebs that clogged his brain. Then he looked up at Conrad and blinked in surprise as he found himself staring down the barrel of the .38. "Don't shoot, mister," he gasped.

Conrad's face was as grim as death as he asked, "Why not? You and your friend tried to kill me."

The man held up a trembling hand, palm out,

and pleaded, "It was just a job. I swear, it was nothin' personal."

"And that's supposed to make me less inclined to put a bullet through your brain?" Conrad asked coolly.

"I'll do anything you want—"

"Tell me who hired you."

"It . . . it was the girl! That blond girl, the one who went into the Palace to lure you out here. I swear it, mister, I got nothin' against you."

"Do you know her name?" Conrad snapped. He had his doubts that Rose Sullivan was her real name.

The man shook his head. "She never told Riley and me her name. She got word to us through a bartender we know, a fella who knows that we do jobs like this."

"You mean who knows that you're hired killers."

The man's face stiffened. He realized he might be talking himself right onto the gallows. "I ain't sayin' nothin' else," he muttered in a surly tone.

Conrad eared back the .38's hammer, making the man's eyes widen in fear again. "Where can I find her, the blonde who hired you?"

"I got no idea, and that's the truth, I swear it. All Riley and me knew was where to meet her and talk about the job."

"How did you wind up with my friend as your prisoner?"

"That skinny hombre? He was spyin' on the girl. She spotted him in the place where we met and had me and Riley lay for him outside in the alley."

"If he dies, you'll hang. I'll see to it."

"That ain't fair!" the man howled. "I never shot him!"

"Your partner did, and he's dead. That just leaves you to swing for it."

Before Conrad could say anything else, a loud, authoritative voice ordered, "Mister, put that gun down and step away from that man!"

Conrad glanced over his shoulder and saw that a couple uniformed Denver policemen had arrived on the scene. He lowered the Smith & Wesson and nodded toward the man lying at the edge of the street. "This man and another one tried to kill me. The other one is lying over there. I shot him in self-defense. There were plenty of people on the street. I'm sure you can find witnesses to back up my story."

"That's fine," one of the officers said, "but until then you'd better hand over that gun."

Conrad hesitated. He didn't want to be unarmed.

Before it became an issue, Bat Masterson walked up, breathing heavily. "I can testify . . . that my friend Mr. Browning . . . is telling the truth. I saw what happened . . . with my own eyes."

The attitude of the police officers changed. "Are you sure about that, Mr. Masterson?" one of them asked. Clearly, they knew Bat and were familiar with his reputation as a lawman.

Masterson nodded. "I'm certain." He seemed to be catching his breath.

The policemen looked at each other. One of them shrugged and said, "In that case . . ."

Conrad knew they were going to take Masterson's word for it.

"My friend was wounded in the shooting." Conrad pointed toward Arturo. The doctor had cut strips off of Arturo's shirt and wadded them up to use as pads to try to stop the bleeding. "He needs to get to a hospital."

"We'll send for an ambulance wagon," one of the officers said with a nod. "And we'll take this one into custody."

Masterson said, "If you need to talk to Mr. Browning or me, we'll be in the Palace."

"All right, Mr. Masterson, that's fine."

Masterson put a hand on Conrad's arm. They turned toward the theater and gambling parlor.

"You followed me out anyway, didn't you, Bat?" Conrad asked quietly as they walked toward the big building.

"It's a good thing I did, I'd say."

"I knew when I saw the shot crease that bastard's hand and make him drop his gun, it had to be you who fired it."

Masterson laughed. "You're giving me too much credit, Conrad. That shot was pure luck. I was aiming at his body. I wanted to ventilate the son of a bitch!"

"Luck or skill, I'm glad you showed up when you did. He had a bead on me."

"Let's get a drink, and you can tell me what this is all about," Masterson suggested. "I assume it has something to do with those missing children of yours."

Conrad nodded, feeling a moment of bleak emptiness go through him. "It must."

A short time later, they sat at a table in a small

private room off the gambling hall with a bottle of whiskey on the table between them. Conrad sipped the drink Masterson had poured. He still had a poker tournament to take part in, and he didn't want to muddle his brain.

"I reckon you went after Rose when you saw her shooting at me," he said.

Masterson nodded. "That's right. I wasn't sure what was going on, but I knew she couldn't be your friend if she was trying to put a bullet in you. Unfortunately, she's considerably younger and faster than I am. I chased her for a few blocks, but she gave me the slip. What's going on here, Conrad? I thought she worked for Ellery Hudson."

Conrad explained the suspicions he'd started having about Rose. The frown on Masterson's face deepened as he listened.

"How could Pamela Tarleton have planned so far ahead as to set up all of this?" he asked when Conrad was finished.

"Pamela was a genius when it came to revenge. I've seen plenty of evidence of that over the past few months. I'm sure she tried to plan for every contingency she could think of. We've only seen the schemes that actually came to fruition."

Masterson shook his head. "This Rose Sullivan seems to be almost as cunning. She came close to killing you several times."

"I know." Conrad nodded.

"Now that you've exposed her for what she is, you shouldn't have to worry about her anymore."

Conrad hoped that was the case, but he wasn't so

sure. Certainly it wouldn't be as easy for her to try to kill him, but she had gotten away. He wasn't convinced she would just give up. Pamela must have paid her to kill him. Rose, or whatever her real name was, might feel she had to honor that bargain.

"What are you going to do now?" Masterson asked.

"Find out where Arturo was taken and make sure he's all right. Then I'll take my place in the tournament again. Have there been any more winners?"

"A couple. You really intend to carry on with it?"

"I know there's a connection between McKinney and Pamela, and I still have a hunch he knows more than he's been willing to admit so far." Conrad smiled faintly. "When the time comes for the next round, I'll be ready."

Chapter 19

It took only a short while to discover where Arturo had been taken. When Conrad arrived at the hospital he learned the bullet wound in Arturo's arm had been cleaned and dressed, and thick rolls of bandages were wrapped around the arm, making it hard for him to move it. Of course, he didn't need to be moving it anyway, the doctor said. He also had a bandage around his head where he had an ugly gash from the blow of the gun butt that had knocked him out.

The shock of being shot had caused him to pass out, and the loss of blood had kept him unconscious for a while. Once his senses returned Conrad was able to talk to him, although the doctor cautioned him to make it short and not tire the patient too much.

Arturo explained how he followed Rose to the grimy little restaurant called Luigi's and eavesdropped on her conversation with the two hired gunmen. His story agreed with what Conrad had been told by the derby-wearing killer.

"I'm sorry, Conrad. I thought I was being so sly and resourceful by following Miss Sullivan. Instead I walked right into a trap that could have wound up getting both of us killed."

"You got hurt a lot worse than I did," Conrad pointed out. "And yet you still tried to warn me."

"When I regained consciousness in the carriage, I realized it was still moving, so I thought they probably hadn't carried out their plan yet. I stayed absolutely still and didn't let them see that I was awake. Then when we stopped and Miss Sullivan got out, I was sure they hadn't struck yet. I waited until I heard her voice again, and that's when I made my move, as they say."

Conrad had to grin at that. "I heard that fella in the carriage—Riley, his name was—let out a howl. What'd you do, bite him?"

"Actually, yes," Arturo replied with a solemn expression on his face. "When I tried to get out the door, he grabbed me, and one of his hands was within reach. I hated to do something so unsanitary, but it seemed like the best course of action at the time."

"Maybe you won't catch hydrophobia from him, even though he was a skunk, sure enough." Conrad chuckled.

"He yelled and let me go," Arturo went on, "and I made it out the door and called to you. Then I heard a shot, and that's the last thing I remember until I woke up here."

"I thought he'd killed you. It was a big relief when I found out he hadn't."

"For me as well," Arturo said in all seriousness. "I owe you an apology, though, sir."

Conrad frowned. "How do you figure that?"

"I allowed myself to be captured so that I could be used against you. Not only that, but now Miss Sullivan has escaped."

"It's not your fault she got away, and at least now we know for sure that she's been plotting against me."

"But wouldn't it have been better if she wasn't aware you were on to her schemes?"

Conrad shrugged. "Who knows? This way there's no chance of her fooling any of us again. The one who really lost out is Ellery Hudson. He'll have to find somebody to take her place."

A nurse came into the room and insisted that Conrad leave. Arturo needed his rest. Conrad agreed, and returned to the Palace, hoping Masterson hadn't been forced to delay the start of the tournament's second round because of him.

Stifling a yawn as he went into the building, he pulled out his watch. It was after midnight. He'd had only a couple hours sleep in the past forty-eight hours, and was starting to wear down. Despite that, he had to press on and do whatever was necessary.

One of the hostesses was coming down the stairs as he was going up. She recognized him and said, "Oh, Mr. Browning, Mr. Masterson said that when you came in, he wanted to see you right away."

Conrad nodded. "Thanks. I was just on my way to look for him. Do you know if the second round of the tournament is ready to get underway?"

The woman shook her head. "We're still waiting for the winner to be determined at one of the tables."

That news made Conrad feel a little better. He hadn't held things up. After checking in with Bat and making sure nothing else had come up, he might still have time to get a little sleep.

He found Masterson in the big room where the tournament was taking place. As the hostess had said, only one game was still going on, with two men each doggedly trying to clean out the other. Some of the players were sitting around drinking, eating, or dozing. Masterson was talking to several of them, but he broke off the conversation and came over as soon as he spotted Conrad. "How's Arturo?"

"Doing as well as can be expected," Conrad replied. "He has a headache from being pistol-whipped, and that wounded arm will keep him in the hospital for several days. But it looks like he's going to be all right."

Masterson smiled. "That's good news. How about you?"

"Other than being a little tired, I'm fine," Conrad shrugged. That wasn't strictly true. He was more than a little tired.

"We can do something about that. The room you used before is empty. I made sure of that. Go get some sleep. It'll be a while before the next round of games gets underway."

"I don't want any special favors, Bat."

"And I'm not offering you any. You're one of the winners. I want you to be rested and at the top of your game when play resumes." Masterson paused.

"Anyway, don't be so damned stiff-necked. If somebody offers you a little help—which I'm not—there's nothing wrong with accepting it. Your father's the same way, always determined to go it alone."

Conrad smiled. "All right. Thanks. I *am* tired."

"Go turn in. I'll see to it that you're awake in plenty of time for the next round."

Grateful for the respite, Conrad went along the hall to the room and stretched out on the bed as soon as he had kicked off his boots and taken off his coat. Despite everything on his mind that he thought might keep him awake, he was asleep as soon as he closed his eyes.

A soft rapping on the door woke him later. He sat up, yawned, and swung his legs off the bed. He went to the door and opened it, finding one of the pretty hostesses standing there. She smiled at him. "Mr. Masterson wanted to let you know the next round of the tournament will begin in about an hour, Mr. Browning."

"Thank you," Conrad said, covering up another yawn as he did so. "Do you know what time it is?"

"Almost six o'clock, sir."

Conrad frowned. "In the morning?" That would mean he hadn't gotten much sleep at all.

"No, sir. Six o'clock in the evening."

"Oh." That made more sense. His deep, dreamless sleep had lasted more than twelve hours. A sudden growl from his belly confirmed that. He was ravenously hungry. "Thank you. Could I get a basin of hot water?"

"Certainly, sir."

After he had shaved and cleaned up, Conrad slapped as many of the wrinkles out of his clothes as he could and went to join the others in the tournament room. He found a sense of anticipation in the air. Even though only eight players would be continuing the game, many of the men who had taken part planned to stay and watch.

Bat Masterson was standing beside the table of food and drink. Conrad went over to join him and began filling a plate. One of the hostesses poured a cup of coffee for him.

"Feeling better?" Masterson asked.

"Almost human again," Conrad replied, smiling.

"You were worn out, and I can't say as I blame you. By the way, I paid a visit to the hospital earlier to check on Arturo."

"How's he doing?"

"Trying to tell the doctors and the nurses how they can run things better." Masterson chuckled. "That fella's got opinions on just about everything, doesn't he?"

"And he doesn't mind expressing them. I'm glad to hear it. It sounds like he's getting back to normal in a hurry."

Masterson grew more serious as he went on, "I took the liberty of hiring some men to sit outside his room and keep an eye on him."

"Guards, you mean?"

"That's right. I don't think that woman would try

to hurt him while he's in the hospital, but you never know."

Conrad thought about it and nodded slowly. "You're right. That was smart of you, Bat, and I appreciate it. Arturo can testify that she was trying to have me killed. Of course, so can the man who was arrested, not to mention you and me."

"She can't get to him in jail or to us," Masterson pointed out. "Arturo was out there defenseless. Not anymore, though."

The food and coffee made Conrad feel better, not to mention what Masterson had told him about Arturo. He looked around the room, searching for Rance McKinney, but didn't see him. With a slight feeling of alarm, he asked where the rancher was.

"One of his men showed up a few hours ago with a message from his foreman," Masterson explained. "Some sort of trouble at the ranch, I expect. Rance said he'd have to go and take care of it but insisted he'd be back in time to take part in the next round." The former lawman frowned. "Come to think of it, he should have been here by now. I warned him if he wasn't here when we were ready, he might have to forfeit his place in the tournament."

Conrad's worry grew. "You can't do that, Bat."

"I know why you want him to be here, Conrad, but there are other players who put up a lot of money to take part in this. I have a responsibility to them, too."

"I know that. I'd just hate to think that it's all been for nothing."

"You might wind up winning a lot of money,"

Masterson pointed out. "But that doesn't really mean a lot to you, does it?"

Conrad didn't answer. He didn't have to.

A few minutes later, his worry eased as Rance McKinney came into the room. The rancher still wore his black outfit and the black-and-white cowhide vest. Obviously he hadn't taken advantage of the opportunity to get some fresh clothes. Conrad supposed he had been busy with whatever had taken him away from the Palace in the first place.

He didn't really care what that might be. The important thing was that McKinney was back.

Bat Masterson called for everyone's attention and had the eight big winners from the first round come forward. Conrad didn't know any of them except McKinney. One of the hostesses brought out the same big white hat they had used for drawing lots a couple days earlier.

"As per the rules of the tournament established before it began, in this round there will be two tables with four players at each one. Step up, gentlemen, and draw for your table assignments."

Conrad wished that Masterson could just put him at the same table as McKinney, but that would go against the rules everyone else had accepted, and it would look suspicious, as well. Even so, he had to suppress a groan of disappointment as he drew a chip marked with a numeral 1 and McKinney drew one putting him at the second table.

"Take your seats, gentlemen," Masterson said, "and best of luck to you all!"

Chapter 20

The other three men at Conrad's table introduced themselves as David Carruthers, Adam Neville, and Steven Gray. Carruthers was a tall, distinguished man with a fringe of white hair around his head and a white goatee. Neville was lean and dark-faced, with deep-set eyes. Gray matched his name, a bland, colorless man, but Conrad knew not to underestimate him because of that. All three men had triumphed in the first round of the tournament, so he knew they had to be excellent card players.

They knew the same thing about him and would be approaching him warily. Hand after hand went by with the pots remaining fairly small. Nobody won or lost much. Conrad and Carruthers were slightly ahead, but that could change in a matter of minutes.

Concentrating on his cards and his game didn't leave Conrad any attention for the other game, so he didn't know how McKinney was doing. All he could do was hope that he and McKinney emerged as the winners, so they would face off in the final showdown. Luck had been running against Conrad lately, not in his cards but in the things that really mattered to him, so he hoped Fate would look kindly on him.

By the time the four men took a break at midnight, Carruthers had pulled farther ahead. Conrad was about even, Neville and Gray struggling a little more. The pots had increased gradually. It wouldn't take two days to determine the winner, Conrad sensed. The game might be over by morning.

Bat Masterson came over to him and commented, "The cards seem to be running pretty good for you, Conrad."

"Not as good as they are for Carruthers."

"David's a fine player, all right." Masterson nodded. "But so are the other two. They could get right back into this with just a few lucky hands."

Conrad was well aware of that. As the stakes grew higher, so did the potential for sudden shifts in the game.

Play resumed and continued on through the wee hours of the morning. Neville's luck never turned. Around four o'clock, he threw in his cards at the end of a hand and muttered, "That's it for me. I'm busted."

"Too bad," Carruthers said smoothly. "You played a good game, Adam."

Neville shrugged. "Not good enough."

There was no disputing that.

Neville shoved back his chair and left the table.

"Why don't we take a break, gentlemen?" Carruthers suggested. Conrad and Gray nodded in agreement.

Masterson wasn't around, so Conrad got a cup of coffee and sat down on one of the armchairs, stretching out his legs in front of him. Play continued at the other table, so without being too obvious about it, he watched Rance McKinney. The rancher was betting heavily, and the stacks of chips in front of him were smaller than those in front of the other players. Conrad felt like sighing. If it kept up, he wouldn't be facing McKinney in the final round. In that case, he wouldn't have lost anything except some time, and as Masterson had pointed out, he might be considerably wealthier when all was said and done.

But money didn't mean anything to him. The only important thing was finding his children.

When he and Carruthers and Gray resumed their game, a certain recklessness began to crop up in Conrad's play. He was aware of it and tried to rein it in, but the stress of the past few days—the past few months, really—had all his nerves on edge.

He had been prepared to spend the rest of his life as Kid Morgan, drifting from place to place, a loner and a fast gun. But then had come the hellish ordeal in Hell Gate Prison, followed by the discovery of the plot against him by Roger Tarleton, Pamela's cousin, and then the most shattering blow of all, the revelation of the twins' existence and their role in Pamela's evil plan. Since then he had carried out his search for them, only to encounter deadly traps almost every step of the way. It was too much for one man to cope with, he thought, especially for a man who already had to come to grips with his wife's murder.

He was tired of it. He wanted it over. He wanted to be united with his children *now*, so he could put all the dreadful past behind him.

Unfortunately, life didn't seem to be paying any attention to what he wanted. It went along on its bitter way, dealing out more heartbreak and tragedy.

He took a deep breath as he realized he had just pushed twenty thousand dollars worth of chips into the center of the table to call a bet. He had two pair in his hand, nines and fives, but Carruthers took the pot with a flush.

Conrad's jaw tightened as he studied his chips. He still had a good stake, plenty big enough for him to continue, but he couldn't afford to lose any more on careless, distracted plays. He saw the faint smile on Carruthers' face. The man thought he was losing his edge and would be easy pickings from here on out.

Carruthers was about to find out just how wrong he could be.

Coolly, almost emotionlessly, Conrad continued playing, and the chips began to flow back in his direction. It was a trickle at first, then a steady stream. He folded when he didn't have a good hand, stuck with his cards when he did, bluffed every now and then just to prove he could. Surprisingly, Steven Gray matched him almost hand for hand, and it was Carruthers who began to be squeezed out. Conrad saw the desperation growing on the man's face.

He had lost track of the time. Was it morning yet? He didn't know and didn't care. Bat Masterson was back in the room, moving from table to table to watch the play. Conrad wondered fleetingly how McKinney was doing, but he didn't take his eyes off his cards and his fellow players to check.

He tried to fill a straight and failed, winding up with a pair of threes to show for it. When he looked across the table at Carruthers, who had about twenty thousand left, instinct told him to see what would happen if he raised. "Five thousand."

Gray saw the bet and upped it five more. Carruthers stayed in.

"I'll see that, and ten thousand more," Conrad drawled as he pushed the stacks of chips to the center of the table.

Gray shook his head and tossed in his cards.

Carruthers had gone pale at the size of the bet. It would cost him everything he had left to call. But if he folded, it would be a simple matter for one of the others to force him out on the next hand. That would just be postponing the inevitable. "Call," he said as he pushed in everything.

Conrad put down his pair of threes.

Carruthers let out a deep groan as his fingers tightened on his cards until they started to bend. With a visible effort, he forced his hand open and dropped the cards faceup on the table . . . a pair of twos, a seven, a jack, and a queen.

"I thought you were bluffing," Carruthers rasped.

Conrad shrugged. "I was. I just wanted to see how far I could push you."

"And you wound up pushing me all the way out." Carruthers dragged a deep breath into his lungs and blew it out in a sigh. "Well played, Browning. I didn't think you had it in you. Your nerves must be made of steel."

Conrad didn't know about that, but he knew his nerves had been tempered by all the gunfights he'd been in during the past couple years.

"Very good," Carruthers went on as he pushed back his chair. "Congratulations to you both. I'll be interested to see what happens now."

Masterson came over, shook hands with Carruthers, and invited him to have a drink. Conrad and Gray stood up and stretched. Conrad checked the time. It was a little after eight o'clock. In the morning, he supposed. He didn't think he had lost *that* much track of the time.

A glance at the other table showed him that only two players remained there, and to his surprise, one of them was Rance McKinney. Obviously, the rancher had staged a comeback. He and the other man looked to be about even.

Conrad went over to Masterson and asked, "Do you think you could send someone over to the hospital to see how Arturo is doing, Bat?"

"I figured you'd want to know," Masterson said with a smile, "so I did better than that. I stopped there myself a little while ago. It's before visiting hours, so they didn't want to let me see him at first, but I can be pretty persuasive when I want to."

"Plus no one wants to say no to the famous Bat Masterson."

Masterson's smile widened into a grin. "What's

the point of having a reputation if you can't take advantage of it?"

"So how's Arturo?"

"Considerably stronger. They'll probably let him out of there in another day or two. He'll have to wear a sling for a while, the doctor says. But his arm should be all right."

Conrad nodded as a feeling of relief went through him. Their journey had turned out to be more dangerous for Arturo than Conrad had intended.

"Just you and Gray now, eh?" Masterson went on.

Conrad nodded. "That's right."

"And it's down to McKinney and Jack Lawlor at the other table. Things may work out for you yet, Conrad."

"I hope so. I've got a lot riding on this."

A short time later, he and Steven Gray returned to the table. Since Conrad had won the last hand, he had the deal. He called five card draw.

After he'd won a couple small pots, Gray took the next hand and changed the game to seven card stud. Conrad wasn't as comfortable with that but had no choice but to go along.

Gray won several hands in a row, and Conrad felt his nerves growing taut again. As if sensing that, Gray started pushing with bigger and bigger raises. Conrad told himself to settle down.

At the other table, Rance McKinney suddenly burst out, "Yes! Hot damn!"

Conrad glanced over and saw the dejected slump of the other player's shoulders. The man shook his head and spread his hands, indicating that he was out.

"How about it, Browning?" Gray asked. "Are you in?"

Conrad saw the arrogant grin on McKinney's face. He turned to look at the cards in his hand, and once again the blood in his veins seemed like ice water.

"Oh, I'm in."

To the very end.

Chapter 21

After that, Conrad's nerves didn't bother him anymore. His goal was in plain sight. All he had to do was reach it. He played with a cool-headed resolution, taking chances when his instincts told him it might pay off. Most of the time he was right. The pile of chips in front of him began to grow as the chips in front of Gray dwindled.

With McKinney emerging victorious at the other table, theirs was the only game left. Men gathered around the table to watch. They were careful not to get too close and distract the players, but Conrad and Gray were definitely the center of attention. McKinney came over and watched several hands with a sneer on his face.

Conrad ignored him. He raised two thousand. Gray called. Conrad took the pot with two pair.

He won the next two hands as well. On the next hand he got two eights and two jacks on the deal. He bet ten thousand. Without hesitation, Gray saw the bet and raised it five grand. Conrad discarded

the three that had come with the eights and the
jacks and dealt himself a third jack. He bumped the
bet up ten thousand more.

Back and forth the bet went, each man grim faced
with determination as the pot grew to staggering
proportions. If he lost that hand, Conrad realized,
he wouldn't be out of the game, but his chances
would be severely crippled. The same was true of his
opponent.

Gray knew that, too. He said, "There's no point in
dragging this out." He waved a hand toward the
chips he had left. "Everything. I'll bet it all."

It was a desperate move. Conrad counted quickly.
He was a thousand dollars short of being able to
cover the bet. He had to fold in order to have anything left for the next hand.

A chip sailed onto the table and landed on the
pot. "It's on me, Browning," Rance McKinney said.
"Call him."

Conrad turned his head to look at the rancher.
"Why would you want to help me out?"

"Because you're the one I want to face, not this
pasty-faced tinhorn."

Anger kindled in Gray's eyes. He leaned forward,
about to say something, but Bat Masterson stepped
up to the table.

"Gentlemen, let's not have any trouble here." The
former lawman's voice was calm and quiet, but it
had a steely edge to it. He reached down and picked
up the chip McKinney had thrown into the pot.
"Sorry, Rance. Stakes are limited to what each man
has on the table."

McKinney looked like was going to argue, but Gray spoke up first. Clearly, his pride was stung. "With your permission, Bat, I'll withdraw a thousand dollars from my bet. Browning can call now."

Masterson looked at Conrad. "All right with you?"

Conrad pushed his chips forward and said flatly, "I call."

Gray turned his cards over. "Full house, tens over threes."

Conrad's pulse thundered in his ears. He laid his cards faceup on the table. "I have a full house, too. Jacks over eights."

Gray stared at the cards for a second, then closed his eyes and sighed. When he opened them, he said dully, "The pot is yours."

Cheers and applause erupted from some of the spectators. Men leaned forward to pound Conrad on the back. McKinney looked on sullenly. No one had congratulated him like that when he won.

Gray picked up his lone remaining chip and tossed it across the table onto the pile in front of Conrad. "I don't see any point in playing another hand. The game is yours as well, Mr. Browning."

Conrad glanced at Masterson, who nodded in agreement. The outcome of the next hand was a foregone conclusion. Playing it out would have been a waste of time.

Masterson drew out his watch and checked the time. "It's just after noon," he announced. "The final round will begin at six o'clock this evening, if that's agreeable to the players."

"Fine by me," McKinney said.

Conrad nodded. "All right." He needed food and rest again. The tournament had turned into something of a marathon.

"Six o'clock, then," Masterson said as he snapped his watch shut. "And may the best man win."

McKinney's sneer made it clear he had no doubt who that was going to be.

Despite the weariness that gripped him, Conrad told Masterson to have one of the hostesses wake him in three hours. "There's a barber just down the street. I want to get cleaned up, and if there's time I'll go to the hospital and see Arturo."

"Just be careful when you leave here," Masterson advised. "Rose Sullivan is still out there somewhere. She might make another try for you."

Conrad shrugged. "I doubt that. Now that she knows we're on to her, she's probably left town." He wasn't completely convinced of that, even as he said it. He didn't really know what Rose was capable of.

The three hours of sleep blunted his exhaustion, and after a hot bath and a shave, he felt considerably better as he dressed in fresh clothes he'd had sent over. His spirits perked up even more when he reached the hospital and saw how much better Arturo looked.

He was sitting up in bed with his left arm in a black silk sling. A tray of food was in front of him and he was pushing the remains of a meal around listlessly with a fork. He smiled, his mood visibly brightening as Conrad came in. "It's good to see you, sir. Does this mean the tournament is over?"

Conrad shook his head. "No, but the final round

will be starting before much longer. Me against Rance McKinney."

"That's what you wanted, isn't it?"

"Yeah. I'm going to see if I can't get McKinney to talk about Pamela."

"You don't expect him to admit much about her in front of everyone who'll be watching, do you?"

"All I want to know is whether or not she had the twins with her when she was here in Denver before. And if she did, whether he knows what she did with them." Conrad took a deep breath. "But that's enough about my problems. How are you feeling?"

Arturo looked down at his tray with disdain. "I'd be much better if they had some decent food here. I'm not sure but that I could have gotten a better meal at Luigi's."

"I can see if I could get something sent over from there," Conrad offered with a smile.

"No, no, that's not necessary," Arturo said quickly. "I don't expect that I'll be staying here much longer. I can put up with hospital food until then." He started to shrug, then stopped short and winced. "Otherwise I'm doing quite well, as long as I remember not to move this arm very much."

"I'm glad to hear that."

Arturo lowered his voice and asked, "Is there still a gunman out in the hallway?"

"You mean the guard that Bat sent over?" Conrad nodded. "Yeah, somebody's still out there keeping an eye on you."

"Do you really think that's necessary?"

"As long as Rose Sullivan, or whatever her name is, is loose, I don't think it'll hurt anything."

Arturo sighed. "Very well. I don't see that I represent much of a threat to Miss Sullivan, but I suppose you know more about this sort of thing than I do. After all, a lot more people have tried to kill you."

"That's the truth."

Conrad visited with Arturo for a while longer, then looked at his watch and saw it was time he needed to be getting back to the Palace.

"If you find out anything, let me know right away," Arturo said. "Any time of the day or night."

Conrad smiled as he put his hat on. "I doubt if the nurses would let me in here in the middle of the night."

"Oh, I doubt that. I never saw a place yet you couldn't charm your way into."

Conrad laughed and lifted a hand in farewell as he left the room. "I'll see you tomorrow," he promised.

He was solemn again by the time he reached the Palace. Before the night was over, he might know more about the fate of his children. Or he might discover that the whole thing had been an exercise in futility. With the way the search had gone so far, it was hard to know what to expect.

The main room of the gambling hall was crowded. A roar of acclaim went up as Conrad went in, which took him by surprise. Obviously most of those people recognized him and knew he was one of the finalists in the tournament. As he made his way across the room, men crowded around to shake his hand, slap him on the back, and wish him luck. Conrad tried to be gracious about it, but he quickly found himself growing impatient with the display.

Bat Masterson rescued him, showing up to put an arm around Conrad's shoulders and lead him toward the private room, saying in a loud, cheerful voice, "Let us through, folks, let us through! The cards are waiting!"

Quite a few of the men who had taken part in the tournament were in the private room, drinking and smoking. Their ten thousand dollar buy-in had bought them that privilege. They would be allowed to witness the conclusion of one of the biggest poker games ever held west of the Mississippi.

All the tables had been cleared out except the one where Conrad and McKinney would play. Their chips were stacked up neatly on each side. McKinney was already at the table, slumped and brooding in his chair. When Conrad came up and rested his hand on the back of the opposite chair, McKinney's eyes rose to lock with his for a second.

A hatred much deeper than a man would normally feel for an opponent in a game burned in McKinney's gaze. Once again, Conrad wondered what had caused the rancher to feel that way about him. It had to have something to do with Pamela.

"Do either of you need a drink or something to eat before we begin?" Masterson asked.

McKinney shook his head. "Let's just get this over with."

"I could use a cup of coffee," Conrad said.

Masterson motioned for one of the hostesses to bring the coffee, then reached inside his coat and brought out a sealed pack of fresh cards. He slit the seal with a thumbnail, removed it, shuffled the cards deftly, and placed them in the center of the table.

"Cut for deal, gentlemen."

Conrad nodded to McKinney. "Go ahead."

McKinney reached out and took some of the cards off the top of the deck. He cut the queen of hearts.

"Conrad?" Masterson said.

Lazily, apparently completely at ease, Conrad leaned forward and cut the deck as well.

He turned up the ace of spades.

"The deal is yours," Masterson said. "Good luck, gentlemen. Let the game begin."

Chapter 22

There hadn't been a lot of talk during the previous games. Some men liked to have some conversation along with their cards, but most serious players had little to say except things that had to do with the game. The men taking part in the high-stakes tournament were all serious players, no doubt about that.

McKinney was almost completely silent and uncommunicative. He said how many cards he wanted and announced whether he was calling or raising, and that was it. He sullenly ignored Conrad's attempts at small talk.

It wasn't going to be easy to get McKinney to spill whatever he knew about Pamela. Conrad was going to have to figure out a way to make it part of the game.

He won the first few hands. The trend made McKinney scowl darkly. Then the rancher took a good-sized pot, and for a second, a triumphant grin flashed across his face.

"Maybe your luck is changing," Conrad commented.

McKinney grunted. "Luck's got nothin' to do with it. It was only a matter of time."

Conrad took the deal right back by winning the next hand. McKinney's features darkened with rage. His brief taste of winning made losing even more difficult for him to swallow, Conrad thought.

Even though he had decent cards Conrad folded the next two hands. The pots weren't huge, and his stake was big enough he could afford to lose them. McKinney felt better again.

As the next hand got underway, Conrad looked at his cards and said, "I'm curious about the time you spent with Pamela while she was here in Denver."

McKinney grunted and didn't make any other reply as he studied his hand.

"Why don't we sweeten the pot a little?" Conrad suggested. "You tell me more about her visit, and I'll take that in lieu of a raise."

"You're loco," McKinney growled. "That's none of your business."

Conrad saw some of the spectators exchanging puzzled glances. His suggestion definitely *was* odd. He pressed ahead with it, anyway. "You can't blame me for being interested. She and I were engaged at one time, you know."

"Not when I knew her," McKinney snapped.

"No, but that doesn't mean I didn't care about her anymore."

"Care—" McKinney repeated before he choked off the rest of the response. He shook his head and snarled, "Five thousand," as he pushed chips into the middle of the table.

"I'll see that and raise five," Conrad added a couple stacks of his own chips to the pot.

He didn't say anything else about Pamela as that hand continued. After a couple more raises, Conrad called and won the pot with four nines. McKinney threw in his cards disgustedly.

"You could have saved yourself some money if you'd taken me up on my offer," Conrad pointed out.

"Go to hell," McKinney snapped.

Conrad's natural pride made him stiffen at that insult. The men gathered around the table watched in rapt silence. Normally in the West, such a comment would result in trouble, a fist fight at least and quite possibly gunplay.

Conrad got control of his temper and smiled faintly. "Too late. I've already been there."

He didn't offer any further explanation, and McKinney didn't ask for one. Instead, the rancher asked, "Damn it, are we here to play cards or to gossip?"

In answer to that, Conrad began dealing the next hand.

He won several hands, and was well ahead of the game before he brought up the subject again. "Did you visit Pamela at her hotel while she was here?"

"You've sullied the woman's good name enough," McKinney said. Losing had made him edgier and more short-tempered.

"I didn't say anything improper happened," Conrad replied. "I just wondered if you met her children." He watched McKinney's dark, hooded eyes. There was no flicker of response in them, and

Conrad's heart sank. Was it possible his instincts were wrong? Could McKinney have been telling him the truth all along?

"I don't know anything about any kids," McKinney said. "Give me two cards, blast it."

Conrad dealt the two cards. "What about the nurse traveling with her?"

McKinney ignored the question as if he hadn't heard it.

The pot rose steadily as the two men traded bets. The spectators were quiet and attentive. Enough chips were in the center of the table that the hand was serious business.

"Twenty thousand more," McKinney said as he pushed out the chips. That drew a few murmurs from the other men in the room.

"That's fifty to me." Conrad didn't look at his cards. He knew what sort of hand he held. "I'll see the bet and raise ten."

"See it and twenty more," McKinney snapped.

Conrad didn't hesitate. "Make it an even hundred thousand."

No one said anything. The room was so quiet it was like Bat Masterson and the other spectators weren't even breathing. If McKinney saw the bet, more than half a million dollars in chips would be piled in the center of the table.

Conrad saw a gray pallor under McKinney's permanent tan. The rancher looked at his cards, looked at the big pile of chips, looked across the table at Conrad. Finally, between clenched teeth, he declared, "I'll call," and pushed out the chips to make it official.

Conrad laid down four queens.

McKinney's fingers involuntarily clenched on the cards in his hand. Breathing hard, he forced his fingers open and let the cards drop on the table. All of them were hearts . . . the two, three, seven, nine, and jack. The flush was a good hand, but not good enough to beat Conrad's four ladies.

Just like that, McKinney's stake was down to about two hundred thousand. Conrad had three-quarters of a million in front of him, once he'd pulled in the pot.

"You couldn't be that lucky," McKinney grated between clenched teeth.

"Careful, Rance," Masterson said before Conrad could reply. "I was watching every move the two of you made. So were all these other fellas. There was nothing shady about that hand."

Murmurs of agreement came from the other men.

"Then you won't be that lucky again," McKinney snarled. "Deal 'em."

"I think we'll have a new deck first," Masterson said. "You, ah, sort of bent some of those cards, Rance."

McKinney didn't apologize for ruining the deck. He sat impatiently while Masterson got out a new one and broke the seal.

With the new cards in play, Conrad dealt. As he sent cards floating across the table to the rancher, he said, "If you want to stay in the game, maybe you'd better consider my offer, McKinney. Tell me the truth about Pamela Tarleton."

"I've told you all I know."

"I don't believe you."

McKinney started up from his chair. "You're callin' me a liar?"

"Rance!" Masterson snapped. "Sit down." He looked over at Conrad. "You're supposed to be playing a game here, Conrad."

Offending Bat Masterson was the least of Conrad's worries. He sensed McKinney was about to crack. He just needed to apply a little more pressure. "What's the bet?" he asked as McKinney settled back down in his chair.

"Let me look at my damn cards." McKinney snatched up the hand Conrad had dealt him. After a moment, he said, "I'll open for twenty."

"I'm in," Conrad said. "Cards?"

"Three," McKinney choked out.

Conrad dealt the cards and drew one for himself. McKinney didn't miss that, he noted.

He had tried for a full house but failed, leaving him with three nines. McKinney bet ten thousand, and Conrad folded. He could have stayed in easily and possibly won, but he wanted to offer McKinney a shred of hope . . .

And then snatch it away.

With the deal again, McKinney's confidence appeared to rise slightly. Conrad opened for twenty thousand. McKinney matched it. After the draw, Conrad raised five. McKinney saw that and raised ten more. Conrad kept the pressure on with small raises that McKinney obviously felt like he had to match. His raises were reckless. The bet went back and forth, and almost before anyone knew what was happening, the pot was big enough that McKinney was forced to push in the rest of his chips. With his face haggard and drawn, he waited to see if Conrad was going to match the bet and raise again.

"Everything," Conrad murmured.

"You son of a bitch!" McKinney exploded. He would have come out of his chair if Masterson's hand hadn't dropped firmly on his shoulder and held him down. Panting through teeth clenched with rage, McKinney said, "You know I don't have it. You're not even giving me a damn chance!"

"Yes, I am. The truth about Pamela Tarleton will cover the bet."

"I've told you the truth!"

"I want to know about the children," Conrad insisted.

The two of them locked eyes across the table. The atmosphere in the room was one of breathless anticipation. Finally, after what seemed like long minutes but was probably a matter of seconds, McKinney said, "Fine. I'll tell you what I know. But not until after the hand."

Conrad shook his head. "Not good enough. You could be lying about knowing anything."

McKinney's lips drew back from his teeth in a grimace. "Two children, right? A boy and a girl?"

Conrad's heart slugged in his chest. His hunch had been right all along. McKinney did know something about the children!

"But that's all you're getting until I see your cards," the rancher went on.

Conrad took a deep breath and nodded. "Fine."

McKinney laid down his cards. "A pair of kings."

Startled gasps came from some of the men. McKinney had bet everything on a measly pair.

But the hush fell again when Conrad said, "All I have is a pair, too." He laid down the ace of clubs, followed by the ace of spades.

The black aces were enough.

The game was over.

Chapter 23

Rance McKinney seemed to shrink in his chair, like a balloon with the air leaking out of it. For a split-second, he'd felt a flicker of hope when Conrad said he had only a pair as well. There was only one hand that would beat McKinney's two kings.

Conrad's two aces had done it, and McKinney was wiped out.

Cheers went up from many of the men in the room, indicating that McKinney wasn't well-liked among the group. They were happier to see a relative stranger win. Several of them pounded Conrad on the back in congratulations.

Conrad watched McKinney across the table, shaking his head like he couldn't believe what had just happened. The hate-filled gaze he gave Conrad was even darker than before.

Conrad pushed the chips to the side. "You'll take care of this, won't you, Bat?"

"Of course," Masterson replied. "Do you prefer a bank draft or cash?"

"A bank draft will be fine. Send it over to Ellery's office tomorrow, will you?"

"Sure, if that's the way you want it."

The casual way Conrad talked about nearly a million dollars impressed the crowd. He went on, "Drinks for everyone, and take it out of my winnings."

"You heard the man," Masterson said, raising his voice. The spectators surged out of the private room to head for the bar, leaving Conrad and McKinney alone except for Masterson and a few stragglers.

"I believe you owe me something," Conrad told the rancher.

"You bastard," McKinney said. "If I had a gun—"

"You'd be dead," Masterson cut in, "because if you were armed, Conrad would be, too. Even if he wasn't, *I* am. There'll be no gunplay in here. The Palace may not be my place anymore, but the owner is a friend of mine and I won't have it shot up."

"No gunplay," Conrad agreed. "But you're going to have to pay off your bet, McKinney. Otherwise you'll be known from one end of the frontier to the other as a welsher."

"Fine," McKinney snapped. "I don't know what business it is of yours, but Pamela Tarleton had those two kids with her, along with a nurse. A boy and a girl, like I said. They weren't much more than babies."

Trying not to let McKinney see how deeply the news affected him, Conrad went on, "Do you remember their names?"

"Yeah. The little boy was Frank. The girl was called Vivian."

Conrad felt like he had been punched in the gut. Would Pamela really be that cruel? Would she really have named the children after Conrad's parents?

But she must have, because McKinney had no reason to lie about it. He might know that Conrad's mother was Vivian Browning, but he wouldn't have any idea that Conrad's father was Frank Morgan. That information wasn't strictly a secret, but it wasn't known to very many people, and no one who knew would have told McKinney about it.

"What else can you tell me?"

McKinney shook his head. "That's it. I saw the kids and the nurse one time, and Pamela didn't explain anything about them. I didn't figure it was any of my business."

"They went with her . . . when she left for San Francisco?"

"As far as I know."

"Were they happy? Well cared for?"

"Happy?" McKinney repeated with a scowl. "How the hell would I know if they were happy? They were little kids. But that nurse seemed to be taking care of them just fine."

Conrad nodded slowly. "Anything else?"

"I can't think of a damned thing. Are you satisfied, you son of a bitch?"

"Take it easy," Masterson warned.

Conrad said, "Why wouldn't you tell me any of this before?"

"Why the hell would I want to? I don't owe you anything." McKinney's mouth twisted bitterly. "At least I didn't until now. I can't believe you beat me with a pair of aces."

"You were trying to beat me with a pair of kings," Conrad pointed out. He shoved his chair back.

"Are we done here?" McKinney demanded.

Conrad nodded. "We're done."

Masterson said, "Look at it this way, Rance. All you really lost was the ten grand you used to buy into the game. Winnings come and go."

"Yeah, that makes me feel a hell of a lot better," McKinney snapped as he got to his feet. He stalked out of the room.

Everyone else had drifted away. Conrad and Masterson were alone in the room. Masterson took out a cigar, clamped it between his teeth, and asked around it, "Do you believe him?"

"I think so."

"Was it worth it? You spent days playing poker and risked a small fortune, and what did you really learn?"

"That I haven't reached the end of the trail yet. I didn't overlook the place where Pamela hid the children. She left here with them and headed on to San Francisco."

"There's still lots of rough country between here and there," Masterson pointed out. He snapped a match to life and set fire to the cigar in his mouth.

Conrad nodded. "I know. And I plan to check at every place along the railroad, just to make sure I don't overlook anything. But my gut is telling me that I won't find the twins until I reach the coast."

"San Francisco is a big town. Lots of places to hide a couple young'uns."

"That's true." Conrad smiled. "But I have nothing but time to look for them."

Masterson extended a hand. "Good luck." Conrad shook with him, and the former lawman went on, "What now?"

"As soon as Arturo is in good enough shape to travel, we'll head west again."

"You could leave him here," Masterson suggested.

"I know I could. But he's come this far with me and risked his life to help me. I reckon he deserves to be in on the finish."

"That'll give you a while to rest up after this tournament, I suppose."

"I could use it," Conrad admitted. "Playing for such high stakes will wear a man out. I think I'll go back to the hotel, have a good meal, and then sleep for another twelve hours or so."

"I'll walk over to the Lansing House with you."

Conrad lifted an eyebrow. "Worried about me, Bat?"

"I'm sure the word's already getting around town that you won almost a million dollars tonight."

"Which you're going to have delivered in the form of a bank draft to my lawyer tomorrow."

"Wrong. I'm not going to have it delivered, I'm going to hand it over to Ellery Hudson myself. I don't trust that much money to anybody but me."

"That's fine. I'm glad to hear it."

"Not everybody who hears about your big win will know that you don't have the cash," Masterson continued. "So we're not going to take any chances."

"Fine. I won't argue with you." Conrad tried not

to yawn. "Anyway, I could use the company. It'll help keep me awake."

The two men got their hats and left the Palace. Conrad knew he should be glad he had finally gotten more information from McKinney, but he felt strangely empty inside. Masterson was right; he hadn't really learned all that much, especially considering the strain of the past few days. And he had no way of *knowing* that McKinney had told him the truth, even though the rancher hadn't seemed to be lying.

"You said that McKinney has a pretty good-sized spread?" Conrad asked as he and Masterson walked toward the Lansing House.

"That's right. The Double Star is northwest of Boulder."

"Pretty rugged country?"

"Some of it." Masterson shrugged. "McKinney's range runs from the plains through the foothills and on up into the mountains. He's got a mighty tough crew and runs the place like it's his own little kingdom."

"In other words, you could hide a couple small children there without much trouble."

Masterson looked over sharply at him. "What the hell? You think Pamela stashed the kids with *him*?"

"I can't rule it out. I know there was a connection between the two of them. Maybe his reluctance to talk was just part of Pamela's game. Maybe he was trying to fool me all along."

Masterson frowned and shook his head. "No offense, Conrad, but you're thinking too blasted much.

You talk about Pamela like she was some sort of, I don't know, evil genius."

"You're not far off the mark there, Bat."

"When you think like that, you wind up just going around and around in circles. You can't ever trust your instincts, because Pamela might have anticipated that and made allowances for it."

Conrad rubbed his chin and frowned in thought. "You're right," he admitted. "But she's been two or three steps in front of me the whole way, Bat. How can I not consider every possibility?"

"Well, consider this possibility," Masterson said as they reached the Lansing House and paused in front of the hotel's entrance. "If you start poking around McKinney's ranch, you're liable to get yourself shot full of holes."

"That's a chance I may have to take."

Masterson looked at him for a long moment, then nodded. "If you decide to take a ride up there, let me know."

"You want to come with me?"

"Damn right I do. I don't like McKinney much, either. If he's got those kids stashed away, then he deserves whatever he's got coming to him."

Conrad smiled and clapped a hand on Masterson's shoulder. "Thanks, Bat. I'll let you know."

"You do that."

Masterson tipped a finger to the brim of his hat as Conrad went into the hotel. He got his key from the clerk and went up to his room. He walked past a gray-haired, stoop-shouldered maid and had his key in the door of his room before he realized a maid probably wouldn't be working that late at night.

He turned swiftly, but he was too late. Rose Sullivan stared out at him from under the gray wig, and the little pistol in her hand was pointed right between his eyes.

Chapter 24

"Don't make me kill you, Conrad," Rose warned.

Instinct made him clamp down on his nerves. He didn't want to do anything that would startle her into pulling the trigger. She was just out of easy reach, but not far enough away that he could dive out of the line of fire. A little more pressure of her finger on the trigger would put a bullet in his brain.

In the back of his mind, he was cursing himself for getting caught. The strain of the poker tournament and the things Rance McKinney had told him had filled up his head to the point that, while he hadn't forgotten about Rose, he hadn't taken the threat she posed seriously enough.

Coolly, he said, "I thought you wanted to kill me, Rose. You've been trying hard enough to do just that ever since I've been in Denver."

A faint smile curved her lips. "Things have changed."

That was interesting. He couldn't think of anything that had changed since the last time he'd seen her, but if there was something that kept her from pulling the trigger, that was fine with him.

"What do you want?"

"Go ahead and unlock the door, then go into your room. Don't make any fuss about it. If you raise a commotion and anybody sticks his head out to investigate, I *will* kill him. That person's blood will be on your hands."

"Take it easy." He started to turn toward the door.

"Carefully!" she ordered.

Taking it slow, Conrad finished unlocking the door and turned the knob. He swung the door open. The room inside was dark.

"Go on!" Rose ordered in a low voice.

As Conrad stepped into the darkened room, he sensed her rushing up behind him. He knew she probably wanted to knock him out, so he threw himself forward into that darkness and twisted aside at the same time. He flung an arm out behind him and snagged the sleeve of the nondescript dress she wore in her disguise as a maid. Closing his hand on the material, he dragged her with him.

She cried out as they went sprawling on the floor. Conrad kicked the door closed, figuring she wouldn't start blazing away blindly. The shadows were his friends. He rolled over onto his belly, then held his breath and lay absolutely still.

Silence greeted his ears. Rose knew any noise she made would tell him where she was. And yet they couldn't lie there forever, trying to wait each other out. Sooner or later, somebody would have to move.

A little light from the gas streetlamps outside

penetrated through the tiny gap in the curtains over the window, and more light seeped under the door from the corridor. Conrad's eyes began to adjust. He could make out the vague shapes of the sitting room's furniture.

His guns were all in the next room, but he couldn't reach them without betraying his presence. Still, he needed to be closer so he wouldn't have as far to go to get them when the showdown came. He slid a couple inches in that direction, the carpet on the floor making his movements silent.

A carriage team suddenly clattered by in the street outside. Rose might use that noise to cover up any sounds she made, Conrad thought. He lifted his head to look for her and saw a flicker of motion to his right. That gray dress she was wearing! It loomed in the air as she leaped at him.

Conrad whirled to meet the attack, surging to his feet and lifting his hands to grapple with her. He reached for her arm and tried to grab the wrist of her gun hand so he could keep the pistol pointed away from him.

He caught hold of empty fabric.

He heard the springs on the divan sag under a sudden weight, then something crashed into his back and drove him forward on his knees. In the split-seconds as he was falling, he knew Rose had slipped out of the dress and thrown it in the air to lure him into moving, then leaped onto the divan and from there onto his back. As he landed on the floor with her solid weight on his back, the impact drove the air from his lungs. The next instant, one of her arms looped around his neck and closed on it with incredible strength, keeping him from drawing a breath.

"You think a woman can't fight?" she said in his ear. "You think we're all weaklings?"

He didn't recall ever saying that, and he certainly wouldn't say it about Rose Sullivan, or whatever her name was. She obviously took her job as a hired killer seriously and was in superb shape. The lack of air was making his head spin as unconsciousness threatened to overwhelm him.

But he was bigger, heavier, and stronger than her, he told himself. He had to be able to break loose from her grip. He got a hand under him, then a knee, and heaved himself off the floor, taking her with him. Pitching to the side, he sent them crashing into the writing table against the wall of the sitting room.

Rose cried out in pain and her arm came loose. Conrad dragged air into his body as he twisted around and reached for her. A small but hard fist slugged into his face as she struck out blindly. Her other hand tried to claw at his eyes, and her knee dug at his groin. She was constantly in motion, and it was like trying to fight a wildcat.

The wig had come off, and he could tell she had tied her blond hair up in a tight knot on top of her head. He grabbed her hair to hold her still. Before she could pull away from him, he hit her.

She went limp, and even after everything that had happened, he felt bad about hitting a woman. As she sprawled onto her back and her arms fell out to her sides, he pushed himself to a knee and stood up over her.

Her foot came up with blinding speed and slammed into his groin.

Pain exploded through him, bringing with it the knowledge that Rose had been pretending to be stunned. She had fooled him, and he cursed himself bitterly as the agony forced him to double over and fall to the floor.

He heard the door of the suite open, and a harsh voice asked, "What the hell happened in here? You were supposed to get the drop on him."

It took a moment for Conrad to realize through his pain that the voice belonged to Rance McKinney.

"Don't worry about that," Rose snapped. "Just take care of him."

"Oh, I'll take care of him, all right," McKinney said with obvious anticipation.

Conrad wished he had a gun. Although he might not have been able to see straight to fire it, he would have tried anyway.

But he didn't get the chance. A dark shape loomed over him, and the world fell on his head, making everything else go away.

Sometimes just being alive came as a great surprise, which was how Conrad felt as awareness seeped back into his brain, along with a great deal of pounding agony.

He had been knocked out before, so he knew what it was like to feel as if a band of demons was inside his skull, slugging away at it with balpeen hammers. That was actually his pulse, and pain shot through his head with every beat of it.

But that meant his heart was beating. When he'd passed out, it had been with the grim acceptance of death. Rose and McKinney would probably slit his throat while he was unconscious.

Instead he was alive, and he gradually became aware that he was moving. The rough surface on which he lay swayed back and forth underneath him.

A musty stink filled his nostrils, and something scratchy rubbed against his face. After a few moments, he realized he was wrapped up in a blanket and probably lying in the back of a wagon. The roughness of the ride told him the vehicle wasn't rolling over Denver's paved streets.

So he was out on the trail somewhere, he thought. The fact that McKinney had been in his hotel room along with Rose Sullivan gave him a pretty good idea where he and his captors were headed.

They were on their way to McKinney's Double Star ranch.

Despite the pain in his head, Conrad forced himself to concentrate on the predicament in which he found himself. He remembered how Rose had slipped into the hotel in disguise and gotten the drop on him. The exchange she'd had with McKinney proved the two of them were working together. Conrad didn't know if that had been the case from the start, or if Rose had gone to McKinney for help after her true identity as a hired killer had been discovered.

It didn't really matter, he told himself. What was important was that two very deadly enemies of his had teamed up . . . and he was now their prisoner.

So far he hadn't budged as awareness came back to him. He remained as motionless as possible. The wagon's bumps and jolts made him move a little, but he kept his muscles limp so that would look natural. The longer he could keep them from realizing he had regained consciousness, the better.

When he got a chance to make a break for freedom, he wanted to take them by surprise.

He wondered how long he had been out cold. It seemed like a long time, hours, maybe, but he knew that feeling could be deceptive.

Along with the hoofbeats of the team pulling the wagon, he could hear other horses. Outriders, more than likely. Maybe McKinney himself, since he struck Conrad more as the type to ride a horse than sit on a wagon.

Rose would be on the wagon. He considered the possibility of throwing off the enshrouding blanket, grabbing her, and using her as a hostage.

It wouldn't work, he decided. For one thing, he was too likely to get tangled up in the blanket and slowed down by it. For another, just because McKinney and Rose were working together didn't mean that he gave a damn what happened to her. If Conrad threatened to kill her, McKinney might just laugh and tell him to go ahead.

Anyway, he wasn't the sort of man who used a woman as a shield, even a dangerous woman like

Rose Sullivan. He would have to find another way out of the mess.

And it would have to be soon, because he heard McKinney say, "There it is. The Double Star ranch. The last place that bastard Browning will ever see."

Chapter 25

It was too late to make a move before they reached the ranch. Conrad swallowed his disappointment and remained still. A few minutes later, the wagon came to a stop and he heard a gate being opened. The wagon rattled into motion again.

Several more minutes passed before the wagon stopped. Saddle leather creaked as men dismounted. McKinney said, "Let me give you a hand," and Rose replied, "Thank you." Obviously, he was helping her down from the wagon seat. Conrad felt the vehicle shift on its springs.

"Get him out of there," McKinney ordered.

The wagon's tailgate dropped open with a racket. Strong hands reached into the wagon bed and took hold of the blanket-wrapped figure. Conrad felt himself being dragged toward the back of the wagon.

As they lifted him clear of the vehicle, McKinney said, "Dump him out."

The men let the musty blanket unroll. Conrad tumbled free, but instead of crashing limply to the ground as an unconscious man would have, he caught himself lithely on his hands and feet. Blood pumped hard through his veins and he forgot all about how badly his head hurt as he sprang up and swung a fist at the man closest to him.

It was still night. Oil lamps burned on the porch of the big house in front of which the wagon was parked, so he was able to see the cowboy. The blow landed solidly on the surprised man's chin and sent him flying backward.

"He's awake!" McKinney yelled. "Grab the son of a bitch!"

Conrad knew the odds facing him were mighty high. If he could break away from them and get his hands on a gun, he might be able to capture McKinney. Rose wouldn't make a good enough hostage, but the rancher was a different story. Conrad knew McKinney's men wouldn't blaze away at him if McKinney was in the line of fire. He was going to fight until he couldn't fight anymore, and get his hands on Rance McKinney if he could.

One of the Double Star punchers who had accompanied the wagon leaped at him, swinging a roundhouse blow. Conrad ducked under the whistling fist and hooked his right hand into the man's belly. The cowboy folded up as the short but powerful blow drove the air from his lungs. Conrad's left hand shot out and snagged the gun from the holster on the man's hip.

"Look out!" somebody else shouted. "He's got Jonah's gun!"

"Shoot him!" The shrill cry came from Rose.

"No!" McKinney bellowed. "I want him alive!"

Conrad heard a rush of footsteps behind him and bent forward sharply. The man who tried to tackle him sailed over his head. Conrad twisted away from another man. He spotted McKinney standing in front of the porch steps with Rose and lunged in that direction.

A man yelled, "Hyaaah!" and suddenly a horse loomed up on Conrad's right, crowding in on him. He tried to get out of the animal's way, but its shoulder slammed into him and knocked him off his feet. He managed to hold on to the gun as he sailed through the air and came crashing down on the ground, but before he could swing it toward McKinney, another man rushed in and kicked his arm. Conrad's fingers opened involuntarily and the gun flew free.

The cowboy tried to kick him again. Conrad grabbed the man's foot and heaved, sending him falling over backward with a startled yell. Conrad rolled away and scrambled to his feet, ramming into the solid obstacle of a horse's flank. Something dropped over his head and tightened around his neck.

"I got him!" the rider shouted. "I got a loop on him!"

"Don't kill him, damn you!" McKinney roared.

Conrad had no idea why McKinney was so dead set on keeping him alive, but he didn't have time to ponder the question. He clawed at the lasso around his neck, trying to get his fingers under it. The rope was already tight enough that it cut off his air. The way the horse was dancing around, if it bolted the noose would probably break his neck as surely as if he'd dropped through the trapdoor of a gallows.

Men crowded around him and grabbed his arms. Some of the pressure went off his neck as the rope was cut. A fist crashed into his jaw and rocked his head back. In the chaos that surrounded him, Conrad couldn't tell exactly what was going on, but he heard McKinney say, "Hold him," and felt the man's hot breath against his face.

A fist slammed into his belly. Conrad felt sick, but there was nothing in his belly to come up. McKinney hit him again and again, pounding him like a side of raw meat while the cowboys held him up.

Conrad had endured beatings before. He knew how to put the pain aside and pretend that it didn't exist. Blow after blow battered him, until McKinney stepped back and said with vicious satisfaction, "I reckon that knocked all the fight out of him. Let him go."

The men released Conrad. He tried to stay on his feet, but his legs wouldn't support him. He fell to his knees and stayed there.

McKinney stood in front of him, looking dark and huge in that cowhide vest. The rancher grinned and rubbed his swollen knuckles with his other hand. "You may have won the card game, you son of a bitch," he gloated, "but you lost everything else. And you're just gettin' started learning how much you've lost."

He nodded to someone behind Conrad. A booted foot hit Conrad in the back and drove him forward, facedown in the dirt. He coughed as dust clogged his mouth and nose. He knew he was about to pass out again and fought to hang on to consciousness, but it was a losing battle.

A darkness as black as those aces he had used to defeat McKinney closed in around him and took him away.

When Conrad woke up, he was lying in a soft, comfortable bed between crisp, clean sheets. The shock of those surroundings was so great it was almost like someone had thrown a bucket of cold water in his face. He gasped before he could stop himself.

"Browning's awake," a man said somewhere close by. "Go tell the boss."

A door opened and closed, and it was followed by a sound Conrad knew all too well: the sound of gun hammers being drawn back.

He opened his eyes, wincing a little as light struck them. Sunlight slanted in through a window with the curtains drawn back. As his vision cleared, he saw two men standing at the foot of the bed. Each man had a double-barreled shotgun pointed at him, and the weapons were cocked and ready to fire.

"Better . . . be careful . . . with those scatterguns, boys," Conrad husked. "If they go off . . . at this range . . . there won't be . . . much of me left. Your boss . . . won't like that."

"Mr. McKinney said we was to go ahead and kill you if you try anything else," one of the men said with a sneer. "I reckon he's damn sick and tired of your tricks, mister."

Conrad felt too weak for any tricks. He closed his eyes again and lay there, trying to regain some of his strength as he took a quick inventory of his aches, pains, and bruises. Yep, he decided after a moment, he hurt pretty much from head to toe.

Footsteps sounded in the hall outside the room. Conrad opened his eyes. A second later the door swung open and Rance McKinney marched in. The rancher looked pleased with himself as he grinned down at his battered prisoner. "Well, I'm glad to see you're not dead. You'd be gettin' off too easy if you were."

Conrad's voice was stronger as he said, "What the hell are you talking about, McKinney? I never did anything to you except beat you at a game of cards."

McKinney waved his left hand. His right rested on the walnut butt of the Colt holstered on his hip. "I don't care about the money. It's what you did to that poor woman you got to pay for, Browning."

"Poor woman?" Conrad repeated in confusion. "You mean the woman calling herself Rose Sullivan?"

McKinney snorted in contempt. "Not her. That gal can take care of herself better than any I ever saw. She could probably whip half my crew, and out-shoot 'em, too." He drew in a deep breath and glared in hatred at Conrad. "I'm talking about Pamela Tarleton."

"I never—"

Conrad stopped short. He'd been about to say he had never hurt Pamela Tarleton, and that was true in a physical sense. But he had broken their engagement, and although he and Frank weren't truly responsible for her father's death, Pamela blamed them for it. She'd been hurt, all right, and that had allowed the vengeful monster she had been all along to escape.

"I don't know what she told you," Conrad said to McKinney, "but chances are, it was a lie."

"That woman never told a lie in her life," McKinney snapped.

The conviction in the rancher's voice told Conrad that Pamela had worked her magic on him, had woven a spell like some latter-day Circe and convinced McKinney to believe whatever lies she laid out for him. She had probably taken McKinney to bed. She had been able to make any man believe anything when the falsehoods were accompanied by soft, sleek flesh and softer kisses.

"She explained everything to me," McKinney went on. "She told me how you went loco and threatened her, and how she had to break off your engagement and run away from you just to save herself. She told me about how you've been trying to kill her ever since then and how she had to hide out. She didn't dare tell you about those kids, because she knew that would make you even worse. She said if you ever found out, you'd try to track her down, and she made me promise that if the trail led you to me, I'd stop you." He jerked his head in a curt nod. "So that's just what I'm gonna do."

Conrad felt a surge of despair well up inside him. The story Pamela had told McKinney bore a passing resemblance to the truth. But she had changed a few things, like the fact that it was he who had ended their engagement, not her, and twisted others until everything was backward. McKinney thought he was protecting Pamela, and that explained the man's reaction when he found out who Conrad was.

"You've got it all wrong," Conrad said wearily, knowing it probably wouldn't do any good. "I just want to find my children."

"So you can mistreat them like you mistreated their mother?" McKinney shook his head. "Not a chance in hell, Browning. I know what I've got to do. You're never gonna leave this ranch alive." A cruel smile twisted the rancher's mouth. "But we're gonna have some fun makin' sure you wind up dead."

Chapter 26

The vengeful expression on McKinney's face and the cruel anticipation in his voice made it clear what Conrad was dealing with. It was true Pamela had duped McKinney as she had duped so many others, but the rancher had had a mile-wide streak of viciousness and evil in him before he ever met her. Conrad had seen that for himself the first night he had run into McKinney, during that altercation in the Palace. He might have built a successful ranch for himself, but he was still a cold-blooded killer at heart, and the hardcases who worked for him weren't much better.

Conrad wasn't sure exactly where Rose Sullivan fit into things, but he knew she was working with McKinney. That increased the odds against him.

"You can't get away with kidnapping me. When I disappear, too many people will ask questions. They know you had it in for me. They'll come looking for me, and this ranch is the first place they'll look."

McKinney laughed. "Let 'em look. Nobody on the

Double Star will talk. My men are all loyal to me. By the time anybody actually searches the place, the buzzards will have picked your bones clean and the coyotes will have scattered them all over hell and gone."

That was certainly a grim prediction, and Conrad knew it had a good chance of coming true. But he didn't intend to let that happen without putting up a fight.

"Get up and get dressed," McKinney went on, and for the first time Conrad realized he was naked. McKinney added to his men, "When he's got his clothes on, bring him downstairs."

"And if he tries anything, boss?" one of the guards asked.

"Blow him to hell." McKinney grinned at Conrad again. "You see, Browning, I'd rather carry out what I've got planned for you, but as long as you wind up dead I reckon I can accept it." As he left the room he added, "Don't let him get too close to you. He's fast and tricky."

The cowboys nodded in understanding and backed off, keeping the shotguns leveled at Conrad. "You heard the boss," one of them said. "Get out of bed and get them clothes on." The man motioned slightly with the twin barrels of his Greener.

Conrad looked in the direction the man indicated and saw a pair of denim trousers and a plain work shirt draped over a chair. He pushed the sheets back and swung his legs out of bed, grimacing at the pain of stiff, sore muscles from the beating they had given him. "I don't see any boots."

"If the boss wanted you to wear boots, there'd be some boots there. Now hurry up, damn it."

Conrad sensed their nervousness. They were afraid he would try something. At the same time, they hoped he would. Then they could pull the triggers on those scatterguns and have it all over and done with.

He didn't want to give them any excuse to do that, so he moved slowly and carefully as he stood up, went to the chair, and started pulling on the clothes McKinney had provided. When he was dressed, one of the guards opened the door and backed out through it, keeping his shotgun level. The other two guards flanked Conrad.

He smiled at them. "You realize that if you shoot me now, you'll kill each other, too."

The guards' eyes widened, and one of them said, "Damn! He's right!"

Conrad laughed coldly. "Don't worry. I'm cooperating . . . for now."

He had looked around enough to see that the room was simply but comfortably furnished, and as he stepped into the hall and felt a thick rug under his bare feet, he saw the same seemed to be true of the rest of the house. A few yards away, the hall opened onto a balcony that overlooked a large room on the first floor. Conrad hadn't known until then that he was on the second floor.

He figured he was in McKinney's ranch house. The outer walls were made of logs, and there was dark, heavy wood almost everywhere he looked. The horns of deer, moose, antelope, and elk adorned the walls. It was the sort of house that would be built by a man who had carved an empire out of the frontier.

Some men did that sort of thing honestly and honorably. Conrad had a strong hunch Rance Mc-Kinney was not that kind of man. It wouldn't surprise him a bit if most of McKinney's first herd had been acquired by the light of a rustler's moon.

One of the guards backed away in front of Conrad while the others followed him. "They're waitin' for you downstairs."

"They?" Conrad repeated.

"The boss and that gal."

Rose, Conrad thought. Maybe that really was her name, although it didn't seem to fit her.

Not too many gals went by Medusa, though, he told himself with a faint smile, remembering some of the classical literature he'd read back in his college days.

He went down a broad staircase with banisters made from thick, heavy beams. At the bottom, he looked across the big room and saw a table sitting in front of a massive stone fireplace that was cold at that time of year. The table was set for breakfast, and the aromas of hot coffee and food made Conrad's stomach clench as a reminder of how long it had been since he'd had an actual meal.

McKinney sat at one end of the table, Rose at the other. Her pale, wavy hair was loose around her shoulders, which were left partially bare by the low-cut blue gown she wore.

McKinney grinned as he got to his feet. "Glad to see that you've decided to join us, Browning." He waved at an empty chair halfway between him and Rose. "Have a seat."

"You're putting me in the middle so that if your men cut loose with those Greeners, none of the buckshot will hit you or Rose, I take it." Conrad walked to the chair. He kept his face coolly impassive and didn't let them see how much he hurt all over.

McKinney chuckled. "That's right. Sit down."

Conrad sat. The coffee had already been poured in his cup, and the plate in front of him was piled high with steak, eggs, and biscuits.

He turned to look at the woman and nodded politely. "Good morning, Rose. Or would you rather I called you by some other name?"

"Rose will do fine," she told him, without indicating one way or the other whether that was her real name. "You really shouldn't have put up such a fuss, Conrad. It would have been much easier on you if you'd cooperated."

"Guess I always was too stubborn for my own good."

"That's the truth," McKinney said. "Otherwise you would've given up Pamela when you had the chance and not turned loco."

Conrad started to tell the rancher again that he was making a big mistake, but he gave it up as a waste of breath. After everything that had happened, McKinney would want him dead even without the lies Pamela had told him. McKinney's arrogance would have demanded revenge for that humiliating defeat at the poker table.

"Dig in," McKinney said. "You might as well enjoy your last meal."

Conrad picked up the coffee and took a sip of the strong, black brew. As he did, it occurred to him that McKinney might have had the coffee and food drugged. But why would he do that? He already had Conrad completely in his power. Conrad drank some more of the coffee, making him feel better right away.

The food helped even more. He was hungry enough that he wanted to wolf it down, but he forced himself to eat slowly and deliberately. "Just what is it you have planned for me, anyway? I know you're going to kill me, but how?"

McKinney cut off a bite of his steak, popped it in his mouth, chewed and swallowed. "Nobody ever claimed that Rance McKinney wasn't a sporting man."

"What does that mean?"

From the other end of the table, Rose said, "He's going to do something foolish. He's going to give you a chance to fight for your life."

Conrad had hoped McKinney might be leading up to something like that. He would stack the odds against him, sure, but the idea of leaving Conrad one single shred of hope before crushing him would appeal to the rancher.

Conrad turned his head to look at Rose. "I suppose you'd rather just put a bullet in my head."

"That's right," she said without hesitation. "I was paid to see to it that you wind up dead." Her sleek shoulders rose and fell in an elegant shrug. "But since you and that Italian friend of yours ruined all my other plans, I wound up having to go to Mr. McKinney for help. He's calling the shots now."

"Damn right I am. And what we're gonna do is have ourselves a little hunt."

Conrad looked back at him. "What do you mean by that?"

"The Double Star is a big place. My range runs for miles back up into the foothills. My men are going to take you out there and leave you, just like you are now, no gun, no boots, just the clothes on your back . . . and then we're going to track you down and kill you like an animal."

Conrad's eyes narrowed. "That doesn't sound like a very sporting chance to me."

"It's better than you'd get with that devil." McKinney nodded toward Rose at the other end of the table. She didn't appear to take offense at the characterization.

"You're probably right about that," Conrad agreed. He ate some more of the food and washed it down with the coffee, making an effort to stay calm.

He had said people would come looking for him, but he didn't know if that was true. He wasn't sure who it would be. Arturo was still in the hospital, but he wasn't any sort of frontiersman. Bat Masterson would deliver the bank draft for Conrad's winnings to Ellery Hudson, to be deposited in one of Conrad's accounts, but neither of them would have any reason to suspect something had happened to him in time to help him. Nobody else in Denver cared one way or the other about him.

He was probably on his own, he told himself. Alone, on foot, weaponless, with a horde of killers coming after him . . . that was the fate McKinney had in mind for him.

McKinney didn't know it yet, Conrad thought without an ounce of bravado, but the rancher had made a bad mistake by not killing him right away.

At that moment, the man sitting at the table calmly eating his breakfast before being taken out to be hunted down like an animal might still look like Conrad Browning . . .

But Kid Morgan was back.

Chapter 27

The Kid enjoyed the meal and ate plenty. One
thing a man on the drift learned in a hurry was to
eat when he got the chance. You never knew when
the opportunity might come around again.

McKinney started to get impatient. "There's no
use in you stalling, Browning. Things are gonna turn
out the same no matter what you do."

The Kid drained the last of the coffee in his cup
and set it down on its saucer of fine china. "Do what
you have to do, McKinney," he said coolly.

"Damn right I will." McKinney gestured toward
the guards who had stood by during the meal. "Get
him on his feet," he ordered.

The Kid stood up without waiting for the men to
force him to leave the table. He wanted to get out of
there, wanted to have a chance to move around
again and plan his strategy to turn the tables on the
rancher.

The first order of business would be to get his
hands on a gun but that would have to wait. At the

headquarters of the Double Star, he was surrounded by dozens of hardcases toting Colts and shotguns. No matter how good he was, he couldn't buck those odds.

McKinney scraped his chair back, too. "Tie his hands behind him and take him out to the wagon. Be careful. Don't let him try anything."

The Kid smiled faintly. He wasn't going to try anything . . . yet.

McKinney looked at the woman sitting at the other end of the table. "Are you coming along?"

"No, you don't need me. I've done my part. Just make sure he dies."

McKinney grunted. "Count on it."

While a couple men covered The Kid with their shotguns, another of McKinney's punchers came up behind him, jerked his arms behind his back, and lashed his wrists together with several strands of rawhide. The man jerked the knots so tight The Kid's fingers began to get numb right away as the circulation was cut off.

That might prove to be a problem later, he thought, but he would deal with it when the time came.

Once his hands were tied, the guards prodded The Kid toward the front door of the ranch house. He stumbled a couple of times when one of the men poked him hard in the back with a shotgun. The others laughed.

Keep laughing, The Kid thought. The time was coming when it wouldn't be so funny anymore.

They went outside into bright morning sunlight.

A wagon was parked in front of the house. Probably the same one that had brought him out there, The Kid decided. He hoped they wouldn't cover him up with some damn stinking blanket again.

"Get him in the back," McKinney ordered as he followed them out onto the porch.

Men grabbed The Kid's arms and hustled him down the steps and across the yard to the wagon. He didn't put up a fight. The wagon's tailgate was already down. When they reached it, the men took hold of The Kid and literally lifted him and threw him into the wagon bed. His sore muscles protested as he thudded down and rolled across the rough planks.

Awkwardly, because his hands were tied behind his back, The Kid worked his way into a sitting position. A couple of men climbed onto the wagon seat. One of them took hold of the reins while the other turned around and leveled a revolver at The Kid. Other men moved up on horseback, flanking the wagon on both sides. The shotguns had been put away, but half a dozen Colts were pointed at The Kid, and he knew they could shoot him to pieces in a matter of heartbeats.

"You know where to take him," McKinney said from the porch, where he rested his hands on the railing and watched with a satisfied expression on his brutal face.

"Sure, boss." The driver lifted the reins, slapped them against the backs of the team, and called out to the horses. The wagon lurched violently into motion, making The Kid sway back and forth since he couldn't use his hands to brace himself.

The slashing hooves of the team and the swiftly

turning wagon wheels raised a cloud of dust as the
vehicle bounced and rattled away from the ranch.
The guards galloped alongside it, except for one
man who trailed behind the vehicle, eating the dust.
The Kid didn't waste any time feeling sorry for the
man riding drag, since the varmint probably would
be trying to kill him before the day was over.

It was a rough ride. The wagon headed northwest,
toward the foothills and the snow-capped Rockies
beyond that formed a majestic backdrop for the
ranch headquarters. The sky was a brilliant blue with
a few white clouds floating in it. Denver's crowded
streets and the smoky gambling rooms of the Palace
seemed a million miles away, not just forty or fifty.

The Kid sat in the back of the wagon with his head
down. It probably looked like an attitude of despair
to McKinney's men, but it wasn't. He was gathering
his strength and clearing his mind, preparing himself to face what seemed like overwhelming odds.

The way to deal with odds like that, The Kid knew,
was to whittle them down bit by bit. In order to do
that, he had to make them think he had given up, so
they wouldn't be expecting him to fight back later on.

A couple hours passed as the wagon penetrated
deeper into the foothills. The sun climbed higher in
the sky and made the temperature rise. The Kid
didn't bother wishing he had a hat, knowing that
would be a waste of time.

Finally, the driver hauled back on the reins and
brought the wagon to a halt in front of a long line of
rugged gray and brown cliffs about half a mile away.

He turned and told the men on horseback, "All right, get him out of there."

A couple guards dismounted and approached the wagon while the others continued to cover The Kid. They reached into the back of the vehicle, grabbed The Kid's legs, and roughly hauled him out. He fell off the tailgate and landed hard, knocking the breath out of him for a moment. While he lay there half stunned, one of the men drew a knife and bent over to slash the rawhide bonds around The Kid's wrists.

"He's loose!" the man called as he stepped back quickly. "You got an hour, Browning. Then the boss and the rest of us are comin' after you."

The driver moved the wagon away and turned it around, leaving The Kid lying in the dirt. He tried to push himself up into a sitting position, but his hands were like lumps of dead meat and went out from under him. He slumped back down onto an elbow, drawing chuckles from the hardcases who surrounded him.

"Maybe you'd rather we just ventilated you now," one of the men suggested. "It'd sure be quicker, and you're gonna wind up dead anyway."

"McKinney wouldn't like that," The Kid said. "He's got to have his fun."

"We got our orders," snapped the man in charge. "Let's go."

He and the other men who had dismounted swung back up into their saddles. The driver of the wagon whipped the team into motion. Dust billowed and swirled in the air again as McKinney's men headed back the way they had come.

They wouldn't return all the way to the ranch headquarters, though, The Kid mused as he watched them gallop away. The spokesman had said they would come after him in an hour's time. They would rendezvous with McKinney somewhere between there and the Double Star ranch house, and the hunt would begin in earnest.

The Kid flexed his fingers and welcomed the fierce stabbing pain that shot through his hands. The blood was flowing again. He turned his head to gaze at the rugged cliffs. They stretched as far to the north and south as he could see. He couldn't get around them, not in the time McKinney was giving him.

The rancher had stacked the odds in his favor by choosing that place for his men to dump The Kid, planning to drive his quarry toward the cliffs and trap him there. Like an animal, he'd said more than once, and he meant it.

Cornered animals were often the most dangerous, though, The Kid thought as a grim smile touched his mouth. He flexed his fingers again. His hands were starting to work, and he pushed himself up. He made it to his knees, then climbed to his feet.

The rocky ground was rough on his feet as he started toward the cliffs. He ignored the discomfort and lifted his gaze to the heights beyond those cliffs. The terrain rose in a series of bluffs and canyons that climbed steadily into the mountains. He needed that high ground, and as far as he could see, there was only one way to get there.

McKinney probably thought it was impossible for any man to climb those cliffs.

Kid Morgan intended to prove him wrong.

His feet began to bleed before he reached the cliffs, but he didn't slow down. He didn't have much time. He had to get there, find a way up, and make it to the top before McKinney and the rest of the killers returned. If they caught him out in the open, trying to pull himself up a few inches at a time, it would be like target practice for them. They could sit down there and take potshots at him all day until one of them decided to put him out of his misery.

The cliffs seemed to loom higher and higher as he approached them. In reality they were probably about a hundred feet tall, he judged. Although from a distance they looked smooth and sheer, as he came closer he saw that they weren't. They had a slight slope to them in places, and there were rocky outcrops and fissures here and there. If he'd had plenty of time and maybe a rope to help him, climbing the cliffs would be a challenge but certainly not impossible.

He didn't have either of those things, he reminded himself. But even though he couldn't change time, he might be able to do something about the other.

As he trotted toward the cliffs, he stripped his shirt off. The sun was going to blister his skin, but that was a minor worry. The shirt was made of sturdy fabric that resisted tearing, but he was able to get a place started with his teeth and began ripping strips from it. When he had enough of them, he began weaving them together and knotting them into a makeshift rope.

A short time later he reached the base of the cliffs. He estimated that a quarter of an hour had gone by since McKinney's men had galloped off, leaving him with about forty-five minutes before they returned. He tipped his head back and searched the face of the cliff above him.

No handholds were within arm's reach, but he spotted a rocky knob he might be able to catch with the rope he had made from his shirt. From there he could reach other places where he could get a grip and hoist himself higher. If he could angle over a short distance, he might be able to get into a narrow crack he saw zigzagging toward the top. It petered out, but there was another outcropping above it that might give him a handhold.

Quickly, his eyes traced a possible path to the top. Following it would require clinging to the rock with fingers and toes like some sort of human insect and stretching himself almost beyond his ability to reach.

There might be an easier route somewhere else, he thought as he formed a loop in the makeshift rope, but he didn't have time to search for it. It was that way or nothing, and The Kid wasn't anywhere close to being ready to give up.

He had never worked as a ranch hand, but his father had taught him a little about handling a lasso. He gave it a few easy twirls, then cast the loop at the knob that was his target. The loop fell short. The Kid bit back his impatience and tried again.

It took five casts before the loop caught well

enough to support his weight. The Kid leaned hard on the rope to make sure it was going to hold, then began walking up the cliff as he pulled himself along hand over hand.

He had a nervous second as the loop slipped a little. He wasn't high enough to hurt himself if he fell, but he didn't want to waste the time it would take to start over.

The rope held, however, and he continued climbing. A moment later he was able to hang on with one hand and reach higher with the other. His fingers clamped over a rough spot that stuck out far enough for him to get a good grip. He pulled himself up, loosened the rope and slung it around his neck so he could take it with him, and used the knob as a foothold.

The minutes flowed past with maddening speed. The Kid couldn't pull himself up more than a few inches at a time. If he lifted himself an entire foot at one try, it was a huge victory. When he reached the crack he had spotted from below, he realized it was a little bigger than he'd thought. He was able to worm his whole body into it and lift himself by pressing with his feet and back. He left bloody streaks on both sides of the crack as the rocky surface tore and scraped his skin, but what was a little blood when his life was at stake, he asked himself.

And it wasn't just his life at stake. If he was ever going to find his children . . . if he was ever going to make a life for them with him . . . he had to survive.

He had escaped from Hell Gate Prison, he thought, and he had made it through quite a few other or-

deals. He could do this. For his sake . . . for the sake
of little Frank and Vivian . . .

His body was slick with sweat and blood, and he
began slipping. The rocks dug into his flesh as he
caught himself. He had lost track of time and
didn't know how long it would be before McKinney
and the other men who wanted to kill him showed
up. Turning his head, he looked out across the flats
and saw dust boiling up. A groan came from deep
inside him.

They were on their way. And he was only about
halfway to the top of the cliff.

The Kid started climbing again. He reached the
top of the crack and moved onto the face of the cliff
again, clinging desperately to it. He was high enough
that a fall would probably be fatal. Exhaustion made
his muscles tremble. He forced them to work and
pulled himself higher. When he reached an outcropping that was big enough for him to lie down, he
stretched out for a few moments, knowing he
couldn't afford the time but also aware that his body
could be driven only so far without a little rest.

After he had taken about a dozen deep breaths,
he struggled back to his feet and looked up, studying the path that rose above him. He had to use the
rope again to lasso another jutting rock. Above that,
he picked out several handholds and footholds that
would get him almost to the top. He had a chance,
he told himself, a real chance.

He didn't look to see how close McKinney and
the others were. There was no point in it. He would
make it or he wouldn't, simple as that.

After a couple casts, the crude lasso caught the rock. The Kid pulled himself up and was almost there when the rock pulled loose with a sharp cracking sound. For an instant, he seemed to hang in midair as he let go of the rope and his hands shot out to claw at the cliff face. The fingers of one hand caught in a tiny opening. He scrambled to find another hold as his weight felt like it was going to tear those fingers right off his hand.

His toes went in a crack in the rock, his other hand found a grip, and he was safe again. The broken rock bounced and clattered to the ground far below, taking the rope with it.

He didn't need the lasso anymore, The Kid told himself. He could make it from there without it. He dragged in a breath, set himself, and reached higher, ignoring the fear that made his heart hammer madly in his chest.

Ten feet . . . five . . . he could see the top of the cliff, tantalizingly close. He shifted a foot, dug his bloody toes into a narrow opening, and lifted himself. Reaching again, he closed his hand over an outcropping. He was almost close enough to stretch out and grasp the rimrock itself.

It exploded right above his head in a shower of rock splinters and dust as rifles began to crack somewhere below him.

Chapter 28

The Kid fought off the urge to make a desperate leap and try to grab the edge of the cliff. The odds of him being able to do that were so slim he stood a better chance if he continued the climb with the rifle bullets whipping and zinging around him. He clamped down on his nerves and reached for the next handhold.

Firing upward at such a sharp angle was tricky. Most of the slugs struck the cliff below him or sailed over his head. A few pocked the rock face around him, causing little chips of rock to sting his bare torso. He expected to feel the smashing impact of a bullet at any second, but until that happened, he was going to keep pulling himself toward the top.

He got a good hold and pulled himself upward. The rimrock was within reach.

A hundred feet below him, Rance McKinney bellowed, "Shoot him! Shoot the son of a bitch! Five hundred dollars to whoever brings him down! A thousand, damn it!"

The sharp rattle of gunfire filled the air as The Kid stretched his right hand up and closed it over the rocky brink. He shifted his left foot and pushed upward with it. His left hand clamped onto the rimrock as well. He got the toes of his right foot in a tiny crack and put his weight on them, at the same time hauling himself upward with all the strength he had left in his arms and shoulders. A slug burned along his side and struck the rock, almost dislodging him, but he hung on desperately and heaved. His shoulders cleared the top of the cliff, then the rest of his torso, and then he was toppling forward, rolling away from the edge as bullets continued to scream through the air.

But they couldn't reach him. The cliff cut him off from view of McKinney and his men.

He could hear McKinney's livid curses. While The Kid tried to catch his breath and waited for his pounding heart to slow down a little, McKinney turned the air blue with profanity. When the obscene tirade finally ran down, McKinney replaced the curses with swiftly barked orders.

"Get the horses! Get the horses, damn you! We'll get up there and cut him off! He can't get away from us!"

McKinney didn't understand.

The Kid began to laugh. He didn't want to get away. He wanted to meet his enemies on his own terms, at a time and place of his own choosing.

He rolled onto his side, then onto his hands and knees and on up to his feet. Pain shot through him as he put his weight on those lacerated soles. He hobbled toward a sandstone bluff that rose to the mouth of a canyon.

McKinney's reaction told The Kid that what he'd suspected all along was right. There was a trail leading to the top of the cliffs. It had been too far away for him to have reached it on foot in the time they had given him, but on horseback his pursuers could get there a lot faster. He didn't know how much time he had before they would be up there trying to pick up his trail.

Unfortunately, the bloody footprints he was leaving behind with every step meant he would be easy to follow.

Although he hated to take the time to do it, he paused long enough to tear strips of denim cloth from the trousers he wore using a sharp rock. He wrapped those strips around his feet and tied them in place. They served the dual purpose of protecting his feet and slowing down the bleeding, so he wouldn't leave such an obvious trail.

Once he had done that, he was able to move a little faster. While he hurried toward the bluff, he thought about what he was going to do. He needed a gun, a horse, and some boots, not necessarily in that order. He would take them however he could get them, but it wouldn't be easy. His best chance would be to jump McKinney or one of the rancher's men while they were alone. The Kid wasn't sure how many men McKinney had with him, but it stood to reason they would have to spread out some as they searched for him.

If he could overpower one of them without any

shots being fired or an alarm raised, that would be his best chance. Gunfire would bring the rest of them at a gallop, and he would be right back where he started, outnumbered and alone.

He reached the foot of the bluff. It was pretty steep, but some scrubby bushes grew out of it and by holding on to the branches he was able to pull himself up the slope. When he reached the top he found himself looking down a narrow canyon no more than a hundred yards wide. In places it closed in even more than that. Some sparse, hardy grass grew on the canyon floor, and pine trees dotted the rimrock on both sides.

The faint rataplan of distant hoofbeats drifted to The Kid's ears. He couldn't tell if the riders were still below the cliffs or if they had found the trail and reached the top. Either way, he intended to be gone by the time they got there.

Taking a deep breath, he plunged into the canyon and broke into a trot that sent jolts of agony from his feet up through his body with every step he took.

An attractive, middle-aged woman Arturo hadn't met before was at the desk in Ellery Hudson's outer office when he came in. His injured left arm was in the black silk sling, and his face was pale from the strain of being up and around. He had raised a fuss until the doctors at the hospital discharged him on his own responsibility. He hadn't been able to lie in the bed any longer as he worried about Conrad Browning.

True, it had been a little less than twenty-four

hours since Conrad had visited him in the hospital. But most of the day had gone by without a word from his friend and employer, and Arturo had a feeling something was wrong. Conrad would have kept his promise and been by to see him unless something pretty bad had prevented it.

The woman at the desk looked up at him. "Yes, sir, may I help you?"

Arturo took off his hat and held it politely in front of him. "Yes, I'd like to see Mr. Ellery Hudson, please. My name is Arturo Vincenzo."

The woman looked puzzled. "I happen to know you don't have an appointment, Mr. Vincenzo . . . Wait a minute. I know that name. You work for Conrad Browning, don't you?"

"That's right, madam. Is Mr. Hudson available?"

"I can check and see." She got to her feet. "Did Mr. Browning send you?"

"Actually, I was hoping Mr. Browning had been here and you could tell me that he's all right."

"But I haven't seen—" The woman stopped herself and said, "Perhaps you *should* talk to Mr. Hudson."

She hurried through the door behind her, then reappeared a moment later to tell Arturo to come with her. They went along the hallway to the double doors of Hudson's private office.

"Hello, Arturo," the lawyer said as he shook hands. "What can I do for you? This is about Conrad?"

"That's right. He never came to the hospital today."

Hudson frowned. "Well, I suppose he might be busy—"

"You don't understand, sir," Arturo broke in.

"When he left yesterday, he said he would come by today, and then he never showed up. I don't know how well you know Mr. Browning, but I've always found him to be a man of his word."

"Yes, of course." Hudson rubbed his jaw in thought. "Did you check at the hotel?"

Arturo nodded. "That's the first place I went. No one there could recall seeing him all day."

"That's odd," Hudson admitted.

"I went up to the suite," Arturo continued. "Some of the furniture was slightly disarranged, as if someone had bumped into it, and the rug in the sitting room was a bit mussed. I think there was a struggle there."

"But you didn't see any blood or anything like that?"

Arturo shook his head. "No. But I'm still convinced there was some sort of trouble."

"What about the Palace? Have you talked to Bat Masterson?"

"No, I came here first."

"Masterson was here earlier. He delivered the bank draft for Conrad's winnings in that poker tournament, then I prevailed upon him to accompany me to the bank so I could deposit it. I doubted that anyone would bother me while I had the famous Bat Masterson with me."

"And he didn't say anything about seeing Conrad today?"

"Not a thing." Hudson went over to a hat tree and reached for his hat. "Let's go to the Palace and see what we can find out. That is, if you feel up to it. It's only been a couple days since you were shot."

"I'm fine," Arturo said without hesitation. He was rather weak, but he wasn't going to give in to that feeling when Conrad might be in danger.

As they went out, Hudson told the woman at the desk, "I probably won't be back today, Mrs. Moorehead."

"Yes, sir. Is there anything you need me to do?"

Hudson started to shake his head, then paused. "If you hear anything from Conrad Browning, call the Palace Theater and my home. I'll be at one of those places."

"Yes, sir."

Arturo and Hudson walked briskly to the Palace. As they started up the stairs to the main gambling room, Arturo spotted Bat Masterson at the top. Masterson saw them as well and motioned for them to stay where they were. Quickly, he went down the stairs to join them.

"Well, Ellery, I didn't expect to see you again so soon," Masterson greeted them. His expression became more serious as he went on, "There's not any trouble, is there?"

"Perhaps you can tell us," Hudson said. "Have you seen Conrad today?"

Masterson shook his head. "Not at all. I left him in the lobby of the Lansing House last night. That's the last time I saw him. You're not afraid something's happened to him, are you?"

"He promised he would stop at the hospital today," Arturo said, "and he didn't do it."

"Well, plans change . . ." Masterson began.

"He would have let me know," Arturo said firmly. "As Mr. Browning would say, I have a hunch, and that hunch is that something's wrong."

Masterson frowned in thought for a moment before nodding his head. "Let me get my hat. We'll walk over to the Lansing and see what we can find out."

"I've already been there," Arturo told him. "They didn't know anything, but it looked as if there might have been a disturbance in the sitting room of our suite."

Masterson chuckled and said, "No offense, Arturo, but I reckon I've had a mite more experience at getting people to talk than you have."

Arturo shrugged as best he could with his wounded arm. The former lawman was probably right about that, and it wouldn't hurt to have an experienced set of eyes check things out in the suite.

A few minutes later, the three men reached the Lansing House. Masterson spoke to the clerk, who again denied having seen Conrad that day.

"Gather up all your porters and maids and anybody else who was working here last night," Masterson ordered. "I want to talk to them."

For a second the clerk looked like he might protest, but seemed to think twice about the idea of arguing with Bat Masterson. "Of course, Mr. Masterson. It'll take a few minutes."

Masterson nodded. "While you're doing that, I'm going to take a look at Mr. Browning's suite."

"I'm not sure—"

Masterson jerked a thumb toward Arturo. "It's all right, Mr. Vincenzo has the key." He didn't give the clerk time to think up any other complaints, and led Arturo and Hudson to the stairs.

After Arturo unlocked the door and the three of them stepped into the sitting room, Masterson gestured for his companions to stop where they were. "I want to take a look around without anything else getting disturbed," he explained.

It didn't take long for Masterson's keen eyes to study everything in the room. He nodded. "There's been a struggle here, all right. There's a little scratch in the polish on the floor where that writing desk got shoved over hard."

"I noticed the same thing," Arturo agreed. "And someone's been kicking and rolling around on that rug."

Masterson nodded. "You're right. It's a good thing the maid didn't come along and straighten the place up before you saw it, Arturo."

Hudson said worriedly, "That makes it sound as if Conrad has been abducted . . . or worse."

"Let's stay with abducted for now," Masterson suggested. "No sense in borrowing trouble. Let's go back downstairs and talk to the rest of the staff."

When they reached the lobby, they found the clerk had rounded up eight more employees. Masterson began questioning them about anything unusual they might have seen the night before. One of the porters, an elderly black man, lifted a hand and said, "I seen a wagon in the alley behind the hotel, suh. You reckon that could be somethin'?"

"What sort of wagon?" Masterson asked.

"Just a plain ol' ranch wagon. Had a pile of blankets tossed in the back."

A lot of things could be hidden under some blankets. Masterson glanced at Arturo and Hudson, and the expressions of all three said they knew that.

"What time was this?"

"'Long about . . . eleven o'clock, I'd say."

Masterson nodded to Arturo and Hudson. "That was after I left Conrad here." He asked the porter, "I don't suppose you recognized the man driving the wagon."

"No, suh, I'm afraid I didn't. He was just some cowboy. I reckon he works for Mistuh McKinney."

"McKinney!" Arturo exclaimed.

"Yes, suh. Mistuh Rance McKinney. I've seen him here at the hotel, meetin' with important cattle buyers and such. Him and some other fellas on horses left outta here with that wagon I been tellin' you about. And so'd the woman."

"What woman?" Masterson asked.

The porter shook his head. "I never did see her face. She was ridin' up front on the wagon seat, though. Had a coat with a hood on it, and the hood was pulled up so's I couldn't see her face."

Hudson said, "Rose Sullivan. It had to be."

Masterson nodded grimly. "And she's in cahoots with McKinney now. Maybe she always was, for all we know."

"What are we going to do?" Arturo asked. It was clear to him that for some reason, McKinney had kidnapped Conrad.

"I know the way to McKinney's ranch," Masterson said. "I think I need to take a ride out there and have a look around. Are the two of you coming along?"

"I'm sorry, but I couldn't do any good in a place like that," Hudson said. "I'm strictly accustomed to being in the city. My arena is the courtroom."

"I understand." Masterson turned to Arturo. "And you've got that bum wing—"

"I don't care," Arturo said. "Just try and stop me from coming with you."

Masterson grinned. "I wouldn't think of it."

Chapter 29

The Kid followed the canyon's twists and turns for more than half a mile. Once he was between its rocky walls, he couldn't hear much from outside, so he didn't know how close the search was getting. He concentrated on forcing his exhausted muscles to work and ignoring the pain in his feet.

He spotted a narrow game trail, and the sight caused his heart to leap. Animals always knew where water was. The ordeal he'd been through had left him blistered and parched. The trail led deeper into the canyon, which was the way he wanted to go anyway, so he followed it.

A few hundred yards later, he came to a place where brush grew thickly against the canyon's left-hand wall. The game trail angled toward the spot. The vegetation and the trail told The Kid what he would find there, so he wasn't surprised when he parted the bushes and saw a small pool of water that lay against the canyon wall where a tiny spring bubbled out of the rock.

The stone basin that formed the pool kept the water contained. He knelt carefully beside the pool and stretched out a hand toward the surface that seemed to shimmer, even though the sunlight didn't strike directly on it in the narrow defile. He cupped a handful of water, brought it to his mouth, and let it trickle between his lips.

He had never tasted anything so cold and delicious in his entire life.

Throwing himself forward, he plunged his head into the pool. The icy shock of the water sent the blood pumping madly through his veins. He opened his mouth and gulped down a long drink. The bracing effect of it made some of his depleted strength return.

It wasn't easy, but he pushed himself away from the pool. He knew that if he drank too much, it would make him sick. Shaking the wet hair out of his eyes, he wiped his face, and turned around to unwind the rags from his feet. They were glued to his flesh by dried blood. He had to stick his feet into the pool to soak the cloth before he could work it loose.

The cold water numbed his feet and brought blessed relief from the pain. He sat there soaking them for what seemed like a long time. Gradually he became aware of a soft current against his skin. He leaned forward to study the pool. When he saw how clear the water was, instead of fouled by the blood from his feet, he knew there had to be a crack in the rock that carried it away to some underground stream.

It was Eden, The Kid thought in his exhausted half stupor. He had stumbled into paradise.

His next thought was about Rance McKinney. Paradise always had to have a serpent in it, and in that case the low-down snake was McKinney. Lilith the temptress was there, too, in the person of Rose Sullivan.

And if Satan was a woman, Pamela Tarleton fit the bill. Even dead, her hand stretched out to work its evil in his life.

One at a time, The Kid pulled his feet out of the pool and examined them. The water had washed away all the dried blood and cleansed the cuts. Walking on them would just start the wounds bleeding again, he supposed. He would stay off them for as long as he could.

As he looked around, he noticed something at the edge of the pool, where the brush grew up almost to the water. On hands and knees, he crawled over there and pulled the branches back. The rocky wall of the canyon bulged out, forming an overhang. Under that overhang was a small space about a dozen feet long and three or four feet deep. Anybody riding by would never see it, The Kid thought. It would make a good hiding place.

He hadn't gone up the canyon intending to hide. He had been looking for a place where he could ambush one of the searchers. But fate—and that game trail—had led him there. As tired and beat-up as he was, he might not be able to whip a newborn kitten, let alone some tough-as-nails hardcase.

He needed rest, no two ways about it.

He could see all of the cave-like area, but he broke a branch off one of the bushes and raked it back and forth inside the opening anyway, just in case a rattler had crawled in there to escape the heat of the day. When nothing buzzed ominously at the poking stick, he figured it was safe.

The Kid took another long drink from the pool, then crawled under the overhang. Letting the branches he had pushed aside spring back into place, it was soon cool and shady in there, and he felt himself falling asleep right away. He didn't try to stay awake. He let himself go, and within a few breaths, he was dead to the world.

It was the middle of the afternoon before Arturo and Bat Masterson reached Rance McKinney's ranch. They had taken Arturo's buckboard, with Masterson handling the reins since Arturo's arm was injured. As the former lawman hauled the team to a halt in front of the sprawling ranch house, an elderly hostler came out of the nearby barn and stared at them in surprise.

"Lord have mercy," the old-timer exclaimed. "You're Bat Masterson!"

"That's right," Masterson said with a nod. "I'm looking for your boss. Is Rance here?"

The hostler shook his head. "Nope, 'fraid not."

"When do you expect him back?"

"Couldn't say. Him and the crew are out takin' care of a, uh, chore."

Masterson and Arturo exchanged a glance. "What sort of chore?" Masterson asked.

The hoster snorted and said, "You reckon they

tell me anything about what's goin' on around here? I'm just a stove-up old waddy who can't make a real hand no more. Ain't fittin' for nothin' but carryin' water and muckin' out stalls."

Arturo figured the old man would go on feeling sorry for himself and expressing the sentiment at length until someone stopped him, so he spoke up. "What about Miss Sullivan? Is she here?" The tone of his voice made it sound like a natural assumption that Rose was at the ranch.

"That gal who come in with the boss last night?" The holster shook his head. "Ain't seen hide nor hair of her today. Lady like that, you wouldn't expect her to hang around with a worthless ol' bum like me."

"McKinney got back from Denver last night, you said?" Masterson stopped the next wave of self-pity before it could get started.

"Yep. Mighty late, too. I had to get up outta a warm bed to handle the horses and that wagon team. Didn't care much for it, neither."

"Did he have any strangers with him except the woman?"

Suddenly, a cagy look appeared in the old-timer's rheumy eyes. He realized he was running off at the mouth too much. In a surly voice, he said, "I don't know nothin'. I just take care of the horses—"

He stopped with a gasp of surprise when Masterson, in the blink of an eye, produced a gun from under his coat.

"You know who I am," Masterson said coldly. "You know it's not a good idea to lie to me, amigo."

"I . . . I never lied—"

"I don't believe you. McKinney brought someone back from Denver with him, didn't he? Someone besides the woman."

"Perhaps wrapped up in some blankets in the back of the wagon you mentioned," Arturo added, making a guess based on what they had learned so far.

"Dadgum it!" the hostler burst out. "Are you fellas tryin' to get me killed? I can't go 'round blabbin' about the boss's business! Rance McKinney ain't what you'd call a forgivin' man."

"Tell us something we don't know," Masterson muttered. "Better yet, tell us the truth." The barrel of the gun in his hand lifted a little to emphasize the command.

"All right, all right! Take it easy, Mr. Masterson. Ain't no need for you to go shootin' up the place." The old-timer took off his shapeless hat, pulled a red checked bandanna from the pocket of his overalls, and mopped away some of the beads of sweat that had sprung up on his face. "There was a fella in the back of the wagon, all right, and when some of the boys went to drag him out, there was a ruckus. I was in the barn, so I didn't see it all too good. It didn't last too long."

"Was anybody hurt?" Arturo asked tensely.

"I don't know. There weren't no shootin', I can tell you that much. I think they got the fella in the house somehow. That's all I know."

"Did you see him again today?" Masterson asked.

"Nope. But I been stayin' in the barn most of the

time, mindin' my own business. Figured the way things were goin' around here, it was a good idea."

"Where is everybody now?"

"The boss and the rest of the crew rode out around the middle of the day. They ain't come back yet."

"Which way did they go?"

The old man pointed toward the foothills and the mountains beyond them. "West."

Masterson looked over at Arturo again. "Are you up for some more riding?"

"Of course," Arturo replied without hesitation. He wasn't going to admit how much his arm hurt or how tired he was. Not while Conrad was out there somewhere, probably in danger.

Masterson looked at the old-timer again. "There's no reason for you to tell anybody we were here."

"Sure, Mr. Masterson," the man agreed readily. "Whatever you say."

As Masterson got the team moving again and turned the buckboard toward the rugged hills Arturo asked, "Do you think he was telling the truth about not telling anyone we've been here?"

"I doubt it. But I've got a hunch this may be all over before it'll matter."

"What about Miss Sullivan? She may have seen us."

Masterson smiled. "I can't picture her getting on a horse and riding out to warn McKinney that we're coming, can you?"

"I don't know."

But in truth, based on what had happened so far, he wasn't sure there was much of anything he would put past Rose Sullivan.

Chapter 30

Bat Masterson was naturally skilled as a tracker, which had come in handy during his career as a buffalo hunter, army scout, and lawman. But even someone as inexperienced in the ways of the frontier as Arturo could see the tracks left behind by the large group of men who had ridden into the hills ahead of them.

"That has to be McKinney and his bunch," Masterson said. "Nobody else would be out here on the Double Star."

"We are," Arturo pointed out.

Masterson grinned. "Yeah, but there's only two of us."

"Which means, judging by the looks of those tracks, that we're considerably outnumbered."

"We have the element of surprise on our side."

"I hope that's enough." After a moment, Arturo went on, "What do you think McKinney is doing?"

"Well, I've been pondering that. McKinney loves to gamble, we know that. If he and Miss Sullivan kidnapped Conrad, they must want him dead, but I can see McKinney deciding it would be more fun if he gave him a sporting chance."

"You mean some sort of duel? Why bring him all the way out here to do that?"

Masterson shook his head. "No, not a duel. That would be too close to an even break."

"It wouldn't be even at all," Arturo said. "I've seen Conrad draw and fire a gun. There aren't many men faster than him, I'm sure."

Masterson grinned over at him. "You *are* talking to a man who has a certain reputation as a pistoleer, you know."

"I meant no offense, Mr. Masterson, I assure you. But Conrad seems to have inherited a great deal of his father's skill with firearms."

"And there are none better than Frank Morgan. All right, I'll grant you that. But like I was saying, even if he's willing to gamble a little, McKinney will want to stack the deck. Instead of a face-to-face showdown, I was thinking more along the lines of a hunting party."

"A hunting party?" Arturo repeated with a confused frown.

"Yeah. Turn Conrad loose on foot and unarmed, give him a head start, and then McKinney and his men will go after him and hunt him down like a wild animal."

Arturo's eyes widened in shock. "But that's barbaric."

"Barbarism is the natural state of mankind." Masterson shrugged.

"But shouldn't we aspire to more than that?"

"Sure. But in the long run, nothing human beings can do surprises me all that much. That's one of the things years as a lawman taught me."

Arturo was silent for a long moment. "I suppose you're right. What are we going to do?"

"Try to find Conrad first. Then we'll give him a hand and get him out of here. Can you fire a gun?"

"I'm actually a decent shot with a rifle, and since I started traveling with Mr. Browning, I've been involved in several altercations that involved gunplay. But I can't use a rifle with this 'bum wing' of mine, as you called it. I can shoot a pistol, but I'm not sure how accurate I'll be with one."

"Just make sure it's not pointed toward me or Conrad when you pull the trigger, and you'll do all right. You can make McKinney's men duck, anyway. But maybe it won't come to that."

Arturo seriously doubted that. Whenever Conrad was involved, sooner or later things always seemed to involve gunplay.

The buckboard entered the hills. So far they hadn't seen the rancher or any of his men, but the tracks continued to lead in that direction.

Masterson cast a worried glance toward the sky. "Sun's getting lower. There are only a couple hours of light left. I can steer by the stars and find our way back out of here after it gets dark, but we won't have much luck looking for Conrad if we don't find him before then."

"We can't give up. Not if there's a chance we can help him."

"Nobody said anything about giving up." Masterson hauled back on the reins and brought the buckboard to a gradual halt. "But that's interesting." He nodded toward a line of cliffs that rose in front of them.

"What's interesting? I don't understand."

"See those cliffs?" Masterson pointed. "The tracks lead right toward them, but the cliffs run north and south for a long way. From here, there doesn't appear to be any way horses could get up there."

"So why did McKinney and his men ride toward them? Is that what you're saying?"

Masterson nodded. "That's what I'm getting at, all right. It doesn't make sense . . . unless they planned to use those cliffs to help them in their hunt."

"They could drive Conrad up against them, so he wouldn't have any way to escape."

"Exactly. Like cornering a wild animal."

Anger surged up inside Arturo at the thought of his friend and employer being treated that way. He tried to ignore it, knowing he needed to keep a cool head.

"But where are they? We can see all the way to the cliffs. No one's out here."

Masterson lifted his gaze to the higher ground beyond the cliffs. "Maybe they're up there. Maybe Conrad found a way to get to the top after all, and they had to go around to chase him."

"I trust your instincts, Mr. Masterson. What are we going to do?"

"Let's get closer," the former lawman said decisively. "Maybe the tracks will tell us what happened."

That turned out to be the case. The tracks led

almost all the way to the base of the cliff, and from there they went north.

"He made it up there." Masterson grinned as he pointed at the rope Conrad had made from his shirt that was now lying at the bottom of the cliff. "I'd bet my old derby hat on it. Come on." He swung the buckboard along the trail left by the riders.

"We're going to follow them?"

Masterson flicked the reins and got the team moving at a faster pace. "That's right. McKinney's going to lead us right to Conrad, and when we find them . . . well, then I reckon we'll probably see that showdown you were talking about earlier, Arturo."

The Kid had no idea how long he had slept. All he knew for sure when he pried his eyes open was that the light had changed. It was dimmer. Not night yet, certainly, but probably late in the afternoon. He didn't know what had woken him.

Then he heard the deliberate hoofbeats of a horse somewhere close by.

Carefully, The Kid slid closer to the opening. The hoofbeats were louder, sounding like the horse was almost on top of him. He moved one of the branches aside a fraction of an inch to peer out.

A man rode through the circle of brush surrounding the pool. He reined in and looked down at the stone basin. For a second, The Kid couldn't remember what he had done with those bloody rags he'd soaked off his feet. If he had left them where the man could see them, it would be a dead giveaway that he'd been there.

His pulse slowed as he recalled he had balled up the rags and shoved them under a rock. The man might find them if he bothered to search, but he didn't have any real reason to look for them.

The man dismounted and let his horse drink from the pool. He knelt beside the water himself and used his cupped hands to get a drink. The Kid could see the man's profile—an angular, black-stubbled jaw—but that was all. Water dripped off the man's sharp, pointed chin. He turned his head slightly, and The Kid saw that his left eye tended to wander.

He was one of the guards who had pointed a shotgun at him that morning in the Double Star ranch house. Judging by the slow, deliberate way the man had been riding, he had come up the canyon looking for something.

Or somebody. Namely Conrad Browning.

It was the hombre's bad luck that he had found Kid Morgan instead.

The man took off his black hat, and sleeved water from his face. Turning his head toward his horse, he muttered, "I don't think the bastard's up here. We been lookin' all afternoon and ain't found hide nor hair of him. He must've fallen in a ravine or something."

The horse tossed its head, and the gunman laughed. "Oh, you think so, too, do you? Well, I reckon we'll keep lookin' anyway, leastways until it gets too dark to see anything. I can sure as hell use that thousand dollar bounty. Mosey on down to Mexico, that's what I'd do, and find me some little brown-skinned honey to tend to my every need. Yes, sir, my ever—"

The Kid exploded out of the brush at the edge of the pool and slammed into the man's back, driving him forward.

Taken completely by surprise, he didn't have a chance to do anything before he landed face-first in the pool with The Kid on top of him. He had opened his mouth to let out a yell, but that was a mistake. The icy water rushed into his throat.

The Kid looped his left arm around the man's neck and wrapped his legs around the man's torso. He planted his right hand on the back of the man's head and forced it deeper under the water, shoving so hard he felt the impact shiver up his arm as the man's face smashed into the rocky bottom of the pool. Looking into the water he saw crimson streamers of blood twisting snake-like through it. The man bucked and heaved and splashed, but pinned down the way he was, he couldn't throw off The Kid.

The Kid rammed the man's face into the bottom again. The man's struggles weakened. The Kid held him down, waiting for the water to finish him off.

Briefly, it felt almost the same as cold-blooded murder. Normally, killing a man like that bothered The Kid. But the feeling was mitigated by the certainty the man would have killed him without blinking an eye. He thought only about the bounty he was going to collect from his employer, Rance McKinney. The Kid wasn't going to lose any sleep over the hardcase's death.

The man had gone completely limp. The Kid

held his head under the water for another couple minutes just to be sure he was dead, then let go of him and crawled away from the body. The pool was too shallow for the corpse to float. It just lay there, head and shoulders resting on the bottom.

The Kid caught his breath for a minute, then took hold of the man's legs, hauled him out of the water, and rolled him onto his back. The blood in the water had come from the man's broken nose, which had been pushed down almost flat when The Kid hammered it against the stone bottom of the pool.

He hoped that none of McKinney's other men were close enough to have heard the splashing. At least the man hadn't had a chance to yell, before his horse had backed off, spooked by the commotion.

Talking in low, soothing tones, The Kid approached the horse. The animal relaxed slightly and allowed him to take hold of the reins. He tied them to one of the bushes and felt better now that he knew the horse wasn't as likely to run off.

The light in the canyon had dimmed even more as he turned back to the dead man and started stripping his clothes from him. A glance at the rosy sky told The Kid that the sun was setting. Night would fall soon.

The dead hardcase had been about the same height as The Kid but twenty or thirty pounds lighter. He was able to get into the denim trousers and the faded red shirt the man had worn, but the clothes were tight on him. He didn't bother with the black vest.

The man's gunbelt and boots were more important. The gunbelt buckled all right around The Kid's hips. He pulled the Colt .44 from the holster and checked it. The revolver was in good shape, which came as no surprise. A killer's main tool was his gun, so naturally he took care of it. The Kid pouched the iron and picked up one of the boots.

The dead man had been a little skinny, but that didn't affect the size of his feet. The boots were plenty big enough for The Kid. Maybe too big, in fact. But he used the knife he found in the man's saddlebags to cut up the ripped and ragged trousers he'd been wearing earlier, pulled the man's socks on, then padded his feet thickly with the strips of cloth before he pulled on the boots. When he stood up to check how they felt, he found his feet didn't hurt all that much. He would be able to get around without being too hampered by his injuries.

The Kid hung the man's hat on the saddlehorn and looked through the saddlebags. He found a couple dry biscuits wrapped up in some cloth and had to force himself not to cram them into his mouth. He could eat later. There was extra ammunition that would fit the revolver and the Winchester rifle in a sheath strapped to the saddle.

Now that he was armed again, The Kid felt a lot better. He had a grim chore still to do, though. He bent and grasped the dead man, dragging him over to the hidden space where The Kid had slept away the afternoon. He managed to shove the corpse under the overhang where it might not ever be found.

"Sorry, mister," he muttered. "I don't have a shovel or the will to bury you properly. It's just too damned bad you threw in with McKinney." He started to turn away but paused to add over his shoulder, "And I don't like having shotguns pointed at me."

With that out of the way, he went back to the horse and settled the black hat on his head. From a distance, he figured he could pass for the dead man, especially in the fading light. His hope, though, was that none of McKinney's other men were in that canyon. If they had spread out to search for him, it was possible.

He untied the mount and led it out of the brush. Before he swung up into the saddle, The Kid stood for long moments, listening intently. He didn't hear any other horses moving around or men calling to each other. The rugged landscape around him was quiet.

He mounted and turned the horse west, away from Double Star headquarters. Maybe there was nobody close by at the moment, but there were other men in the gathering shadows who wanted him dead. Too many for him to risk trying to get back to the Double Star while it was still light. He stood too great a chance of riding right into trouble.

He needed to find another hiding place, somewhere he could eat the meager supper he'd found in the dead man's saddlebags and rest some more. After that he intended to head for the ranch headquarters. McKinney wouldn't expect him to try anything like that. The Kid knew if he could get his hands on the rancher, McKinney's men would have to think twice about coming after him with guns blazing. Such a daring ploy would be easier once darkness had fallen completely.

Later in the night would be soon enough for the killing to start again, he decided.

The Kid rode up the canyon as gloom settled around him.

Chapter 31

Masterson drove the buckboard along the cliffs as the sun continued to sink lower. Long shadows from the mountains covered the landscape, as the vehicle moved along at a fast clip. Arturo lifted his good arm and put his hand on his hat to hold it on as he bounced a little on the seat.

"Sorry the ride is pretty rough," Masterson said.

"Don't concern yourself with that, Mr. Masterson. We can't afford to waste any time."

"That's what I thought."

After a while they came to a trail that zigzagged its way to the top of the cliff, following a narrow ledge. Masterson brought the buckboard to a stop and muttered a curse as he stared at the trail.

"There's no way we can get this buckboard up there. The trail's plenty wide enough for a man on horseback, but not a wagon."

"Then what are we going to do?"

Masterson rubbed his jaw in thought. "I suppose I could unhitch the team and we could ride up bareback. Or we can walk it, but when we got to the top we wouldn't have any horses."

"I can try to ride bareback," Arturo said, although the prospect of mounting one of the horses and attempting to guide it up that narrow trail was terrifying to him. He would have to ignore his fear, since Conrad's life might be riding in the balance.

Masterson was about to say something else, but a sudden rattle of rocks above them made him stop short. He tilted his head back to look up and whispered, "Somebody's up there, and it sounds like they're on their way down." He slapped the reins against the horses' backs. "Let's get over in those trees until we find out who it is!"

Masterson sent the buckboard rolling swiftly toward a stand of pines about fifty yards along the cliff from the spot where the trail began. Whoever was at the top of the cliffs might hear the hoofbeats from the team and the creaking of the wheels, but that couldn't be helped. Arturo hoped that the sounds of the riders' own descent would cover up the other noises.

When they had circled the trees, and were out of sight of the trail, Masterson brought the buckboard to a stop. He drew his pistol and pressed it into Arturo's hand. "Follow my lead," the former lawman said grimly. "Don't start shooting unless I do."

Arturo nodded. "Rest assured that I won't, Mr. Masterson."

Masterson hopped down easily from the buckboard and picked up the Winchester he had placed in the back of the vehicle. He worked the rifle's lever, throwing a cartridge into the firing chamber.

"Come on," he told Arturo, who had climbed down awkwardly on the other side of the buckboard. "Stick close to me."

The two men moved swiftly but quietly into the trees, working their way toward a spot where they could watch the trail. Masterson pointed out one of the pines and motioned for Arturo to take cover behind its thick trunk. He darted behind another tree.

Arturo edged his head out just enough to see what was going on. A couple men on horseback reached the bottom of the trail and rode out a few yards from the base of the cliff before reining in. Arturo recognized the distinctive cowhide vest that Rance McKinney usually wore. The man with McKinney was one of the rancher's hired gunmen.

He pointed to the ground and said excitedly, "See, boss, I told you I heard something. Those are wagon tracks."

"They damn sure are," McKinney agreed. "Who'd be out here following us?" He reached for the stock of the rifle that stuck up from his saddleboot. "We'd better find out."

Masterson gave Arturo a curt nod. "That's our cue." He stepped out from behind the tree, leveled his Winchester at the rancher, and called, "Keep your hand away from that rifle, McKinney, or I'll drill you!"

McKinney froze with his hand still a few inches

away from the rifle. "Masterson!" he exclaimed. "What the hell?"

"Better warn that gun-wolf of yours not to try anything, either," Masterson warned. "If he does, you'll be dead before you hit the ground."

"Take it easy, Bob," McKinney told the other man.

Arturo stepped forward and pointed the pistol at McKinney. "Where is Conrad Browning?" he demanded.

A harsh laugh came from McKinney. "Is that what this is about? You're looking for Browning? I don't have any idea where he is. But I'll have the law on you for coming on my range and threatening me. You can't get away with this, Masterson, even if you are famous."

Masterson's rifle didn't budge. "That's not going to work. We know you and Rose Sullivan and some of your men kidnapped Conrad from the Lansing House last night. You brought him out here to hunt him down like some sort of wild animal. Because he beat you at cards, or because Pamela Tarleton filled your head with some sort of nonsense about him. Maybe both, with the fact that you're a lowdown son of a bitch thrown in on top of it. But you'd better call it off, Rance, or you're the one who's going to wind up dead."

The hardcase started to say, "Boss, maybe we'd better—"

"Shut up!" McKinney ordered. "Masterson's just guessing. He doesn't have any proof of anything."

"I'll get it, though," Masterson vowed. "Until then, you're coming back to the Double Star with me and

Arturo. Get down off that horse and come over here."

"Go to hell!" McKinney shouted. "If you want to shoot me, Bat Masterson, you go right ahead!"

Something about McKinney's angry bellow sounded odd to Arturo, and with a flash of insight, he realized what it was. "He's trying to warn someone! There must be——"

Guns began to roar above them. Masterson fired, but McKinney had already kicked his feet free of the stirrups and dived out of the saddle as the slug from the former lawman's rifle sizzled through the space where he had been a fraction of a second earlier. McKinney hit the ground and rolled.

Arturo jerked his gun up and saw that several of McKinney's men had crept down the trail on foot and opened fire when they were about halfway down the cliff. Arturo pointed the pistol at them and started pulling the trigger. The gun roared and bucked in his hand. He had no idea if his shots were landing anywhere near McKinney's men, but he kept firing anyway.

Masterson grunted, staggered, and dropped the rifle. Arturo glanced over at him, afraid Masterson had been mortally wounded. He clutched his right forearm and said, "It's just a scratch, but they've got us outgunned."

The hammer of the pistol in Arturo's hand clicked on an empty chamber.

"Hold your fire!" McKinney yelled. He was on his feet again with a revolver in his hand. "Hold your fire!" He pointed the gun at the two men by the trees. "How about it, Masterson? Do you give up, or do we shoot you and your friend to pieces?"

"The law won't let you get away with murder," Masterson said.

"Murder? You two came out here on my range and started shooting at me and my men. Sounds like self-defense to me." McKinney eared back the hammer of his Colt. "What's it gonna be?"

Masterson sighed. "All right, you've got us. Now, what are you going to do with us?"

An ugly grin stretched across McKinney's face in the fading light. "Things haven't quite worked out today the way I planned, but you've given me a new idea. Instead of me hunting down Browning, I'm gonna make him come to me . . . and you two bastards will be the bait in the trap!"

The shadows were thick in the little side canyon where The Kid had stopped to rest. He could see only a narrow slice of sky from where he was, but it had faded from blue to purple and back to a deeper blue that would soon be black. Pinpricks of light were beginning to appear as the stars came out.

He had eaten the two dry biscuits and stretched out on the ground for a while to rest. He didn't allow himself to go back to sleep, because he wanted to head for the Double Star ranch house as soon as it was good and dark. He lay there on his back looking at the stars and thinking.

Maybe it would be best to circle around McKinney's headquarters and head for Denver instead.

McKinney had already revealed everything he knew about the children. They weren't there. Pamela had taken them with her when she left for San Francisco. So why even bother trying to settle the score with McKinney?

Because it wasn't a good idea to leave an enemy who wanted his blood behind him, The Kid decided. McKinney might follow him and try again to kill him.

Besides, a man didn't run from trouble. He faced it head-on and conquered it. That was the example Frank Morgan had set for him, and The Kid intended to follow it.

He sat up sharply as he heard a faint clink, the sound of a horseshoe striking a rock.

Somebody was coming.

The Kid sprang to his feet and moved swiftly to the horse's side. He closed his hand over the animal's muzzle to keep the horse from making any noise. He could hear hoofbeats as the rider moved slowly and deliberately past the mouth of the side canyon, where it opened into the main canyon about twenty yards away.

Another of McKinney's men, The Kid thought, searching for him in the darkness. Maybe even McKinney himself, although The Kid thought it more likely that the rancher would have returned to the Double Star already.

The rider missed the little side canyon, and moved on past it. The Kid knew he could take the man by surprise and whittle down the odds a little more. Leaving his horse where it was, he catfooted along the canyon wall. As he approached the opening, he slid the gun from its holster on his hip.

Silently, he rounded an outcropping of rock at the mouth of the canyon and leveled the revolver at the rider's back.

Only there wasn't any rider. Even by starlight, The Kid's keen eyes could see that the horse's saddle was empty.

That sight set off alarm bells in his brain. The searcher must have spotted the side canyon after all and sent his riderless horse on ahead to draw The Kid out into the open. He whirled and dropped into a crouch. A gun blasted behind him, and he felt the wind-rip of a bullet as it whipped past his ear.

He spotted the muzzle flash from the corner of his eye and sent a slug of his own in that direction. His reaction was so quick that the two shots almost sounded like one. He heard a sharp cry of pain and triggered again at the spot on the other side of the canyon mouth.

He'd already fired before he realized there was something different about the cry he'd heard. It had been higher pitched than he expected. His finger was taut on the trigger, but he didn't fire a third shot. He moved quickly and silently to one side, just in case his assailant got off another round.

A figure pitched forward out of the shadows. A gun thudded to the ground as the person fell. Shock went through The Kid as he saw the fair hair that spilled around the figure's head.

He kept the motionless bushwhacker covered as he approached carefully. When he came to the fallen gun, he kicked it aside, farther out of reach. There was no doubt about it. Even in man's clothes, the shape on the ground belonged to a woman.

Rose Sullivan.

He heard labored breathing. He had wounded her, but she was still alive. Kneeling beside her, he grasped her shoulder, and rolled her onto her back.

His hand flashed out, grabbed her wrist, and shoved her arm aside just as the derringer she thrust toward him cracked wickedly. She cried out again as he twisted her wrist and forced her to drop the little gun. He used the barrel of the Colt in his other hand to bat it aside.

She kicked at him, but he squeezed until the bones in her wrist grated together. A sob came from her. If she meant for the sound to touch his heart, she failed.

He let go of her, stepped back quickly, and pointed his gun at her again. "How bad are you hit, Rose? You'd better tell me, otherwise I'll just let you lie there and bleed to death."

"You . . . son of a bitch," she gasped out. "You put a bullet . . . in my side."

"Stand up," The Kid ordered. "I'll have to see some blood before I believe you."

"Damn you . . ." Rose struggled to her feet. A dark, stain spread on the shirt she wore. She bit back a groan and asked, "Now are you satisfied?"

He backed into the side canyon, keeping her covered as he did so. He didn't know if any of McKinney's men were still in the vicinity. If they were, they were bound to have heard those shots.

"Come on," he ordered. "But don't try anything else."

"Or what? You'll kill me?" She laughed. "Conrad Browning isn't going to murder a woman."

"You want to bet your life on that?" The Kid murmured.

She heard something in his voice that told her how close she was to death. She sighed and followed him as he backed into the canyon.

He circled around and wound up behind her, still covering her with the Colt. "All right. Let's take a look at that wound."

"You want me to take my shirt off, is that it, Conrad?" she asked mockingly.

He flipped the gun around in his hand, raised it, and brought the butt chopping down against the back of her head. He didn't hit her very hard, and her thick hair cushioned the blow, but it was enough to send her to her knees, stunned.

He holstered the Colt, grabbed her arms, jerked them behind her back, and knocked her down. He straddled her hips with his knees, pinning her to the ground, and held her wrists with one hand while he used the other to pull her shirt up. His bullet had scraped a narrow furrow along her side instead of penetrating her body.

"You'll live," he told her. "That's more than you deserve. I'm surprised McKinney let you come out here with him."

"McKinney doesn't know a thing about it. He's a damned fool. He should have just put a bullet in your brain and buried your body where nobody would ever find it."

"That's what you would have done, right?"

"That's right. I was paid to kill you."

"And you take pride in a job well done." The Kid let go of her and surged back to his feet, moving away from her as he kept her covered again. "You can sit up and tear some strips off your shirt to use as bandages. Or you can let that wound keep bleeding. It doesn't matter to me."

"You're a cold-blooded bastard, aren't you?" Rose sat up.

"You get that way when people steal your children and keep trying to kill you."

Rose started tending to the bullet crease as best she could. "What are you going to do now?"

"Are McKinney and his men still out here looking for me?" He didn't know if she would answer the question, or if he could believe her if she did, but he didn't see any harm in asking.

"Some of them are. McKinney and one of the men were headed back to the cliffs, the last I saw of them." Rose snorted in derision. "They think they're such hardcases. They never even knew a woman followed them out here and kept looking after they gave up. I found this little canyon, and my instincts told me you might be holed up in it."

"Pretty smart," The Kid admitted. "So was that trick with the horse. You just weren't quite quick enough to take advantage of it."

"Next time," Rose promised in a frigid voice.

"If I kill you, there won't be a next time."

She didn't say anything.

"But I think I can get better use out of you than that."

"As a hostage?" She laughed again. "McKinney doesn't care whether I live or die."

"But he might care what you can tell the law about him and his little 'sport'. He might want you back just to keep you from talking."

"That would mean he'd rather see me dead."

"Well," The Kid said, "either way it's a distraction, isn't it?"

Chapter 32

While The Kid kept his gun on her, Rose ripped strips from her shirt and wadded up a couple of them to make a pad that covered the wound on her side. She tied the pad tightly in place with more of the makeshift bandages.

"On your feet," The Kid told her when she was finished. "We're going to go see how far off your horse strayed."

"You're going after McKinney tonight?"

"No reason to wait. With it being dark, maybe he won't see me coming."

Rose shook her head. "He's going to kill you, you know."

"He's been trying to. And I'm still here, aren't I?"

"You're as crazy as he is," she spat out.

"Maybe." Let her think that if she wanted to. "Let's go."

The horse Rose had taken from the Double Star hadn't gone very far. They found it less than a hundred yards away in the main canyon, cropping contentedly at the grass. The Kid led the animal back to the side canyon. He wasn't going to let Rose mount up until he was on the horse he had taken from the dead gunman.

A few minutes later, they were riding east toward the edge of the foothills. He knew there was a chance they could run into some of McKinney's men who were still searching for him. If that happened, he would just have to fight his way through them and keep an eye on Rose at the same time. It would be quite a challenge.

As they rode, The Kid indulged his curiosity. "How in the world did a woman wind up being a hired killer?"

Rose laughed. "You think women can't kill?"

He thought bitterly about the havoc Pamela had wreaked in his life. "They don't usually get blood on their own hands. They prefer to have some man do their killing for them."

"Some women are like that, but I always liked to handle my own problems. I started at a pretty early age."

"Killing, you mean?"

"Realizing that some men deserved to die. From there it didn't take me long to figure out that it could be profitable, too. Men are fools. A pretty face and a sweet smile is all it takes to make them believe whatever you want them to believe."

Even though he didn't know the details of Rose's background, he had a hunch it was somewhat similar to that of his friend Lace McCall. She had had a bad time of it as a youngster, and had developed a tough hide and considerable skill with a gun. But she was a bounty hunter and used her talents on the side of the law, at least to a certain extent. She wasn't a cold-blooded killer like Rose.

He might have tried to find out more from her, but just then he noticed an orange glow in the sky up ahead. As he frowned, puzzled by the sight, he smelled smoke. Something was burning.

"Come on." He heeled the horse to a faster pace.

A short time later they reached the cliffs The Kid had climbed earlier in the day. He moved close enough to the edge that he could look down and see a vehicle burning below. The flames had subsided a little, so he got a good look at the charred framework of what appeared to be a buckboard.

If he didn't know better, The Kid thought, he would have taken it for the buckboard that Arturo had driven all the way across the Great Plains from Kansas City.

A cold finger traced an icy trail along his backbone. That *was* Arturo's buckboard, he realized.

"Let's get down there," he grated. "You know where the trail is. Show me."

"What if I don't?"

The Kid turned in the saddle. The Colt sprang into his hand. "You can cooperate, or I'll tie you up and leave you here."

Rose thought for a moment. "All right. Follow me."

She rode north. The Kid trailed behind her with his gun still drawn. After they had gone a mile or so, they came to a ledge that worked its way down the face of the cliff. She continued to lead the way with The Kid covering her as they descended.

They galloped to the burning buckboard. The fire was almost out, but the blackened wood still glowed cherry red in a few places. The team was gone, obviously unhitched and led away before the vehicle was set ablaze.

The Kid spotted something white flapping in the breeze a few yards away. It was a piece of paper weighted down by a rock. He dismounted, keeping his gun pointed toward Rose. Stooping quickly, he pulled the paper free.

The moon was rising, but there wasn't enough light for him to read the words written on the paper. He holstered the Colt and reached into the shirt pocket where the dead gunman had kept his makings. A moment later a match flared as The Kid snapped it to life with his thumbnail.

The glare from the match revealed the words scrawled on the paper.

**I HAVE MASTERSON AND THE ITALIAN.
COME TO DOUBLE STAR AT DAWN
OR THEY DIE.**

The coldness he had felt earlier crept through his veins. The note wasn't signed, but obviously the message was from Rance McKinney. Arturo and Bat Masterson were the rancher's prisoners. The Kid wasn't sure what they had been doing out there—looking for him, more than likely—but that didn't matter. Their lives were in danger, and he was the only one who could save them.

"What is it?" Rose asked as The Kid crumpled the paper and threw it aside.

"McKinney has my friends." The Kid told her about the demand that he come to the ranch head-quarters at dawn.

She laughed. "I guess it's a good thing you have me, then. Maybe you can trade me for them. In a case like that, McKinney might decide he wants me alive after all."

"The hell with that." The Kid drew his gun and lined the sights on Rose. "I'm not waiting that long."

Arturo's arm hurt like blazes. McKinney's men had pulled it out of the sling and yanked it behind his back so they could tie his wrists together. Then they had tied him into the chair where he sat in the big parlor of the ranch house. Masterson was beside him, similarly trussed up.

"McKinney's going to kill us, you know," Arturo commented. He hoped talking would get his mind off the slow, warm trickle of blood he felt making its way down his arm from the reopened wound.

"Oh, sure," Masterson agreed readily. "He can't afford to turn us loose. I don't believe in false modesty. I'm much too famous for him to get away with kidnapping us like this. It'll be better for us if we just disappear. But there's still one thing we have to remember."

"Mr. Browning is still out there somewhere."

Masterson grinned. "Exactly."

They were carrying on the conversation in low

voices because a guard was on the other side of the room, standing by the front windows with a rifle in his hand. Other guards were posted around the house.

The gunman glanced over at them and snapped, "You two shut up that mutterin' over there. I don't know what you're sayin', but you're startin' to get on my nerves."

Masterson raised his voice. "We were just talking about how all of you who survive are going to wind up dancing at the end of a rope. I hope you've enjoyed the wages McKinney has paid you so far, because you won't live to collect any more."

The man pointed the rifle at the former lawman. "Why don't I just go ahead and shoot you?" he snarled. "The famous Bat Masterson! You ain't so high and mighty now, are you?"

"McKinney wouldn't like that," Masterson pointed out. "He wants us kept alive . . . for now."

The hardcase snorted contemptuously. "For now is right. You two are dead ducks, you just don't know it yet."

"On the contrary," Arturo said, "I believe we're well aware of it."

"Well, just shut your traps, or I'll shut 'em for you. The boss may want you alive, but he didn't say nothin' about how I couldn't take a rifle butt to you and bust your jaws."

"You have a point, amigo," Masterson drawled. He looked over at Arturo and shrugged.

They didn't know where McKinney was. Maybe still looking for Rose Sullivan. The rancher had been upset when they got back and discovered that she was gone. It was impossible for Conrad to have taken her, Arturo knew, so that meant she had left on her own. From the way McKinney had gone raging around, he'd had some plans of his own for the beautiful killer.

Footsteps sounded on the porch. The guard turned his rifle toward the door as it burst open, but he lowered the weapon as another of McKinney's men hurried in.

"Where's the boss?" the newcomer asked.

"Upstairs, I think. Damn it, Carter, I came near to pluggin' you! What's so all-fired important?"

"There's a horse comin' in with somebody tied across the saddle. I think it's that girl, and she looks dead!"

"Son of a bitch," the guard said. He turned toward the stairs and raised his voice. "Boss! Mr. McKinney!"

"What the hell is it?" McKinney asked a moment later from the top of the stairs.

"The boys have found that Sullivan woman. Somethin's happened to her!"

McKinney came clattering down the stairs in a hurry, gun in hand. "Show me," he demanded. All three of them went outside, leaving the front door open.

Masterson looked over at Arturo. "Conrad wouldn't have killed her, would he?" he asked quietly.

"Only if she was trying to kill him."

Arturo's head lifted as he heard something behind him, a stealthy sound like someone gliding across the thick rug on the floor. He tried to crane his head enough to look around.

A familiar voice said, "Just sit still, Arturo. I'll have you and Bat loose in a minute."

Before Arturo could even gasp in surprise, all hell broke loose outside.

The Kid got the knife under Arturo's bonds and severed them with one swift, strong stroke. Then he moved over and cut Masterson free as well. The explosion from the barn hadn't taken him by surprise, as it had McKinney and the other men in the yard between the house and the barn. He had known just about how long it would take for the fuse to burn down and had been expecting the blast.

Finding that crate of dynamite in the barn had been good luck. He'd planned to fire the place anyway, but blowing it up was a lot more spectacular and caused a lot more chaos. After tying up the hostler, he had dragged the old-timer a good long distance away from the barn so he'd be safe, then opened all the stalls and led the horses out as well. It had taken time to do all that without alerting any of McKinney's men that something was going on, but The Kid had learned to be patient, as well as how to move as quietly as an Indian when he needed to.

Once the barn was empty, he'd planned to start a fire and lure McKinney's men out of the house that way. Then he'd found the dynamite and grinned as he unrolled a long length of fuse and touched it off. After that, it had been simple to circle through the darkness to the rear of the house, overpower the guard he found there, and let himself in to look for Arturo and Masterson.

He'd been waiting for the explosion on the other side of the dining room door, but something else had happened to draw McKinney and his men outside. He heard the shouting about Rose, and his forehead furrowed in a frown. He had left her tied securely a long way from the ranch headquarters. Clearly she had gotten loose and come to warn McKinney. The Kid didn't understand how, but it didn't matter. The ball was already underway.

As Masterson came up out of the chair, flexing his fingers to get feeling back in them, The Kid thrust a revolver into his hand. He had taken it from the guard he had knocked out.

"You lie low in here, Arturo. Bat and I will deal with McKinney."

Arturo gestured toward the rifle in The Kid's other hand. "I'm already bleeding again. You might as well give me that Winchester."

The Kid didn't hesitate. He grinned and handed the rifle to Arturo. "Let's go. It won't take McKinney long to figure out I blew up his barn."

The three men headed for the front door. The thud of footsteps on the stairs made them stop and swing around. A couple of McKinney's hardcases were on their way down. The men stopped short at the sight of The Kid and the two former prisoners. They spat curses and clawed at their guns.

The Kid and Masterson fired at the same time, their slugs punching into the hardcases and knocking them back against the stairs. One of the men lay there and writhed in his death throes. The other tried to get up but toppled down the stairs, coming to rest at the base with blood welling from the bullet hole in his chest.

The brief, one-sided gunfight had delayed them only a few seconds. They headed for the door again and burst onto the porch. The barn was fully engulfed in flames, casting a hellish red light over the ranch house and the area in front of it. McKinney and several gunmen were gathered around a horse. They had lifted Rose down from the animal and McKinney had an arm around her to support her. She looked past his shoulder, spotted The Kid, and screamed, "Browning!"

McKinney and his hired killers twisted around, but The Kid and Masterson already had their Colts leveled, spouting flame and lead. Behind them, as more gunmen came pounding around the corner of the house, Arturo lifted the rifle to his shoulder and opened fire, working the Winchester's lever, cranking off round after round despite his injury.

McKinney's men were tough. They stood their ground and put up a fight, even as bullets scythed into them. The Kid heard several slugs whine past his head. He placed his shots coolly and carefully, knowing he probably wouldn't have time to reload. Every bullet had to count. Beside him, Bat Masterson was doing the same thing.

One by one, the killers crumpled. As his men fell, McKinney dashed to the side, dragging Rose with him. He emptied the gun in his hand to cover his retreat.

The Kid saw them fleeing and said to Masterson,

"I'm going after McKinney!" He bounded off the porch before anyone could stop him and ran toward the corner of the house where McKinney and Rose had disappeared.

As The Kid hurried after his quarry, he had a chance to thumb fresh cartridges into his gun after all. He stopped at the corner of the house and pressed his back against the wall rather than rush blindly around it.

"Browning!" McKinney yelled from somewhere close by. "Browning, you hear me? I know what happened to your wife. Are you gonna stand by and let another woman die?"

"H-help me!" Rose cried. "He's really going to kill me!"

The Kid didn't believe that for a second. They were trying to trick him again.

But then a gun blasted and Rose screamed. It could still be a trick, The Kid told himself, but it had sure sounded like McKinney had shot her.

"C-Conrad . . . ?" The name was a hoarse whisper. She stumbled into view, blood welling from her mouth and soaking her shirt where she had both hands pressed to her midsection. The Kid's eyes widened in horror.

He realized a split-second later that McKinney was behind her, holding her up and shoving her along. The rancher thrust his gun hand under Rose's arm and opened fire. The Kid threw himself forward as bullets ripped through the air just above him.

The light from the blazing barn was uncertain, but he could see one of McKinney's legs. He fired, drilling a slug through the rancher's thigh. McKinney bellowed in pain and twisted around. The shock of being shot caused him to let go of Rose. As she toppled limply away from him, McKinney tried to line his sights on The Kid, but the revolver in The Kid's hand was already roaring. He fired three times. All three bullets smashed into McKinney's chest and drove the man backward in a macabre, jittering dance. McKinney dropped his gun and fell, landing on his back with his arms and legs flung out. He spasmed, his chest jerking as he tried to drag breaths into his body. His fingers clawed at the ground.

Then he went limp all over as death claimed him.

The Kid scrambled up and ran to Rose's side. He rolled her onto her back. He was still watchful for tricks, but she was beyond that. Life was fading rapidly from her eyes.

"I . . . I don't like to . . ."

That was all she got out before her last breath sighed from her throat. The Kid had a pretty good idea of what she had been trying to say.

She didn't like to leave a job undone. For once, she had failed.

Kid Morgan was still alive.

"Sir?" Arturo said from behind him.

The Kid straightened and turned around. He saw Arturo and Masterson standing there with their guns in their hands.

"McKinney's men who are still alive have scattered," Masterson said. "They're liable to come back, so it might be a good idea to find some horses and get out of here while we can."

The Kid nodded in agreement. "I know where there are horses."

Arturo looked past him at the bodies of Rose and McKinney. "She didn't do her job this time, did she?" he asked, unknowingly echoing the same thought that had just gone through The Kid's head.

"No, she didn't," The Kid said. "And McKinney lost the last hand . . . again."

Aces were the best. Hot lead beats aces, every time.

Chapter 33

Masterson stood next to the new buckboard and grinned up at Arturo. "I wouldn't have thought it, amigo, but you turned out to be a hell of a fighting man."

"High praise indeed coming from the famous Bat Masterson. But it would be perfectly fine with me if I never again have to engage in any of these . . . ruckuses."

Masterson laughed. "I wouldn't count on that happening. Not as long as you're traveling with Conrad Browning."

Conrad, dressed in his usual black suit, black hat, boots, and string tie, finished tying his horse to the back of the buckboard. He would be handling the team until Arturo's arm healed up, a process that had been unavoidably delayed by the battle at the Double Star ranch house.

Denver was still buzzing about what had happened out there several nights earlier. The official theory was that rustlers had raided the ranch. Most of the members of McKinney's crew who had survived had taken off for greener pastures since he was no longer alive to pay them. Conrad had a pretty good idea they had run off most of the Double Star stock in the process, figuring that at least they would get something out of the deal that way. The few who were still there weren't saying much. None of them wanted to implicate themselves in McKinney's murderous schemes.

The presence of Rose Sullivan's body was a mystery. Most folks figured she was McKinney's ladyfriend who'd had the bad luck to be at the ranch when it was attacked.

Nothing tied Conrad, Arturo, or Masterson to the incident, and they were going to leave it that way. Ellery Hudson knew the truth, of course, but the lawyer wouldn't say anything. Conrad was his client, after all, so he was honor bound to keep silent.

As Conrad climbed up to the buckboard seat beside Arturo, Masterson asked, "You're still heading for San Francisco?"

Conrad nodded. "With stops to search along the way. There's still no proof Pamela took the kids with her all the way to the coast. She left here with them, but that's all we know."

"There's a lot of country between here and there," Masterson mused. "I could come along and help you look."

Conrad smiled and shook his head. "You've got a wife and a good life here, Bat. You don't need to give that up. Besides, you said you wanted to try your hand at journalism. Maybe someday you'll write about what happened."

Masterson laughed. "I don't think so. I believe we'll just let this little scrape go unreported. What would be the point in it?"

"That's true." A wistful look came over Conrad's face. "Nothing was really settled, was it? I still didn't find my children."

"It's only a matter of time, my friend, only a matter of time."

Conrad and Arturo lifted hands in farewell, and Conrad got the team moving. The buckboard rolled away, leaving Bat Masterson behind them.

"He's right, you know," Arturo said. "You'll find them. Little Frank and Vivian. They're out there somewhere, and they may not know it, but they're just waiting for their father to find them."

Conrad smiled. The hopeful words comforted him.

But he thought about everything Pamela Tarleton had had waiting for him so far, every bit of treachery and danger, and dark shadows shifted in his eyes.

From bestselling authors William W. Johnstone and
J. A. Johnstone comes a blazing new saga of the
MacCallisters. One family, forging a destiny.
One legacy, sworn to justice. One name,
branded in the heart of America . . .

**TURN THE PAGE FOR
AN EXCITING PREVIEW OF
MACCALLISTER: THE EAGLES LEGACY**

The Scottish Highlands, 1885. Two men,
brandishing knives, attack a young woman outside
a pub. Duff MacCallister steps in and saves her—
killing one of the assailants. Big mistake. The
attacker was the sheriff's son, and now MacCallister
is marked for death. His only hope: America. In the
sprawling land of dreams, Duff hopes to start a new
life with his American cousins. Unfortunately, the
sheriff's deputies are tracking him down—with nine
of the deadliest cutthroats money can buy.
Blazing a trail of blood and bullets all the way to the
Rockies, Duff has to kill his enemies one by one—
or die trying. But, Duff is not alone. He has a new
ally by his side. A living legend of frontier justice.
The gunslinger known as Falcon MacCallister . . .

MACCALLISTER: THE EAGLES LEGACY

On sale now
Wherever Pinnacle Books are sold

Chapter 1

Scotland: Dunoon in Argyllshire

The White Horse Pub in Dunoon had an island bar, Jacobean-style ceiling, beautiful stained glass windows and etched mirrors. Despite its elegant décor and clientele of nobles, it was primarily a place for drinking and most who came behaved with decorum, enjoying the ambiance and convivial conversation with friends. But some, like Alexander, Donald, and Roderick Somerled, sons of Angus Somerled, Lord High Sheriff of Argyllshire regarded their station in life not one of seemliness, but one of privilege. They drank too much, considered all others to be beneath them, and behaved with little restraint.

Duff MacCallister, a tall man with golden hair, wide shoulders and muscular arms was sitting on a stool at the opposite end of the bar from the Somerleds. That wasn't by accident; there was a long-standing feud between the MacCallister and Somerled clans, going back to the time of Robert the Bruce. Although the killing of each other had stopped a hundred years ago, their dislike of each other continued.

Ian McGregor, owner of the tavern, was wiping glasses behind the bar and he stepped over to speak to MacCallister. "Duff, m'lad, I was in the cemetery the other day and I saw marked on the tombstone of one of the graves, HERE LIES GEOFFREY SOMERLED AN HONEST MAN. So this, I'll be askin' ye. Think ye now that there may be two bodies lyin' in the same coffin—Geoffrey *and* an honest man?"

Duff MacCallister threw back his head and laughed out loud. He was wearing a kilt and he slapped his bare knee in glee. McGregor's daughter, Skye, a buxom lass with long red hair, flashing blue eyes, and a friendly smile had been filling three mugs with ale as her father told the joke. She joined in the laughter.

Duff and Skye were soon to be married, and their banns were already posted on the church door. Most of the customers of the White Horse Pub appreciated Skye's easy humor and friendly ways and treated her with respect due a woman. But some, like the Sheriff's three sons, treated her with ill concealed contempt.

"Bargirl!" Donald shouted. "More ale!"

"You know her name, Somerled," Duff said. "And it isn't Bargirl."

"'Tis a bargirl she is and her services we're needin'."

"I'll not be but a moment, Mr. Somerled," Skye replied. She had just put the three mugs on a carrying tray. "I've other customers to tend to now."

"You're carrying three mugs, there be but three

of us," Donald said. "Serve us first. You can get more ale for them."

"I'll not be but a moment, sir," Skye replied.

Donald was carrying a shillelagh, and he banged it so loudly on the bar that it startled Skye, and she dropped her tray.

"What a clumsy trollop ye be!" Donald said. "If you had brought the ale here, as I asked, this no' woulda happened."

"I told you sir, I had other customers."

"Your other customers can wait. Be ye daft as well as clumsy? Do ye know who I am?"

"Donald Somerled, that is my fiancée you are talking to and if you speak harshly to her again, I will pull your tongue out of your mouth and hand it to you," Duff said, barely controlling his voice, so intense was his anger.

"We'll be seeing who is handing who their tongue," Donald said, hitting his open hand with his shillelagh.

Duff put his mug on the bar, then stepped away to face Donald. "I'm at your service."

With a defiant yell Donald charged Duff, not with his fists, but with the raised shillelagh. Duff grabbed the same barstool he had been sitting on, and raised it over his head to block the downward swing of the club. The clack of wood crashing against wood filled the entire pub with a crack almost as loud as a gunshot. The noise got the attention of everyone in the bar and all conversation stopped as they turned to watch the confrontation between a MacCallister and a Somerled.

Donald raised his staff for a second try, but as he held his club aloft MacCallister turned the stool around and slammed the seat into Donald's chest so hard that he let out a loud whoosh as he fell to the floor with the breath knocked from his body.

"You'll be paying for that, Duff MacCallister!" Alexander said. As Donald writhed on the floor trying to recover his breath, his older brother charged.

Duff tossed the barstool aside, then put up his fists to meet Alexander's charge. He parried a wild, roundhouse right, then countered with a straight left that landed on Alexander's chin, driving him back. With a yell of anger, the third of the Somerled brothers, Roderick, joined the fray.

Duff backed up against the bar, thus preventing either of them from getting behind him. He sent a whistling blow into Roderick's nose and felt it break, causing the big man to grab his nose and turn away from the fight. Only Alexander was left, but he was the biggest and the most dangerous of the three. Shaking off the blow to his chin, he raised both fists, then advanced toward Duff.

The two men danced around the barroom floor exchanging blows, or rather, attempted blows. Duff learned early in the fight that he could hit Alexander at will. He was so big and so confident of his strength that he made no attempt to block Duff's blows, willing to take them in order to get into position to return the punches. He seemed to be taking them with no ill effect.

Duff bobbed and weaved as Alexander tried

roundhouse rights, straight punches, and uppercuts, finally connecting with a straight shot that Duff managed to deflect with his left shoulder, thus avoiding a punch to his head. There was so much power in the blow that Duff felt his left arm go numb. He could no longer count on that arm to ward off anymore of the big man's punches.

Knowing he was going to have to end the fight soon, he bobbed and weaved, watching for an opening. Alexander tried another roundhouse right. Duff managed to pull back, and as Alexander completed his swing Duff pulled the trigger on a straight whistling right driving his fist into Alexander's Adam's apple.

He gagged, and put both hands to his throat, allowing Duff to follow with a hard right to the chin. Alexander joined Donald who was getting up but showing no interest in continuing the fight.

For a long moment everyone in the bar looked on with shock and amazement. The Somerleds had a reputation for fighting, something they did frequently. And, because they were the sons of the sheriff, they never had to pay any of the consequences that others of the county had to pay when they engaged in the same activity.

They seldom lost a fight and yet in front of an entire inn full of witnesses, one man, Duff MacCallister, had taken the measure, of not just one of them, but of all three. And at the same time.

"Hear, hear, let's give a hurrah for Duff MacCallister!" someone shouted, and the bar rang with their huzzahs.

"Now, gentlemen, I believe you called for more ale?" The bartender spoke to the Somerleds as if nothing had happened, as if he were merely responding to their request. Donald and Roderick responded with a scowl, and helped their oldest brother to his feet. Then the three men left.

Everyone in the pub wanted to buy Duff a round, but he had already drunk his limit of two mugs, so he thanked them all, accepting their offers to buy for him when next he came in.

"Skye, would you step outside with me for a moment?" Duff asked.

"Ian, best you keep an eye on them," one of the customers said. "Else they'll be outside sparking."

Skye blushed prettily as the others laughed at the jibe. Duff took her hand in his and walked outside with her.

"Only four more weeks until we are wed," Skye said when they were outside. I can hardly wait."

"No need to wait. We can go into Glasgow and be married on the morrow," Duff suggested.

"Duff MacCallister, sure'n m' mother has waited my whole life to give me a fine church wedding, and you would deny that to her?"

Duff chuckled. "Don't worry, Skye. There is no way in the world I would start my married life by getting on the bad side of my mother-in-law. If you want to wait then I will wait with you."

"What do you mean you will wait with me? What else would you be doing, Duff MacCallister? Would you be finding a willing young lass to wait with you?"

"I don't know such a willing lass. Do you? For truly, it would be an interesting experiment."

"Oh, you!" Skye hit Duff on the shoulder Alexander had hit in the fight. He winced.

"Oh! I'm sorry. You just made me mad talking about a willing lass."

Duff laughed, then pulled Skye to him. "You are the only willing lass I want."

"I should hope so."

Duff bent down to kiss her waiting lips.

"I told you Ian! Here they are, sparking in the dark!" a customer shouted. With a good natured laugh, Duff and Skye parted. With a final wave to those who had come outside to see the sparking, Duff started home.

Three Crowns

Duff Tavish MacCallister was the fifth generation to live on and work Three Crowns, the property that was first bestowed by King Charles II upon Sir Falcon MacCallister, Earl of Argyllshire and Laird of Three Crowns. Falcon was Duff's great great great great grandfather. The title passed on to Falcon's eldest son, Hugh, but died when Hugh emigrated to America. The land stayed in the family, passing down to Braden MacCallister, who was Duff's great great great grandfather. The land passed through the succeeding generations so that it now belonged to Duff.

Three Crowns got its name from three crenellated hills that, with imagination, resembled crowns. The family cemetery was atop the middle crown where

Sir Falcon MacCallister and all succeeding generations, down to and including Duff's father, mother, and only brother, lay buried. Duff was the last Mac-Callister remaining in Scotland.

Duff raised Highland cattle on Three Crowns. He liked Highland cattle, not only because they were a traditional Scottish breed, but also because they required very little in the way of shelter, enjoying conditions in which many other breeds would perish. Cold weather and snow had little effect on them and they seemed to be able to eat anything, getting fat on what other cattle would pass by.

Duff had read of the great cattle ranches in the American West, and how they required many cowboys to ride herd on the huge number of cattle across vast areas. Because the Highland cattle were so easy to manage, and he had only three hundred acres, Duff was able to manage his farm all alone. He did have something in common with the cowboys of the American West, though. He managed his herd from the back of a horse.

He saddled his horse, and as the sun was rising, took a ride around his entire three hundred acres, looking over his cattle. It was a brisk morning and he and his horse blew clouds of vapor into the cool air.

His horse whickered as he rode through his small herd of cattle, distinctive with their long hair and red coloring. The cattle were grazing contentedly, totally unresponsive to the horse and human who had come into their midst.

As Duff rode around his herd, he imagined what

it would be like when he had a son to help him run the ranch. He and Skye had spoken often of it.

"What if our first child is a girl?" Skye teased.

"Then we shall make her a princess, and have a son."

"But if we have only girls?"

"Then I will make them all tomboys, and they will smell of cattle when they go to school."

"Oh, you!" Skye had hit him playfully.

Duff also planned to build a place for Skye's parents so they could live on Three Crowns with them. For now, Skye's father, Ian McGregor, enjoyed a good living running the White Horse Pub, but there would come a time when he would be too old to work. When that time came, Duff promised Skye, Ian could retire in comfort in his own house, right beside them.

As Duff reached the southern end of his property he saw a break in the fence. Ten of his cattle had gone through the break and were now cropping the weeds that grew on the other side of the Donuun Road. Duff slapped his legs against the side of his horse, riding at a quicker pace until he reached the break in the fence.

"Who told you cows you could be over here?" Duff said as he guided his horse through the break and across the road. He began rounding the cattle up and pushing them back across the road toward the break in the fence. It wasn't a particularly hard thing to do, Highland cattle were known not only for their hardiness, but also for their intelligence and docile ways. He had just gotten the last cow pushed back through the break, when Rab Malcolm rode up. Malcolm was one of Sheriff Somerled's deputies.

"Your cows are trespassing on county property," Malcolm said. "You could be fined for that, you know."

"My cows were keeping the weeds down along the side of the county road. I should charge the county a fee for that."

"Making light of the offense does not alter anything. I saw your cows on the road. That is a violation and you could be cited."

"Cite me or ride away Rab Malcolm," Duff said. "I'll not be listening to your prattle."

Malcolm lifted a billyclub hanging from his belt, and used it as a pointer, pointing it directly at Duff. "With your wild carryin' on last night, 'tis an enemy you have made of the sheriff. In this county, 'tis not a smart thing to make the sheriff your enemy."

"Sure 'n the Somerleds and the MacCallisters have been enemies for two hundred years and more. I doubt there is anything I could have done last night that would make it more so."

"You will see. The sheriff was very angry. I've never seen him more angry."

"Be gone with ye, Malcolm. 'Tis enough of your mouth I've listened to today."

"See that your fence is mended, Duff MacCallister. I will not have commerce along this road disturbed by the likes of your cattle," Malcolm said, just before he rode away.

Because the cattle frequently pushed through the fence at one point or another around his ranch, keeping them mended was an ongoing operation.

Duff had long ago acquired the habit of carrying in his saddle bags the tools and wire he would need to perform the task. Dismounting and taking out his tools and wire, Duff's horse stood by patiently for the fifteen minutes or so it took to make the repair.

Chapter 2

"I'll not be playing the pipes at my own wedding," Duff said that evening at the White Horse Pub. "For sure now, and how would that look? My bride would come marching in on the arms of her father, finely dressed in her bridal gown, looking beautiful, but there is no groom standing at the chancel waiting for her. 'Where is the groom?' people will say. 'Poor girl, has the groom deserted her at the altar?' But no, the groom is standing in the transept playing the pipes."

Skye laughed. "No, I dinnae mean play the pipes at the wedding. But afterward, at the reception you could play the pipes. You play them so beautifully, 'twould be a shame if ye dinnae play them."

"A fine thing, Ian," Duff said to Skye's father behind the bar. "Your daughter wants me to work on my wedding day."

"Duff MacCallister, for you, playing the pipes isn't work. It is an act of love and you know it. Sure'n there's no a man alive can make the pipes sing a more beautiful song than you."

"So the two of you are doubling up on me, are you?"

"And if we need another, there's m' mother," Skye said. "For she would want to hear you play as well. Say you will, Duff. Please?"

Duff laughed. "Aye, I'll play the pipes, for how can I turn you down?"

"Best you be careful Duff, m' boy, lest you let the lass know how much power she has over you."

"Ian, do you think she doesn't already know?" Duff asked. He put down his empty beer mug, then stood. "Best I get home. Skye, would you be for stepping outside with me?"

"No need for that, Duff MacCallister. The only reason you want me to step outside is so I will kiss you good night, and I can do that right here."

"In front of everyone?"

Skye smiled sweetly. "Aye, m' love. In front of God, m' father, and everyone else."

Skye kissed him, and the others in the pub laughed, and applauded.

Before stopping by the White Horse Pub, Duff had picked up his mail. Not wanting to read it in the pub he waited until he got home. Settled in a comfortable chair near a bright lantern, he looked through the mail.

Dear Cousin Duff,
My name is Andrew MacCallister, and yes, we are cousins, though I'm certain that you have never

*heard of me. I have heard of you only because I
hired someone to research my family's past with
particular emphasis on any of my family that might
remain in Scotland. That brought me to you.*

*You and I share a great great great great
grandfather, one Falcon MacCallister from the
Highlands of Scotland. You might be interested to
know that I have a brother named after him, and, I
am pleased to say, Falcon has done the name proud.*

*My twin sister Rosanna and I are theatrical
players, and on the fifth of April we shall be
appearing at Campbell's Music Saloon on Argyle
Street in Glasgow. It would please us mightily if you
could attend the performance as our guest.*

> *Sincerely,*
> *Andrew MacCallister*

White Horse Pub

"I thank you for the invitation, Duff," Skye said in
response to Duff's invitation for her to accompany
him to the play. "But 'tis thinking I am, that you
should go by yourself, for they are your kinsmen."

"And soon to be yours as well. For when we are
married, my kinsmen are your kinsmen."

"Aye, but we aren't married yet, so they are not
my kinsmen now. And they dinnae invite me. They
invited you."

"That's because they know nothing about you. I
will introduce you, then they will know you."

"I think it would be better if I dinnae go," Skye
said. "Besides, after we are married, I will no longer

work for my father, so I feel I should give him all the time I can."

"If you won't go, then I won't as well."

"Duff Tavish MacCallister, how dare you do that to me! Don't saddle me with the responsibility of you not going."

"I just meant—"

"I know what you meant," Skye said, interrupting him. "Duff, you must go to the play. I will be very upset if you do not. Go, then come back and tell me all about it."

"I'll do better than that. If you won't go to meet my kinsmen, then I shall bring them here to meet you."

Skye smiled. "Aye, now that I would like. I have read of them in the newspaper. They are quite famous in America, you know."

"They are?"

"Aye. 'Twill be a grand thing to meet them, I am thinking."

Campbell's Music Saloon on Argyle Street, Glasgow, April 5

Duff MacCallister was a reserve captain in 42nd Foot, Third Battalion of the Royal Highland Regiment of Scots. As such, when he arrived at the theater he was wearing the kilt of the Black Watch, complete with a *sgian dubh*, or ceremonial knife, tucked into the right kilt stocking, with only the pommel visible. He was also wearing the Victoria Cross, Great Britain's highest award for bravery.

He went inside the theater to the will call counter.

"The name is MacCallister. I am not certain, but I believe you may have a ticket for me."

"Indeed I do, sir," the clerk replied. "Just a moment, please." The clerk called one of the ushers over. "Timothy, would you be for taking Captain MacCallister to the green room? Introduce him to the stage manager, Mr. Fitzhugh. He will know what to do."

"Aye. Come, Captain."

Duff followed the usher down a side corridor to an area behind the stage.

"I heard Mr. Service call you MacCallister. Be ye a kinsman to Andrew and Rosanna MacCallister?"

"I am told that is so, though I confess I have never met them," Duff said.

"They are quite famous in theater. We are very lucky to have them come to Glasgow to perform."

They came to a large room with chairs and sofas, also tea and biscuits.

"'Tisn't green," Duff said.

"Beg pardon, sir?" Timothy asked.

"He said take me to a green room. This room isn't green."

The usher laughed. "It's what they call the room where the actors can gather off stage. I think the first one must have been green. Now 'tis the name for all."

"Makes no sense to me."

"Aye, nor does it make sense to me. There is much about the theater that makes no sense to one who is not in the business. But 'tis a good job to have."

There were several men and women standing about in costumes and stage makeup, talking among themselves in words and phrases that were unique and exclusive to their profession.

"George was out on the apron, corpsing while we were working out the blocking. He had me so flummoxed that I didn't know whether to go stage left or stage right," a young woman was saying.

"Had it been me, I would have just given my exit line and stepped behind the backcloth," a young man said, and they all laughed.

"Mr. Fitzhugh, this is Captain MacCallister," the usher said, introducing Duff to an older, bald-headed man who was wearing square-rim glasses which were situated far down on his nose. He was looking at notes he had fastened to a clipboard.

"Ah yes, Captain," Mr. Fitzhugh said. "Mr. MacCallister was hoping you would come. If you would wait here, sir, I shall summon him."

"Thank you." Duff moved over to one side of the room, separating himself and the players in costume and makeup. He noticed that one or two of the young women seemed to be paying special attention to him, and he looked away self-consciously.

Suddenly all the conversation stopped.

"Mr. MacCallister, can I do something for you?" someone asked.

Duff looked up, thinking the person was talking to him, but saw she was talking to a man in his early fifties, carrying himself with great dignity. Like the others, he was in costume and makeup.

"No, thank you. Relax, relax," the man said. Spying Duff, a broad smile spread across his face. "Cousin

Duff, how good of you to come." He extended his hand.

"It was good of you to invite me," Duff replied, appreciative of the man's firm grip. "You would be Cousin Andrew?"

"I am."

"Ma'am," someone said, and as they had with Andrew, all stood in respectful silence as a very attractive woman, also in costume and makeup, came into the room.

"Sister, come and meet our Scottish kin," Andrew called to her. "Cousin Duff, this is Rosanna."

Rosanna stuck out her hand and Duff bowed his head slightly, then raised her hand to his lips for a kiss.

"Oh, my! How gallant!" Rosanna said. "Andrew, do pay attention to our young cousin, perhaps you will learn a thing or two."

"Timothy?" Andrew spoke to the usher.

"Yes, m'laird?" he replied.

"Please take Mr. MacCallister to the orchestra, row five, center seat." Andrew smiled again at Duff. "I may have just sown the seeds of my own disaster. That is the best seat in the house. If I stink up the stage with a poor performance, there will be no hiding it from you. The play we are presenting tonight is called *The Golden Fetter*, by Watts Phillips. I do hope you enjoy it."

"Oh, I am certain that I will greatly enjoy the performance," Duff replied.

* * *

When Duff was escorted with great pomp and circumstance to his seat in the theater, he was aware of the reaction of the others when he, a Highlander in the uniform of the Black Watch took the best seat in the house.

"Who is he?"

"Perhaps a relative of the Queen?"

"He is someone of great importance, of that we can be certain."

"Aye, he is wearing the Victoria Cross. That alone should be enough to warrant the best seat in the house."

The lights in the theater dimmed, but were brightened on the stage. Before the curtain rose the sound of a storm was heard, and as the curtain drew up a flash of vivid lightning was seen, followed by a loud clap of thunder. On stage was the interior of a village barber shop, fitted up with the usual paraphernalia.

Duff enjoyed all three acts of the melodrama, feeling a sense of pride in that his kinsmen were indeed the stars of the performance. After escaping many perils and dangers, Andrew and Rosanna were the last two actors on the stage.

ANDREW (as Sir Gilbert): Look up—look up, dearest! With his own hands he has broken the fetter, and you are mine now, *(embraces her)* you are mine!

ROSANNA (as Florence): *(as her head sinks on his shoulder)* Forever, Gilbert, forever.

The curtain came down to thunderous applause, then it rose again so the players could take their curtain call—in groups for the lesser players, then singly for the more principle roles. Finally Rosanna, who curtsied, then left the stage for Andrew, who bowed. He held out his hand to call Rosanna back so they could take the final bow together as, once more, the curtain descended.

Duff remained seated in his seat as the others in the audience began to exit the theater. He wasn't entirely sure what was expected of him. Was his only obligation to come and see the show? Should he go back to the green room and wait? Or would that be too presumptuous on his part?

Not until he was the only person remaining in the auditorium did he stand and start to leave. Timothy appeared from the same side door Duff had gone through when he visited the Green Room.

"Captain MacCallister?" Timothy called.

"Aye?"

"Mr. MacCallister's compliments sir, and he asks if you will join him in his dressing room.

Duff followed Timothy along the same path he had traversed earlier, passing through the green room, which was more crowded than it had been before. The cast and the stage hands were gathered there, babbling in excitement as they came down from the exhilaration of the production. They walked down a long hall to one of two doors, each of which had a star just above the name. The sign on one door read MISS MACCALLISTER. The sign on the other door read MR. MACCALLISTER. It was upon this door that Timothy knocked.

"Mr. MacCallister? It is Timothy, sir. I have Captain MacCallister with me."

The door opened and Andrew stood just on the other side, his face white and shining with some sort of cleansing lotion.

"Thank you, Timothy. Come in, Duff, come in," Andrew said. "I shall be but a few minutes longer, then perhaps you would honor Rosanna and me by allowing us to take you out to dinner."

"No," Duff said.

"No?" Andrew had a surprised expression on his face.

Duff smiled. "I was your guest for the wonderful play. Now I insist that you and Rosanna be my guests for dinner."

Andrew smiled and nodded his head. "We would be delighted."

Duff watched in fascination as Andrew sat down at his dressing table and, using a towel, wiped his face clean of the cleansing lotion. Gone, also, were the dark lines that had been around his eyes, and the dark outline of his lips.

"You must wonder what kind of man would put makeup on his face," Andrew said, glancing at Duff in his mirror.

"No, I—"

Andrew's laugh interrupted his response. "I know, I know, my own brothers tease me about it. But one must outline the eyes and the mouth when on stage, for next to the voice, those are the most important instruments in an actor's profession. With them we exhibit surprise"—Andrew opened wide his eyes and mouth—"anger"—he squinted his eyes and drew his mouth into a snarl—"sadness"—he managed to make his eyes droop and his lips curl down—"and happiness." Again his eyes were wide, though not quite as wide, and his mouth spread into a big smile.

Duff laughed, and applauded. "That is very good."

"Yes, you could see it because you are here with me, in the same room and but a few feet away. On stage, however, the audience member in the farthest row from the stage must be able to see those same reactions. In order to do that, we must use makeup."

"I can see how that would be so."

There was a light knock on the door and a woman's voice called through. "Andrew, are you decent?"

"Why, sister, I am one of the most decent people I know," Andrew replied.

"That had better be more than a joke, because I am coming in," Rosanna said, pushing the door open and stepping into the room. Her makeup and costume had been removed but she was still a very attractive woman. She smiled at Duff. "Did Andrew tell you we want you to be our dinner guest tonight?"

"I told him, but he refused," Andrew said.

"What?" Rosanna replied in surprise.

"It turns out he wants us to be his guests."

Rossana laughed. "I hope you accepted."

"Of course I did," Andrew said.

Chapter 3

Duff took his two cousins out to dinner at the King's Arms restaurant.

"It is Scot you are, so Scot ye shall eat," Duff said.

"We defer to you, cousin," Andrew said.

Duff ordered a rich, Scotch broth to start the meal, then a hearty pot-roasted chicken with potatoes, as the main course. He finished it up with clootie dumplings covered in a rich custard sauce.

During the meal Andrew explained how they were related.

"Our father, that is mine and Rosanna's, was Jamie Ian MacCallister the Third. He was captured by the Shawnee Indians in 1817 on his seventh birthday and raised among them so that he was more Indian than white. He learned the warrior's way and when he was only nine, he shot a deer with a bow and arrow he had made himself. If that wasn't enough, he fought off two wolves for the carcass. That earned him the name Man Who is Not Afraid."

"Father was at the Alamo," Rosanna added. "He

was the last courier Colonel Travis sent out before
the final battle."

"There is a statue of him in the town of MacCallister, Colorado. The statue was made by the noted
sculptor Frederic Remington," Andrew continued.

"My with a history like that, a statue and a town of
the same name, your father must have been quite a
successful man," Duff said. "I'm sure you are very
proud of him."

"We are," Rosanna said. "He was one of the true
giants of the American West, and founder of the city
that bears his name."

"His father was Jamie Ian the Second," Andrew
said, continuing the narrative. "He was one of the
early settlers and a successful farmer in Ohio. My
great grandfather was Jamie Ian the First, and he
was truly a giant. He made the trek West with Lewis
and Clark, and became a mountain man, living and
trapping on his own for many years before returning
to civilization.

"My great great grandfather Seamus MacCallister, was a captain during our Revolutionary War. He
was with Washington at Valley Forge, crossed the
Delaware with him, and was at his side at the final
Battle of Yorktown. In doing family research, I came
across a letter written to him by George Washington
in which he praises Seamus for his military skills and
courage.

"My great great great grandfather, Hugh MacCallister, was a captain in the service of Governor
Joseph Dudley of Massachusetts during the Queen
Anne War. Hugh MacCallister was the first of our

family to emigrate from Scotland, and was the brother of Braden MacCallister, your great great great grandfather. Both were sons of Falcon MacCallister, and that, my dear cousin, is where our family lines cross."

"You said in the letter that you have a brother named Falcon," Duff said.

"Indeed we do," Andrew said. "I hope you will forgive the familial pride, but Falcon is one of the most storied people in our American West. Have you heard of General Custer?"

"Of course. I have read much of him."

"Falcon was with Custer on his last scout."

"But how can that be? I thought all who were with Custer were killed."

"Custer divided his forces into three elements," Andrew explained. "All who were with him were killed, that is true. But most of the other two elements survived."

"I must confess that when Uncle Hugh took the MacCallister name to America it sounds as if he, and all who followed, have done the name proud," Duff said.

"Do you know much of our mutual ancestor, Falcon?" Andrew asked.

"Aye," Duff responded. On February 7, 1676, Fingal Somerled and his clan set out to destroy the MacCallisters and steal all their cattle. But our mutual grandfather, Sir Falcon MacCallister, Earl of Argyllshire, learned of the threat and set a trap for the Somerleds. When Somerled and his men entered Glen Fruin, he encountered a large force of men led by Falcon MacCallister. Somerled tried to withdraw but found his exit blocked by a strong force that Falcon had put into position for just that purpose. The Somerleds were trapped with MacCallisters in front and at the rear, and the walls of the glen on either side. They were completely routed, many were killed, and Fingal barely managed to escape with his life. That was the start of a feud between our two families that continues to this day."

"You mean you are still killing each other?" Rosanna asked.

"Oh no. Thankfully we have put that aside." Duff thought of the recent fight he had with Donald, Roderick and Alexander Somerled, and he chuckled. "But we do still have our moments."

"Do you know the history of any of your other ancestors?" Andrew asked.

"Oh yes. We have kept an oral history as part of our lives, so much so that I feel I actually know ancestors whom I never met. Duncan MacCallister is an interesting ancestor, but I'm afraid my great great grandfather, Duncan fought against your great great grandfather Seamus in your revolutionary war. He was with General Cornwallis at Yorktown. As a result, he was part of a surrender. I am proud to say, however, that he fared much better at Waterloo, where Napoleon was defeated. Duncan was a sharpshooter with the 95th Rifles, part of the Duke of Wellington's army.

"My grandfather, Alair MacCallister was a Brigadier with Sir Harry Smith in India when Ranjodh Singh was defeated. My father was a captain with General

Simpson during the Crimean War, at the Battle of Sevastopol."

"And you?" Andrew said.

"Ah, yes, my uniform. I am a captain in the reserves."

"You may be in the reserves now, but I know for a fact that you are not wearing the uniform of the Black Watch merely for show," Andrew said. "You took part in the battle of Tel-el-Kebir in Egypt. That is where you received the Victoria Cross you are wearing."

Duff smiled self-consciously. "You have done your homework, haven't you, Andrew?"

"I wanted to find out as much as I could about our Scottish cousin," Andrew said. "And while, admittedly, the blood lines that connect us have grown thin with succeeding generations, I believe the spark of kinship can quite easily be fanned into a flame of genuine friendship."

"For anyone else, the blood might be too thin at this point to claim kinship," Duff said. "But not for the MacCallisters. Sure'n we are as kin as if ye were my brother." He glanced over at Rosanna. "And a more beautiful and talented sister I could scarcely envision."

Rosanna extended her hand across the table and, once more, Duff raised it to his lips for a kiss.

After they enjoyed their dinner, Duff took them to the White Horse Pub. Duff was greeted warmly by nearly every customer in the pub. Ian was behind the counter, and smiled broadly as he saw Duff arrive with Andrew and Rosanna.

"Ian, my friend, may I introduce to you my kith and kin from New York," Duff said.

Ian, who had been drying glasses, put the towel over his shoulder and extended his hand toward Andrew. "Sure'n 'tis a pleasure to meet the American cousins of my dear friend, and soon to be son-in-law, Duff Mac-Callister." He looked toward Rosanna. "And what a beautiful woman you be. 'Tis no wonder you are so successful in the theater."

"Are all Scots so gallant?" Rosanna said.

Ian laughed. "'Tis our way."

"Where is Skye?" Rosanna asked. "I must meet my cousin's fiancée."

"She is there waiting on yon table," Duff said, pointing her out.

"Oh, my," Rosanna said. "What a beautiful young woman she is. Duff, I can see why you are so smitten with her."

"As can I," Andrew said. "What I can't see is why she should be smitten with you." Andrew's jibe drew a laugh as Ian put mugs of ale on the bar in front of each of them.

Andrew reached into his pocket for money, but Ian held up his hand. "This is on the house. Surely I can furnish a beer to m' own cousins now, can't I?"

"Cousins?" Andrew looked at Duff. "Did I not go far enough in my genealogy research?"

"We aren't cousins yet," Ian said. "But when my Skye marries Duff, 'tis cousins-in-law we shall be."

Andrew chuckled. "I suppose that is true, isn't it?"

Skye returned to the bar then and was introduced to Andrew and Rosanna.

"'Tis most pleased I am to meet such famous theater people," Skye said with a little curtsy as she greeted the pair.

"It is true that we strut and fret our brief hour upon the stage," Andrew said. "But thus far, fame has eluded us."

"He is being modest, Skye," Duff said. "You should have seen the high esteem in which they were held by the people of Glasgow when I visited there to see their show."

"The people of Glasgow were uncommonly kind," Rosanna said. "Certainly they treated us with more deference than we deserve."

"I think not," Skye said. "I read of you in our newspaper. I have the article here." Skye reached under the bar then pulled out a newspaper that was carefully folded to display the article that held her interest.

She began to read:

> Campbell's Musical Saloon has occasioned many theatricals and musicales of note, but rarely have the boards been so crowned as to be trod by that magnificent pair of thespians, Andrew and Rosanna MacCallister. Brother and sister they, the MacCallisters have long been the object of attention and admiration in New York. Should one be fortunate enough to attend a performance in which these two appear, they will indeed regard the evening of entertainment as time well spent.

She put the paper down. "If the paper writes that of you, then you are truly famous."

"You read very well, young lady," Andrew said. "You would make a fine thespian yourself."

Skye blushed at the flattery.

At that moment Sheriff Angus Somerled came into the tavern and much of the laughter and conversation grew quiet as he stood just inside the door, perusing the place with dark and brooding eyes.

"Skye, lass, see if we can be of service to the sheriff," Ian said quietly.

Skye approached the sheriff, then curtsyed. "Sheriff, may we serve you?"

Sheriff Somerled looked over at Duff, then pointed at him. "Is it true that, last week, you fought with my sons for no reason?" he asked.

"That is not true," Duff replied.

"How can you say it is not true when with my own eyes I saw the bruises you inflicted upon them."

"I am not saying that I didn't fight with them," Duff said. "What I dispute is that I fought with them for no reason. I fought with them because they attacked me."

"There are three of them and but one of you, yet they are the injured ones. Would you be tellin' me, Duff MacCallister, that they attacked you first, and yet you bested the three of them? Because that I am not believing."

"You should believe it, Sheriff, for Duff is speaking only the truth," Ian said. "All who were here that night will bear witness to the fact that your sons attacked MacCallister."

"Aye, Sheriff, 'tis true enough," one of the other patrons said. "Your sons started the fight."

The sheriff said nothing in direct reply, but a blood vessel in his temple began to throb, a visual display of his anger. He looked at Andrew and Rosanna. "Are you the theater people I have heard about?"

"I don't know if, or what you might have heard of us. But it is true that we are theater people," Rosanna replied.

"Why dishonor yourselves by standing with one who is known to be a brigand?" Angus Somerled asked.

"Duff MacCallister is my cousin," Andrew replied. "Were he at the gates of hell, I would stand by him."

"You make claim that he is your cousin?"

"Aye, of the selfsame blood as Falcon MacCallister, he who defeated your ancestor at Glen Fruin," Andrew said, perfectly adopting the Scottish brogue.

"*Ochh.* It is worthless you are, the lot of ye." Sheriff Somerled spun on his heel, and left the tavern.

"And it is good riddance to ye, Angus Somerled!" Ian McGregor called out after the sheriff left. It wasn't loud enough for the sheriff to hear, but it was loud enough for all in the pub to hear, and they laughed out loud.

Two days later, Duff went to Glasgow to tell his cousins good-bye.

"We have had a wonderful visit," Rosanna said. "Especially so since we met you and were able to reconnect our family after all these years. And how wonderful it was to meet Skye. She is such a delightful young lady. I am sure the two of you will be very happy."

"Thank you. I am sure we will be as well. I enjoyed meeting both of you," Duff said. "It was an interesting experience, finding out what happened to those of my family who went to America."

"You should come to America as well," Andrew said. "Yes, come to America after you have married, and bring your bride with you."

"Perhaps I will," Duff said. "I would like to see America, and I would like Skye to see it with me."

"But if you come, you should come to live, not just to visit," Andrew said. "You would love it in America, and Americans would welcome you. We are that kind of people."

"I have land here," Duff said. "If I were to come to America, how would I live? I have no land there."

"Land is easily acquired," Andrew said. "We have so much land in America that we give it away. It is called homesteading. All you have to do is move on to a piece of unoccupied property, work it, and file a claim. Then it becomes yours."

"Aye, that is an interesting proposition, but Skye still has her family here. I think it might be difficult to persuade her to undertake such an adventure."

"Perhaps not as difficult as you may think," Rosanna said. "Skye strikes me as a young woman with an adventurous spirit. She may want to come. But, whether you come to visit or to live, you must spend some time with us."

THE EAGLES SERIES BY
WILLIAM W. JOHNSTONE

__Eyes of Eagles
0-7860-1364-8   **$5.99**US/**$7.99**CAN

__Dreams of Eagles
0-7860-6086-6   **$5.99**US/**$7.99**CAN

__Talons of Eagles
0-7860-0249-2   **$5.99**US/**$6.99**CAN

__Scream of Eagles
0-7860-0447-9   **$5.99**US/**$7.50**CAN

__Rage of Eagles
0-7860-0507-6   **$5.99**US/**$7.99**CAN

__Song of Eagles
0-7860-1012-6   **$5.99**US/**$7.99**CAN

__Cry of Eagles
0-7860-1024-X   **$5.99**US/**$7.99**CAN

__Blood of Eagles
0-7860-1106-8   **$5.99**US/**$7.99**CAN

Available Wherever Books Are Sold!

Visit our website at **www.kensingtonbooks.com**